MW00390050

Whistler's

Mother

To
Lisa,
Thank you for your
interest in my novel!
I hope you enjoy it, and
look forward to your thoughts and
opinions in your review!

Jon Kearney

"Whistler's Mother"

A Novel by Jax Kearney

Published by BookBaby

www.BookBaby.com

Copyright © 2008 Jax Kearney

Published 2022

All rights reserved. No portion of this book may be reproduced
in any form without permission from the publisher, except as
permitted by U.S. copyright law.

For permissions contact: JaxScript@Gmail.com

Cover Design Art by: RebecaCovers

Original photo licensed by Alamy 2022

ISBN: 978-1-66785-845-6

Printed in United States

First Edition

Acknowledgements

This novel is a work of fiction. Although several real towns in Connecticut are mentioned, the street names and highway numbers are often intentionally fictionalized.

Any resemblance to actual events or persons, living or dead, is entirely coincidental.

Special Thanks

I would especially like to thank all the readers in my inner circle who over the years have read my early drafts, and helped me improve as a writer and storyteller.

Your input has been invaluable. THANK YOU!

Whistler's Mother

A Novel

by

Jax Kearney

©2008 All rights reserved.

ONE

Summer 2005 - Coastal Connecticut

So far, the weekend had been quiet. Friday night passed without any elevated "incidents" as they officially called them. The house appeared peaceful and serene; the way Jim liked it. Earlier in the day they had one somber check-in, which unfortunately meant severe drama someplace else. The female staffers always handled the check-ins, as it made their unexpected guests more comfortable. Most women that ended up at the Gildersleeve Women's Shelter probably wouldn't appreciate a man on the premises at night, so he stayed hidden as much as possible. He was only there in case of trouble, but sometimes even the serenity tests his nerves.

From the outside, you might never realize that this quiet old Victorian house on the edge of town served as the county's only safe haven for battered and abused women. Blending in with other older houses of similar style in the neighborhood, all of which seemed like they could benefit from some minor repairs. The house itself just missed being listed on the national historic registry by a few years. Like the other time-worn homes nearby, it could benefit from a new coat of paint, and some landscaping. The foundation that ran the shelter liked the somewhat rundown appearance of the house, claiming that it helped the house to not draw any undue attention.

The old home sat all by itself on what used to be a dairy farm. The yard usually looked rather unkempt, but they never let it become a complete jungle. Sometimes the girls would cut the grass themselves, anything to make it more like a real home, even if it meant manual labor. The large vegetable garden in the back grew some vegetables and flowers. Working in the soil became a form of therapy for some of the "guests", and the activity made it look like a normal family might be living there. The milking barn used to stand near the back of the property, but the dilapidated structure partially collapsed. They tore it down as a safety precaution. A small shed out back holds some small garden tools, supplies, and other lawn equipment. Oddly, no one ever seemed to tame the entire acreage. There's a difference between the need for normalcy and mowing down three acres of grass with a push mower.

The city inherited the old house when the old dairy farmer, who long before stop producing milk or any other farm produce, refused to sell to anyone and finally fell victim to back taxes. The house was scheduled to be demolished, when the foundation stepped in to rescue it. They were honestly surprised by how much money they raised to restore the old residence, which turned out to be twice as much as they needed, and helped to establish the operating budget. Of course, like any public facility, the endowment has dropped significantly since.

The house has two oversized round gables over windows in the front and rear of the house that gave it a castle like appearance, but nobody here expected a knight to ride them off into the sunset. A widow's walk adorned the apex of the home's three stories, which Jim had not seen since helping with the restoration five years ago. Everyone loved the view from the roof-top gazebo, and it quickly became a favorite of the residents who were unlucky enough to have to spend time here. It added level of security to be able to stand in the equivalency of a lookout tower, and survey the surrounding country in every direction. You would have to dig a tunnel to get near the house without being seen. Even the most paranoid of the women, not that any woman staying here didn't have a right to a healthy amount of nervous apprehension, felt better after seeing the widow's walk. Nearly twenty-four hours a day you would find at least one of the "guests" unofficially manning the gazebo styled turret. It was also a popular spot among the sleepless, as there were a lot of restless nights in a place like this.

Jim stopped reading, and put down the book, and ran his hand through his short black hair. Running his fingers through his locks, he could not shake the general uneasiness inside him. Whereas he never thought of himself as a big man, he stood six feet tall. Proud of his fit body, and doing the work to keep his physique toned. People routinely pegged him to be ten years younger than the thirty-five years he carried now. Although he still didn't consider himself a fighter, he studied Taekwondo the past twenty years, and became quietly competent in the style. You can only take so many beatings before you decide you've had enough. And thanks to his tortured teenage years, he understood the female residents in that regard. The martial arts changed Jim's life. At first, it was for self-defense and confidence, but later he learned to appreciate the discipline, and the culture that spawned it. Understanding and control were the linchpin to everything, and part of his stability had been undermined.

The previous weekend, an abuser followed one of the new check-ins to the house. Fortunately, Jim convinced the man into leaving without incident, and possible arrest. He got lucky the intruder was one of those suddenly "apologetic after the fact" types so it never got ugly. The man left his ugliness all over the face of the woman he forced into residency. The breach made everyone who worked and particularly those who stayed at the house feeling exposed. An abuser knew the location of their sanctuary, and they feared it would become common knowledge among the community, and therefore accessible to other violators. The widow's walk became more popular than ever.

The only man ever allowed in the house was Jim, and he never went past the rooms in the front hall. Inside the door of the house, with its small viewing window still adorned with a hand painted depiction of a farmer milking a cow from the original owner, a short hallway leads to one of several sitting areas. The staff office greeted visitors immediately to the left of the entrance, which in turn led into the small night duty room where Jim was attempting to read. On the right side of the hall sat was the counseling room. This is where he and the other therapists would do their best to reinstall the confidence and self-reliance in the women, along with other skills they would need to leave this place and return to some semblance of a normal life. As one of the most respected counselors in the state working with the abused, Jim graduated from Yale University's prestigious school of psychiatry, and owns a host of commendations that would make other doctors jealous. Not one to brag about his achievements, he never displays his accolades, but gave several of them to his mother, who like any proud mom shows them off with great pride. You won't find any of them in his private office in town either, nor in his own home nearby. The walls of his offices are covered with the letters and thank you notes of appreciative patients, as he put it, "Those are my real awards".

The hallway stretched into the house a good fifteen feet, until you hit "The Line". A thick red stripe painted on the floor at the end of the main hall, right before it opened up into the main sitting room. No males were allowed past this point, except for emergencies, including Jim. One night they had to call the police after a nasty fight broke out between two of the ladies staying there. Evidently, after comparing their sad stories, it became tragically apparent that they were both guests at the house thanks to the same abusive man. It might have been comical, had it not taken place in a shelter for battered woman and centered on the despicable acts of an insecure male. The station sent over their only female officer on the force back then. They roused her from a restful sleep to respond to the call. Even the cops were respectful of the line, as much as possible. That made the women feel safer, and keeping them safe was the whole purpose of the women's sanctuary

Due to the recent compromise of the location, a portion of that protective comfort they worked so hard to maintain evaporated. With no way they to ascertain if the abuser in question had told anyone, they agreed it would only be a matter of time before he told someone. Eventually, the address of their refuge would become common knowledge. Because of this, the foundation was working on a plan to increase the security for the women. It seemed their only option would be to hire a private company. Having a few big strong guys might make them physically secure, assuming they were trustworthy men, but it would erase the comfort provided by the refuge of their no men policy. Jim felt betrayed. In the five years since he and the rest of the Connecticut Foundation for the Safety of Women established the shelter, and they never had an on-site incident involving a male yet. They were proud of their flawless record, as well as the depressingly long list of unfortunate ladies they helped these past few years. These were the ones who wrote the notes of appreciation adorning the overwhelming percentage of the wall space of Jim's offices. But now that the shelter's location might be known throughout the county, even the steady and unshakable Jim Whistler became more wary and cautious than usual.

Saturday night pushed its way past the witching hour, and was nearing two a.m. when he saw the lights of a car enter the long circular driveway leading up to the house. Slipping into the office and peering through the window blinds, he let out a sigh of relief when he recognized the car. Well, what little solace as the situation allowed, knowing full well they were about to receive another resident. Hearing a key turn in the otherwise, always locked door, he peeked into the front hall through the small reception window. Opening the door, Karen ushered in a petite young woman with a split lip and face swelling that would soon be a black eye. Scurrying back to the duty room, he closed the door the behind him as quietly as he could.

Jim hit it off with Karen the very first time they met. She was as dedicated as they come, and like a lot of female counselors, a former battered woman herself. When she reached the breaking point in her relationship with her abuser, one night after taking what she called "a standard Friday night beating", which were far worse than the weekday beatings, she pummeled the guy into a coma with a baseball bat. Thanks to a good lawyer, she avoided going to jail and instead ended up doing a few months at a psychiatric hospital, where she learned she could not only help herself, but apparently had the gift of being able to administer to others with the same problems.

Karen Alexander exuded a simple beauty. Never the one you noticed from across the room, she was easy to talk to, with an infectious laugh. And the more that ease and laughter drew you in, the more you were struck with her natural charm, both inside and out. On a sunny day the hidden streaks of red in her dark brown hair seem to illuminate her soft round face, but don't let that pretty face fool you. She'd been through her share of abuse in her twenty-eight years, and people often thought she was older because of the confident way she now carried herself.

Learning to fight at a gym for boxers, she became quite the fighter herself. The staff still reveres her for the time she escorted one of the women from the house to a trial. The man who made the woman's stay at the shelter a necessity tried to hit her at a pretrial conference. Karen stepped up and slugged the jerk, breaking his jaw, and knocked him out cold. She's been a hero to the residents ever since.

Jim heard them enter the front office. She picked her up at the hospital. It was one of the services they offered the girls. Tonight, she would give the young woman the house basics, and do the complete check in tomorrow morning. The foundation and staff believed that the last thing you needed to do after getting abused, was paperwork.

Listening to them through the door separating the office from the duty room, he could hear the depression in the tone of her voice as she stated her name mechanically, Stacy

Johnson. You could tell she was still wound up tight by the way she would talk in spurts, spitting out the words between clenched teeth. A lot of them talked that way when they first arrive, like they expect to be hit for their answer, and don't want to bite their tongue. Everyday Jim hated the fact that women needed a place like this, and he tried not to think of what it would be like if they hadn't opened this home? Then what would these ladies do? Shaking off the thought, he listened to Karen going over the house rules with the young woman. She volunteered that she was twenty-three years old, and legally separated from her soon to ex-husband Jay, but she agreed to meet him to talk about it. Smartly, she insisted on a public place, but it didn't stop her ex from beating the shit out of her to the astonished looks of all the bystanders who did nothing to help. If not for a security officer for one of the stores challenging him, he might have beat her to death right there in the mall. Thanks to the guard's timely intervention, the estranged husband ran off, and they transported her to the hospital where Karen picked her up.

Karen's voice was a natural tranquilizer. Possessing a soothing calm tone that worked magic in making residents comfortable. In a few short minutes, Stacy's speech pattern and demeanor switched from frightened and angry, to one of pure exhaustion. Inside he wanted to help comfort her, but seeing a man might undo all the work Karen had done to settle her down. She would meet Jim in the morning, when it wouldn't be such a shock. Things always looked clearer in the light of a new day. That's what they say anyway, but that doesn't account for the fact that daylight actually solves very few problems.

Sitting back down on the bed, he tried to pick up where he had left off in his book when he saw the lights of a second vehicle approach the house. The complete lack of an exhaust system on the car, let him know instantly that it didn't belong to any of the staff members. When he picked up the phone, Karen was on the line as well.

"I'm on it. I'll let you know if we need you."

He said "okay", and hung up. Through the door, he could hear her calling the police as the car screeched to a loud halt directly in front of the house. Trying to verify the unknown guest, he strained to see who it was, but the window in the duty room faced the side of the house and didn't offer much help in identifying the stranger. His efforts became moot as the intruder loudly announced himself to the entire house.

"STACY!" He roared for all to hear, as he slammed the car door. "Get your ass out here, bitch! We're going home!"

"Oh my God," Stacy whispered trembling. "It's Jay."

"Stay here." Karen told her as she moved out into the hallway to take a look.

Clandestinely pulling back the corner of the blinds that covered the small window in the front door, to survey the scene, only to be met by the sight of a baseball bat coming straight at her face. Ducking to avoid being hit as the man destroyed the small portal with the weapon. As the shattering crash of aluminum and glass rang out, she safely ducked under the fury of shards and wood that sprayed violently down the hall. The man reached through the new opening fumbling around for the lock. Karen grabbed a small chair outside the office door, and slammed the man's arm dangling into the house. Screaming like a wounded animal as he withdrew his limb back to his side of the door, leaving a trail of fresh blood, tearing open his forearm on the jagged edges of the pane still clinging to the frame.

Rushing into the hall to add his support, Jim stepped out to see the man rear back all the way, then strike the door knob with a full stroke of the bat. The thundering ping of the aluminum stung his ears, but it paled to his discomfort as the doorknob, on this side of the door, busting free from the knob's mechanism and rocketing towards him, striking him right between the legs. Blinding white lights dominated his perception as he dropped to his knees, disoriented. Through his painfully obscured vision he saw the man rear back and strike the door again. This time the aluminum bat was too much for the door jamb, and the door swung open.

Karen bravely tried to hit him with the chair, but he met her half-way with a short swing of his bat as he charged through the doorway. The deflected blow still drove it back into Karen's chest, knocking her into the wall and down to the floor. His vision, still a swirling mass of two men he struggled to see as one. The intruder then bashed the office door open with a single devastating swing. If there was anyone left asleep anywhere in the shelter up until now, Stacy's bloodcurdling scream of fear from inside the small room would have torn them from their slumber. The decision was made, he couldn't wait any longer.

Shaking his head to regain as much of his eyesight as possible, he sprang forward in a full charge. The man raised the bat to strike again, but before he could swing it again, Jim slammed his shoulder into his gut. Pushing with all his force, he drove the man backwards out on to the landing. The abuser did his best to back-peddle until the floor disappeared beneath them. As they flew off the porch, he positioned himself to land on top of him and let him absorb the brunt of the impact, because it wasn't going to be pleasant.

As they sailed through the air together, the rank smell of booze dominated the man's rancid breath as they came crashing down on the front lawn like a pair of rocks. Not that this man deserved one ounce of sympathy, he almost felt sorry for him when the weight of his body cracked several of the assailant's ribs as he landed on top of him. Bouncing apart from the kinetic energy of the impact, they both went sprawling out in opposite directions. Jim scrambled to his feet doing his best to look like he was 100% ready to go, hiding the fact that he was totally winded by the combination of the door knob and crash landing. The man reached for the bat on the ground, but he kicked it away from him.

"It's over buddy." He said firmly, trying a little diplomacy. "The police are on their way."

With some effort the man rose to his feet, gingerly holding one side, blood streaming down his forearm.

"I don't know who the fuck you are," he stammered, "but you just fucked with the wrong person."

The man threw a spinning roundhouse kick striking Jim in the head and knocking him down.

"I came here to get my wife, and if I have to go through you to do it," The man stated, "Then so be it."

The ringing in Jim's head continued, but strangely the strike fully restored his vision in time to see the man try to punt his head. Narrowly dodged the blow, he returned fire from his kneeling position with a back fist into the man's ribs. The man let out a shriek, but didn't go down. Instead, the man counter punched Jim in the head knocking him backwards to the ground again.

A small crowd gathered by the door by now. Karen was trying to hold back three or four of the ladies who wanted to assist him. Even Stacy watched the proceeding, peering through the open door, albeit from a hiding spot behind one of the other women.

"We have to help him." One of them offered as she continued to keep them back.

"He'll let us know if he needs our help." She cautioned.

Using the momentum of falling, Jim rolled over backwards, planted his feet and stood up. He settled into a defensive pose for whatever came next, only to see that the angry husband had retrieved the baseball bat.

"Come on motherfucker!" The man shouted. "Come on!"

Hearing the sirens growing in the distance, he knew the cops would be there any second now, and he could stall this guy until they got there, but the throbbing in his head said differently. Now he was angry, but he wouldn't show it to this abuser.

"You do know that aluminum bats are illegal in the major leagues." He taunted as his whole demeanor took on a sinister antagonistic tone. "But I wouldn't expect an amateur like you to know that."

The man moved in close to Jim with the bat, who waved him in closer, defiantly.

"Your move slugger," speaking with utter confidence. "Come on. Come through me."

After stalking each other in a circle, the soon to be ex-husband attacked, swinging wildly at Jim's head. Easily ducking the wounded man's sloppy attack, Jim countered with a powerful sidekick to his broken rib cage. The man dropped the weapon and doubled over in pain. His face now serious and angry, he put all his weight and strength into a vicious uppercut that landed with such violent force, that the blow knocked the husband completely off his feet and laid him out flat on his back on the ground. Dazed, the man slowly turned over and brought himself up to a crawling position, trying to stand, but he couldn't muster the strength.

"This one's for your wife," he mumbled softly and kicked him in the ribs again as he tried to get up. The audible crack of another rib or two breaking almost made him smile. The man collapsed limply on his stomach, and blacked out from the pain.

As the sirens were drawing close now, Jim turned to the collection of women on the porch.

"Is everyone alright?"

"Yeah, we're good," Karen coming down the steps to assess his injuries. "How about you?"

Before he could answer, she was looking in his eyes, shining a small flashlight into them, then nodded approvingly. He smiled at her worrying over him.

"I'll be fine. You might want to look him over." Pointing to the unconscious man sprawled out in the grass. "I'm sure I broke his ribs. Check his breathing and make sure I didn't puncture a lung when I took advantage of that."

Smiling and shaking her head, she knelt down to evaluate the abuser. Jim staggered to the stairs and sat down on the first step. Looking over his shoulder with a faint smile, he addressed the women on the porch.

"I'm sorry about the disturbance ladies, but it's over now. You can go back to your rooms, except for Stacy. I think you'll need to identify him for the police."

"Yeah, especially since you knocked his punk ass out" added one of the girls, to which they all murmured in agreement and approval.

Jim turned to face them. "Please, let's not glorify the violence. Not here. Not after what each of you have been through to end up as our guests. I did what I did because I had to, and I'd do it again in a second, but don't think I enjoyed having to do that," pointing to the motionless body in the grass.

"Sorry Doctor Jim," the woman repented. "You're right."

Turning back to the prone body on the ground, he allowed himself a short smile for his conquest over the abusive husband. Deep inside, in that place where you try not to admit to yourself the things you don't want others to know about you, came an overwhelming wave of approval for a just and righteous victory. And as he looked at the unconscious man laid out in front of him, with his back to all the women, his smile widened a little more.

Stacy pulled one of the girls back into the hallway for some privacy.

Whispering to the other woman, "Who's that guy? How come he was inside the shelter?"

"That's Doctor Jim." The other replied. "He's one of the psychiatrists that run this place. Besides, you of all people should be glad he was here."

"Oh, I am. Trust me." She explained earnestly. "I just thought they don't allow men in here at all, you know, to make us feel safe."

"It doesn't get much safer than having Doctor Jim here. He's a black belt." The other woman continued. "And, besides that, he's gay."

TWO

Detective Frank Carmine is wide-awake now, whereas just a minute earlier, he was lost in his own thoughts for the day. The smell of low tide on Connecticut's Thames River drove the morning fog from his nearly middle-aged brain. Frankie did not command the raw appeal he used to in his twenties, when he first joined the force. All he had to do back then was put on the uniform, and girls would flock to him with his dark wavy hair, olive skin and European intrigue. Now pushing forty, he still possessed a certain charm in a handsomely sturdy way, except for the lines on his face. A smart woman would recognize them as the results of drinking and worrying too much. Most people would still say he is still a catch, and Frank would agree.

The department let him drive around his own car, and came to the agreement that they would pay his mileage, and he would cover the upkeep, and neither side complained. He owned the ultimate "Guido car", an IROC Z28. The "Z" would do 150 mph on the highway like a smooth ride in the country. He knew every nuance of *his* car. The Camaro car was his baby, and he took care of it better than his women. Unfortunately, he never found anything wrong with this, and is just one of the reasons he is divorced.

Back when Frank still walked a beat, the local police union bought modest piece of land on the river. Nothing fancy, but large enough for a small pavilion and some covered picnic tables. Every weekend during the spring and summer, the station would have cookouts on the waterfront.
The cinderblock utility building is climate controlled for rainy days, and smaller winter shindigs. Although not the Taj Mahal, it belonged to the police and the police alone, and it sat right on the bank overlooking the riverside. Their own little refuge from the world. You could look up and down the riverbanks in each direction for over a mile and hardly see a

house, thanks to the fact that most of the riverfront in the area flooded every spring.

Frank often cooked for the events, allegedly to keep up the reputation of fine Italian chefs. Every fourth of July they'd all throw in some extra money, and buy lobster for everyone. They did it up right for their biggest party of the year, and they trusted him as their expert to grill the lobsters. The split-cut, open flame charred way his Sicilian grandfather taught him, is the reigning favorite for their entire division.

The Fourth of July was only three weeks off, and the excitement building among the cops and their families was palpable. Single guys made a fortune taking shifts for the married ones, who's wives would never forgive them if they missed the party. Frank bought new utensils for the big day, and had considered getting a new apron this year, but decided not to break with tradition. His "I'm the REAL ITALIAN! De Niro, Pacino, and Stallone call me for advice!" apron was almost more famous than his flame broiled lobster. He couldn't wait. Every officer in the department were pumped up for the holiday. Guys fought over working the fourth more than Thanksgiving and Christmas.

There were rules to the *Pig Pen*, as they had nicknamed the spot, though no one outside the district was ever allowed to call it that. Friday night was just for the bluecoats, no spouses, and no family. Attendance is not required, but if you show up, you came alone. After all, they deserved the time among themselves, to bond, rejuvenate and sometimes heal. Being a cop has never been an easy job, but everyone agreed these "officers only" nights help make everything a little easier, just cops supporting cops.

Saturday however, was an all-day family event. You weren't permitted to come by yourself, without your wife, girlfriend, partner or children. The volleyball and horseshoes areas are in the open space near the parking lot. The kids played Whiffle and kick ball on the other side, and spend half the day retrieving the balls from the property next door. Farmer Joe's horse pasture bordered the lot on that side of the building. They didn't worry about the youngsters getting hurt by the horses, as the equines were genuinely more afraid of the rambunctious little humans, and gave them a wide berth when they invaded their field for a foul ball.

The children had always loved skipping rocks on the mild waves, but ever since they found out about the national championship, they had to have their own official, annual contest every fourth. This was a very big to-do among the offspring, leading to bragging rights for the rest of the year. They would save stones of promise for weeks in advance if they were smooth, flat, and hefty enough. Hell, even his own son Joey had started putting a few away as far back as Easter. The Fourth of July meant a great deal to the officers and their families. The *Pig Pen* was their haven from the world, held a special place in the heart of every office in town, from the top brass down to the newest rookie.

As he pulled up to the pavilion, he sensed the place had changed. When you're really attached to a place you can tell when the slightest thing is out of order. So, when Frank saw Captain Torres at a crime scene, something that happened about once a decade, he knew something was about to taint their holiday festivities.

Getting out of the Camaro, he slammed the door closed. The pungent odor of tidal stench fouled up the linings his nose. He realized he hadn't been here on a weekday in years, never mind at ten in the morning. Hanson and Torres were standing by the steps down to the riverside. The juveniles never used the stairs, they liked to climb the embankment. The slope isn't very steep, but you hit an age where you want things to be easier. Some of the guys like to fish, not that you could eat anything you caught in the river, and scaling the hill with a tackle box and pole was something of a challenge. So, one weekend they all got together and built a staircase down to the waterside for the adults.

Dave Hanson is a sharp guy. Frank and him clashed a little at first. They both expected to be the center of attention. But, after few months adjusting to one another, when the twin stars figured out how to orbit each other, they became one of the most successful detective partners in the history of the state. They had fewer unsolved cases than Sherlock Holmes. Dave was ten years younger, but they understood one another well, and filled in the gaps in one another's reasoning. Some have said they get along because neither one of them will ever get married, again, not if they can help it.

His senior officer broke off and met him halfway from the car. He didn't like Frank. They tried to make him captain once, but he refused because the desk job would have taken him out of the field. So, they gave the promotion to Torres, who has resented it ever since. When the two of them spoke, it always followed the same standard pattern, short and abrupt.

"I don't know what type of savage leaves a dead body in our backyard, but I want his ass, and I want it quick."

He walked off without saying another word. After several painful months of unnecessary confrontations, he finally learned to hold his tongue and let him walk away. The less they said, the better they got along. They were both commendable at what they did. Even Frank had to admit he was a hell of an organizer, even if a little anal-retentive. And Torres, if being honest, would tell you Detective Carmine could not only find a needle in a haystack, but would be able to tell you how long it had been there, and how many times it was used before they lost it. But neither would ever say this out loud, not in this lifetime.

"Well, I see Torres is in a good mood." Frank mumbled sarcastically, crossing over to Hanson.

"Can't say I blame him this time, check it out." He said pointing down to the riverside, "Jeff Wilson, white male, late twenties, has a record of spousal abuse, and dumped right here where we would find him."

Looking down the embankment, he saw the man's naked and battered body lying by the water's edge. The tide was starting to come in and lap his feet.

"Did you look him over, yet?"

Hanson nodded yes. Frank turned to the two patrolmen and the lab technician standing nearby the body.

"Get him out of the fucking water before he drifts out to sea, for Christ's sake."

"We're on it, Carmine. We were waiting on your word." The tech shouts back. He and the two beat cops start to wrap the corpse. He turned back to Hanson.

"How'd he do him?"

"Interesting choice of words." Dave replied coyly. "Throat's cut, but what makes you assume it was a man?"

"Alright, I'll bite." Frank continued, "What makes you think it was a woman?"

"With a history of abuse, ten bucks says a lot of women out there might be holding a legitimate grudge."

"Okay sure," He agreed "but if a woman's gonna take out an abuser with a knife she'll cut off his dick in his sleep, or stab him outright. Chicks usually aren't into the slice and dice."

"I agree, but he also took it in the ass either before, during or after he died, and from the looks of his rectum, it's not his normal thing."

"Well that explains your, *interesting choice of words* comment. Any semen?"

"I couldn't tell for sure, but you've got to hate a man in a seriously personal way to fuck him in the ass and slit his throat."

"Or slit his throat and fuck him in the ass." Frank added. "Okay, so maybe it is a chick. Why dump him here? Authority problem or they just trying to taunt us?"

"I'm still building a theory on that one."

Silence settled over both of them, as the patrolmen and lab tech carried the dead body over the embankment, and placed it on a stretcher of the waiting ambulance. As the paramedics begin to roll the victim past them, Frank stops them. He opens the body bag. The throat has a single, clean laceration down to the exposed trachea.

"Jesus. That's a pretty deep cut for a chick, Dave."

He closed the zipper, and waves the medics on.

"Thanks guys." Hanson adds. "True, but never underestimate the power of hate."

"How about this? The guy's a closet homo, and this was the culmination of some rough sex thing that got out of hand?"

"Who's to say, Frankie? The pressure to close this one quickly is going to be intense? I mean, fuck, the son of a bitch left the freaking body in the Pig Pen."

"Any chance we could sit on this until after the fourth?"

"Too late." He spoke solemnly, "Sarah was already here."

"God Damn, that bitch!"

"Don't let your mama hear you talking like that." Dave joked. "I don't know what attracted you two together in the first place."

"She's the only girl I had met that was as ambitious as I was."

"So, Frankie, if you're so ambitious why didn't you let them make you Captain? I heard they're gonna make Sarah an anchor."

"Dave, my friend. You and I *are* the anchors. They wanted to make me the station manager."

THREE

"What's the damage?" Frank asked, as he fidgeted with a pencil. Never one to keep still when he spoke on the phone, he squirmed more when he talked to forensics. Coroners had his utmost respect for what they did, but something about autopsies didn't sit well with him. It was not the blood; he'd seen more blood than most doctors. He couldn't handle the dissection of the deceased. Their importance notwithstanding, something in him wouldn't let him reconcile an autopsy. Granted, the clinical exam is the only way to know for sure what ended a human life, but sometimes, to him anyway, still seemed like desecrating the dead. His Catholic upbringing was the most likely cause, and the things the church drove into his head during catechism classes, or he simply wanted those now bereft of life be left alone. This is what motivated him as a detective. No one should die for an unknown reason. Everyone dies of a specific event, which is too often a stupid one. It was important to him to find out why, so their soul can rest in peace.

Carrie McKenna was far too beautiful a woman to be a pathologist, Irish perfection, tall, thin hourglass design, with long curly red hair, and green eyes that made you question everything you were doing with your life. Her stare melted your heart like a wounded puppy, or burned through you like you were on the examination table. She graduated from Yale med school only to shock her parents by going into forensic sciences. I guess they expected a more traditional form of medicine, aka, a higher paying one. She was as smart as anyone Frank ever met, and he respected her, and he didn't respect many women, sadly. A fact he only acknowledged privately. His old school views weren't popular these days, but at least he had learned to keep most of his opinions to himself. It did take him thirty-plus years to accomplish. He always felt almost driven to ask her out, but never did. She made him uneasy with her comfort and ability to perform an autopsy.

Frank no longer dated women he thought had one up on him, having a well-known, high-profile wife is what destroyed his marriage. Yet, every time he heard Carrie's voice, with her low throaty tone with hints of the old country, he wished he was over it.

"I thought you were gonna come for the results in person, Frankie." She cooed in her best sultry voice. "What's the matter? Don't you love me anymore?"

The simple act of asking him if he loved her, even jokingly, disoriented him so fast, he lost his grip on the pencil he was twirling nervously, sending it sailing. He could fall for her hard, if he didn't have so much respect for her. Sadly, he still had to learn to reconcile those two things. The pencil rolled over near Hansen's desk. Frank couldn't reach that far without losing his hold on the phone.

"No, no." He said reassuringly, trying desperately to retrieve his utensil from his chair. "You know I don't like the morgue."

Like any good partner, he was right on top of the situation. He retrieved the scribe off the tiles and presented it back to Frank like he deserved an award.

Dave smiled widely at him. "You must be talking to Carrie."

Frankie snatches his pencil from him and shoots him a bird.

"I knew it." Hansen added, walking away laughing.

"Well, I'm beginning to think it's me, Frank." Her voice on the line snapping him back to his conversation.

"Oh, no, definitely not, I mean..." He argued poorly. "You are the most aesthetically appealing woman I know, Carrie, bar none." The words stuck out in his head instantly, aesthetically appealing, for fuck's sake Frank is that the best you could do?

"Well, since I am secure in the knowledge of my mental capacities, I will take that as quite the complement from such a self-confessed connoisseur of the female species."

There it was again. That special something in her statements obviously meant as encouragement, and yet somehow felt like she slighted you. Frank appreciated her sharp mind, although she intimidated him. Her skill at using language to her advantage never failed to impress him.

"So, what do you have for me, beautiful?"

"Well. Let's just say this guy was not enjoying himself."

"How so?"

"Jeffery Wilson, a.k.a. Jeff, white male, 34 years old, and who judging by the trauma to his anal sphincter and rectum was forcibly raped."

"Are you sure?"

"Positive. The bruises to his wrists and ankles, show that he was previously bound hand and foot. I also found fibers in his mouth and throat, so our perp gagged him with a cotton cloth fabric and then sodomized him. The killing blow appears to be one deep slash with a sharp knife of some sort, somewhere between six and ten inches long. The cut, made left to right, possibly during or after the act, so the suspect is right-handed."

"Oh, that narrows it down."

"The guy was either impotent or didn't ejaculate, as there were no traces of semen or seminal fluid, or prophylactic use."

"Could he have used something as a proxy, like a broomstick, pool cue, shit, a baseball bat?"

"Sure, I suppose so, but we haven't found anything to indicate a foreign object, no splinters, fibers, nothing."

"So how big is this guy?"

"I can't guarantee this was a man yet. Hansen said Wilson has a long history of spousal abuse. Maybe she wore a dildo. A woman with gun can be just as convincing as a three-hundred-pound man."

"Are we looking for a three hundred pounder?"

"No, but assuming he or she did him while they were doing him, they'd be at least 5'9", but probably taller."

"Hmm, technically that would make you a suspect, Red. You're right-handed too, and very handy with sharp blades. Where were you last night?"

"Home, alone, waiting for you to work up the nerve to ask me out."

"What makes you so sure I want to go out with you?"

"Well, let's examine the evidence Detective. First, there is the way you act like a little boy around me all the time, which I find cute coming from a man who finds murderers for a living, and two, Hansen told me."

"I'm putting in for a new partner."

"You'll never find a better one."

Covering the receiver, "What the fuck Dave? You told Carrie that I like her?"

"Everybody knows Frankie. Just admit and go for it."

Frank turned back to his phone conversation, still glaring at Hansen, who found the whole thing funny.

"Maybe I'll find one who can keep his MOUTH SHUT. So, our guy's gotta be 5'10" or better?"

"Or girl?"

"It is definitely not a girl, Carrie. Trust me."

"I think it is a woman Frank, and she's pissed. Too many beatings, she snaps, and goes all Burning Bed on him. Hell, hath no fury and all..."

"Yeah, but girls aren't that violent."

"Yes, but woman *are*. You want to bet on it?"

"Sure, Nancy Drew, what's the stakes?

"If the killer is female, you have to make me one of your famous grilled lobster dinners."

"And if it is a man?"

"I'll cook you dinner, one of my fantastic specialties."

"You might as well start planning the menu, beautiful, because this one's a man. I can feel it in my bones."

"Well, may the best cop win."

"You got a deal." As the words came out of his mouth, he realized in fifteen seconds she managed to guarantee what he never had the courage to do, regardless of how attracted he had been to her all along. She had set up a date.

The moment of silence hung for a moment as both parties assimilated their actions. Smiling, Frank leaned back in his chair and put his feet on the desk.

"I see what you did there. Well played madam. Well played."

Having achieved a major victory, and taking a small moment to smile about it to herself, she brought the conversation back to the topic at hand.

"You ain't seen nothing yet. Oh, yeah, not to ruin the mood, but Sarah was here a few minutes ago."

"Oh God, what'd she want?" All the joviality drained from Frank's voice.

"She was asking specific details about the victim."

"What did you tell her?"

"I told her to go fuck herself."

Frank had known Carrie for around two years now, and never once heard her say the word "fuck" ever. It caught him off guard so badly he lost his balance and fell out of his seat, sending himself, the chair and the receiver sprawling across the floor. Hansen did his best to suppress his laughter, trying not to let his partner see how much he enjoyed his embarrassing display of imbalance.

"Frank!? Frank!? Are you there?"

He was scrambling to retrieve it, before Carrie realized what happened.

"Yeah, I'm here. I dropped the damn phone."

"Sure, if you say so."

"I, ah, don't ever remember you talking like that."

"Of course, that's not what I actually said. I told her to go see you if she wanted any information about the case."

"I gotta admit, Carrie. You really surprised me."

"I've got to do something to get off this pedestal you've put me on Frank. I'll talk to you later."

And then the silky voice disappeared. He wasn't sure when it happened, but she now understood him better than he did, and a part of him liked that.

He hung up the receiver, started to straighten the chair, and was about to climb back into it, when another familiar voice hit him.

"What are you doing on the floor, Frank?"

From his kneeling position, he turned to find his ex-wife Sarah standing there, holding a small datebook. He stands up indignantly, sat down in his desk chair deliberately, and composed himself.

His tone became flat and dry, "I dropped the phone."

"Oh, talking to Carrie again?"

Could every woman in the world read him like a book, or just these two, he thought to himself?

"What do you want Sarah?"

"I want to know about the body at the pig pen."

He looked at her for a moment. Carrie had radiant glamour, but Sarah's beauty is more subtle. Carrie's looks stood out from fifty feet away. Sarah got prettier the closer you got to her, and if you got too close, it felt like being sucked into a black hole. Her appeal pulled you in like gravity, swept up in the simple charm of her dark hair, and soft brown eyes. Her personal magnetism made you want to be near to her. Leaving her was the hardest thing he ever did, a close second, having to explain a divorce to his son Joe.

"What body?"

"The naked one, with the free tracheotomy they found this morning."

"Sarah. We have less than three weeks 'til the fourth. I'd like to keep this under wraps until then. I don't want to spoil it."

"I understand the request, but if every cop already knows, then every spouse and girlfriend will know, and every child over twelve will know, so if it'll keep people on their toes until you find this guy, everyone should know."

She was right, but he couldn't let her win that easily. Not Sarah.

"What are you stumping around for, I thought they were making you an anchor? Might as well, you stopped being my anchor three years ago."

"Four weeks smart ass." She chirped. "Do you want to tell me about the body or do we have to play twenty insults first?"

She exuded her don't try me look on her face sapping all the beauty from it. Carrie didn't have an expression that sucked the allure out of hers, at least not one Frank had ever seen.

"Jeffrey Wilson, of Townsend, White male, in his thirties. Throat slashed. We're probably looking for a guy, but the victim has a history of spousal abuse, so we're not ruling out the possibility of it being a woman."

"Was he raped?"

"What makes you think he was raped?"

"Look, I'm not a coroner, but even I could see some sort of rectal bleeding."

"Internal injuries. We're not sure what caused them yet."

"You're yanking my chain, Frank. I can tell because you're trying not to look at me. What really happened?"

He stared at her for a moment, deciding his next move. He did not like to lie to people, even when it was necessary, and lying to a woman you married and loved for seven years was futile at best.

"Who's asking, the nosey ex-wife, or the channel five viewing public?"

"Alright then, just the nosey ex-wife."

Frank nodded solemnly. "He was raped, but there's no sample."

"Before or after he was killed?"

"During or after. We're not sure. You happy now. Now, go tell everyone to be on the lookout for either a man or a woman who likes to rape men and slit their throats. That should kick up the ratings."

"Sometimes it's not about ratings, Frank. We are informing people so they can protect themselves."

"You keep telling yourself that Sarah. Maybe you'll believe it."

"The police aren't the only ones who serve and protect."

"Yeah, right. Run it by Joey after he learns we found the body right where they hold the rock skipping contest."

"I'll do that, Frank. Right after I finish teaching him not to be intimidated by successful woman."

She turns quickly and heads for the door. He stood up to say something, but let her go. He knew when to let them walk away. Woman will always figure out a way to have the last word if they want it. Besides, he had a murder to solve, and there was a good chance of that happening long before he figured out women.

FOUR

You could not hear Jim Whistler's car while running. He owned a charcoal gray Mercedes 380SL. Most people of his financial ability would have bought a new model, but he liked the lines of the old 380s and the little dip in the roof of the car. It was one of the few luxuries he allowed himself visible to the public, besides everyone expects a doctor to own an upscale vehicle. No one ever gave him grief about his sports car, and he took good care of it. Not him personally, he didn't know diddly about engines, but he understood people. So, he chose a mechanic who loved cars and treated each one like one of his children, and Jim didn't mind paying him more than average for good service. He treasured driving as his way of escape. Nothing cleared his thoughts more quickly than a few minutes cruising Route 12 at 50mph with a little light music playing. Nothing loud, but never slow, and it had to be positive and upbeat. The custom stereo would fill the car with ambiance until the motion and sound became one, and the world disappeared. The ebb and flow of the road, tied to the fluency of the tunes melted troubles big and small until they were manageable again. It was Jim's favorite form of relaxation, and something of a tradition coming and going to his mother's house.

Elizabeth Whistler was a strong woman. Far stronger than her small 5'4" frame would lead you to believe. Jim towered over her physically, but always felt small around her. She had stature and presence a Hollywood actor would have traded their soul to possess, and the quiet fortitude one might expect in a librarian. His mother had run the county library as far back as he could remember, and he owed his love of reading to her. He owed everything he was to her. Always fair and steady in the face of trouble, she handled herself with grace under pressure. He only remembered her crying twice in his lifetime. Once when he came out to her as homosexual, but she never tried to convince him otherwise. Her tears were followed by years of quiet acceptance and unconditional support, that hid a difference of opinion and philosophy. Never once did she say out loud that she disapproved of Jim's gay lifestyle, but he knew, and sensed her silent disapproval. Oh, she supported him, discussing problems with boyfriends and offering sound advice, but it lingered, the unspoken doubt in the background. A tacit killer that kept them from ever truly showing the love they had for each other. Instead, they lived on mutual respect. No one was prouder of his accomplishments and choice of careers than her. Jim helped and defended the female species, and that would make any mother proud. He also healed women, and that always touched her, even if he couldn't heal the one woman, he wanted to reach the most, his mother.

The other time he witnessed his mother cry he will carry with him for the rest of his life. He was only six years old when it happened, but the vision still lived in vivid detail in his memories.

He got off the bus in front of the library like he did every day after school. To this day, his mother is still the head librarian. One of the oldest buildings in the state, the library's stone edifice stood tall in the middle of the mostly rural town. Jim liked the old building, although it scared him sometimes. But on this day, the imposing structure didn't occupy his thoughts, but the fact his mother did not meet him out front near the bus stop. If his mom was occupied, she would have Suzy, her assistant to greet him. Maybe they didn't need to wait for him, because he was grown up now, after all, he went to real school now, not kindergarten.

On busy days he usually found his mother toiling away at the front desk amid a flurry of people who required her assistance. People always needed her aid finding texts to make them smarter. No one in the world knew more about books than his mother, and everybody must have known that, because they always asked for help. Sure, her sidekick helped some people find a specific book, but his mother could locate anything in the building, at least that's what he thought.

As he entered the old building through the oversized front doors, Suzy sat alone at the welcome desk. Jim pushed the door all the way until it hit the doorstop. Last year he couldn't always get the door open by himself, which always frustrated him. He would always push the door all the way to the rubber stopper now, just because he was strong enough to do it.

The subtle thud of the door made the assistant look up to find him standing there. She always greeted everyone with a smile. She was a nice lady, especially to him.

"Hey there young man. How was school today?"

"Okay I guess, we worked on math stuff."

"Hmm, math stuff. That can be very important. You'll never know what you have if you can't count it, now can you?"

Jim shrugged. He never put it together back then, but Suzy did have a knack for pointing out the importance of something in a simple and plain way he could understand.

"Where's my mom at?" noticing very few people in the building that day.

She leaned in close. "She's down in the basement with the old books." Using her most ominous voice. "She's doing some math stuff to make sure we have all the old books we're supposed to have. You can go down there if you'd like. You know where the stairwell is. She should be right in the first room down there. You know, the one with the spooky paintings."

"They're not spooky." Jim explained, not even fooling himself. "They're ugly."

Suzy laughed at his false bravado. "Well then, I think you know the way. Just be careful on the stairs."

He tossed his little knapsack of school books behind the counter and headed for the stairwell.

The cellar was like that of any old building in New England, chilly, damp, and poorly lit. He could feel the temperature dropped a few degrees, as he descended the stone stairway. The old wooden banister felt cold to his touch. Even with the lights on, the lower level was still predominantly dark. They only had three light fixtures for the entire length of the hall. They installed them long after they built the building, and it left many shadowy nooks and crannies for a child's imagination to hide monsters in.

He'd been in the library basement many times, although it's still tested his nerves, it got easier each time. The scary picture whose eyes followed you as you walked across the room, didn't seem as creepy as they did the time before. They still gave him the willies though, especially the one near the broken light in the front room. The fixture had been like that as long as Jim could remember, and the guy in the painting would stare at you from out of the shadow like a specter. The offset lighting made him more life-like in the dim illumination filtering in from the other side of the room. His eyes stared with more intimidation than before and an uneasiness settled over him as his mother was not where Suzy said.

"Mom?" He called out low, as his voice seemed to fail him, and didn't get a reply.

He thought he should go get Suzy, but he didn't want to act like a baby. She must be in one of the other rooms with old books, probably counting the really valuable ones. They were so old they didn't let most people use them anymore. His mom said they would fall apart if they weren't handled properly.

Jim crossed the room trying not to pay any attention to the eyes of the paintings following him to the door on the far side. Never before had he been past the first room, to the others at the end of the basement.

He peered slowly around the door and down the hallway. The high ceiling stretched all the way to the back of the building. It made the first room look well-lit in comparison. The three lights tried to illuminate the long hall, but every doorway had a shadow that wouldn't allow Jim to know if the doors were open or closed. The long creepy passageway was longer than any of the halls at his school.

Putting his hand on the cold wall, he started to walk slowly down the chamber. The touch of his fingers along the old bumpy texture of the walls, were like a comforting braille, as he made his way to the first group of doors. They were closed.

Continuing forward, three more sets lay further down the hall, each having one door on opposite sides of the corridor. He approached the next pair. They were set back from the wall in a small alcove, so you couldn't see them until he stood right in front of them. They too were shut.

The third duo lined up to one of the small fluorescent fixtures above, and the door was open. He inched his way closer, but no light came from inside. Standing only a few inches away, he could see nothing within the room itself. Jim swallowed hard as he slipped through the doorway. His imagination started taking over as he conjured up any number of monsters lurking in the darkness behind the door, and he was about to panic when he heard the voice, a stranger's voice.

The man's voice boomed from one of the last two rooms. It was deep and angry and yet controlled as if he was trying not to be too loud. The shrieking squeal of an old door opening ricocheted off the stark cellar walls. Oh no, he thought, he's coming out!

Quickly backing into the nearest cranny to hide, only to realize he chose the open door to the unlit room. Jim fell awkwardly backwards into the dark room, as the man stepped out into the hallway. This time he awoke the old hinges. They squeaked loudly as he dropped to the floor of the room. His heart raced as he plunged into the dark. He crawled towards the beam of light coming through the space between the door and the frame. As he peeked nervously into the corridor, he spotted a large man walking towards where he was hiding.

Scampering deeper into the dark room, Jim's sight diminished among the limited beams of light filtering through the shelves. Where could he hide, maybe in a bookcase? No, they were too full of books for that. He had to make a decision quick or the man was going to find him.

The sounds of footsteps coming closer as he squeezed behind one of the bookshelves. He watched the door intently from his hiding spot, but he thought, *if I can see him, then he can see me.*

He was petrified now. His heart beat furiously, and he began to cry silently, afraid that the slightest noise would give him away. The man moves to the door cautiously. Jim bit his lip to keep his mouth shut and prevent any sound from escaping.

As the man pushed the door open, some light rushed into the room giving a little more of a view of the contents. It was then he found salvation in a surprise ally. The biggest book he had ever seen, standing three feet high on its custom stand that held it upright, nearly as tall as himself. He quietly scampered behind the giant text, as the man entered the room. The menacing voice rang out again.

"Who's in here?" The man asked with authority, making Jim tremble in fear.

The man reached up and pulled the cord to the old hanging light in the room. It flashed brightly illuminating the room for a brief second and then burned out in an even brighter flash. The outline of the man lingered like a ghost against the wall in the renewed darkness.

The man looks around the room carefully, while the passage of time seemed like an eternity to Jim. He bit harder on his lip to keep quiet, tasting blood as the teeth cut into the soft skin. He was doing everything he could to fight back the fear. The tears streamed down his face, but he refused to make a sound.

Then the unthinkable happened, the man turned and left the room closing the door behind him, instantly plunging the room into utter darkness. Jim had seen dark in his room under his covers, but there he always had a faint glow from the hallway, or a nightlight, or the trusty old street lamp on the corner, but this was different. This was the complete absence of all illumination, thanks to the room having no windows. At first, he closed his eyes out of fright, but when he forced himself to open them, nothing but blackness surrounded him. He fought back the urge to start whimpering, praying the man couldn't hear him. Feeling for the edge of the book in front of him, he carefully peaked around it to survey his situation.

He slithered on his stomach towards the wisp of light coming from under the doorway. Reaching up for the door handle, he was struck by dreadful thought and stopped. What if he was still in corridor? Surely the old hinges of the door would give him away when he opened it. As he surveyed the room, ghostly images danced in pitch blackness, unpleasant leftovers from the light bulb's last gasp at incandescence. His fears started to openly fight each other. The monsters that began to take shape in the dark, versus the mysterious man in the hall. They both struck fear into his young soul.

He shut his eyes tightly in hopes of making them disappear, but it didn't work. The ethereal spots moved inside his own eyelids somehow. There was only one choice left to him now, to open the door.

He turned the knob slowly, and managed to crack the door ajar a fraction of an inch without creating a sound. It let in just enough light in to disperse the ghosts, and allow him to peer down the hallway cautiously.

The man stopped at the furthest doorway and looked into the room menacingly.

"You think long and hard about what I said." He told someone in that room, and with that he left, ran up the back stairway, and out a back door to the parking lot behind the building.

Jim quickly swung the door open and bolted out into the passageway, running as fast as he could to the room at the end of the hall. He must have been speaking to his mother. Who else would be down here? Did he hurt her? For the first time he was not afraid for himself. What if this man had done something to his mother? It dominated his thoughts as he ran down the corridor, until he reached the last alcove.

As he rounded the corner he found his mother, and an image that would be burned into his memory forever, she was curled up in a ball crying. The vintage texts were tossed all over the room. They were strewn about like a tornado blew through the library. She was lying on top of the scattered books. Her dress was torn near the hemline and her stockings were in pieces around her ankles, but all he noticed at the time was his mother crying. He had never seen his mother cry before, even when her mother died the year before Jim entered kindergarten.

Approaching her slowly, he knelt down beside her.

"Mommy?" He said softly while reaching out to touch her gingerly.

She snapped back to awareness, and pulled away from him quickly.

"NO!" She shouted at him, pulling away from his grasp.

Why did she yell at him? Did he do something wrong? Then she recognized him.

"Jimmy, oh god, Jimmy" Yanking him close to her in a hug so tight it cut off his wind.

"I can't breathe."

She relaxed her embrace, but would not let go of him.

"Jimmy, Jimmy, Jimmy." She repeated over and over, holding him, rocking back and forth.

"It's okay Mommy. The man left. I saw him go out the back door." Instinctively he stroked her hair like she did when he was upset, and for a split-second he wasn't the baby. For the first time ever, she seemed small to him. He didn't know what else to do, so he hugged he with all the strength he could muster.

She suddenly forced him backwards to examine him, giving him a once over for injuries.

"Are you alright? Did he hurt you?" She blurted out in a panicked voice. "Oh my God, your lip's bleeding. Did he do this to you? Did he do this to you!?" Shaking him involuntarily.

"No, Mommy. I was hiding in the other room, and I was scared, and I bit my lip."

"Did he see you?"

Jim shook his head no.

"Are you sure?"

"I hid behind the big book, and he didn't find me."

"Oh, thank God." She murmured. "Thank God."

"Who was that man, Mommy?"

"Just a bad man who doesn't like Mommy, that's all."

"If he comes back again, I'll shoot him." Jim crowed with all the courage he had left in his six-year-old frame. "Then he'll never be able to hurt you again."

She stared crying and pulled him close again, holding him like that for a few minutes. After a tender moment they got up slowly, and she wiped her tears on the torn sleeve of her garment. Reaching down, she tore off a small piece of the ripped fabric, and addressed the blood on Jim's lip, gently dabbing the drops off his lips and chin.

"I never did like this old dress." Standing up like nothing had happened. "Will you help me pick up these books?"

Jim nodded yes.

"But what about that man, mommy?"

"He won't bother us again, I promise." Using that motherly authority that makes children believe, and Jim believed her.

"So, I guess I don't really have to wait outside for you at the bus stop anymore." She used the small rag to wipe away the remnants of tears from Jim's cheeks.

"Yeah, that was okay when I was a little kid in kindergarten, but now I'm pretty old and can do that by myself now."

She looked at him for a moment. That look of having to surrender a small part of yourself as your child grows up, a forced acknowledgment of them becoming more independent. It was comforting and sad at the same time. Little six-year-old Jim saw both the approval and sadness in the expression. She shook her head solemnly.

"I guess you're not a baby anymore."

He didn't realize it at the time, but for both of them, their innocence died that day.

FIVE

Within a few weeks of *the event*, his mother moved herself and Jim to a different town several miles away. She said she wanted to be out in the country, but he always knew the change had something to do with the man in the cellar that day. Years would pass before she would tell him what happened.

About a year later the nightmares started, thanks in part to the incident, but also due to a regular ole childhood fear of monsters. She swore him to secrecy as to the events that transpired that day. Finally, all the bad dreams ended the day he came home from school, and she told him about the present in his room.

Racing upstairs, and bursting into his room he found it. Sitting on a stand like a phoenix rising from the ashes, was the enormous book he hid behind for safety in the basement. He had no idea how she managed to get it to the house. The tome was far too heavy for her to lift, not to mention being over a hundred years old and belonging to the library.

To this day it sits in the corner of his bedroom, projecting a sense of safety, and on a bad day you can still find him sitting in the Papasan chair with one hand on the text that came to represent security in his life.

Thinking about that day made him cry again. As the tears rolled down his face, he cranked up the tunes, shifted into fifth gear, and let the music and road become one.

The Mercedes glided into the driveway as Jim arrived at his mother's house. At some point, although he couldn't remember exactly when, he stopped calling it "home", and started using "his mom's house." This was his residence for over ten years until he went off to college. The house was old and Jim's appreciation of it grew, as he himself got older. The wrap around porch, the bay windows in the living room, and even the old cellar appealed to him now, especially since he had developed a taste for wines. He did what he could to keep the place in shape, besides; his mother was definitely not helpless. She could still do almost anything herself. She would read about it, learn it, and do it. Elizabeth would tackle any project she thought she felt strong enough to physically complete, and proudly displayed the scars from her many small wounds she amassed completing them. Pulled muscles, small breaks, various cuts and bruises, for all her talents she always found a way to overestimate them. She's finally slowing down, having reached an age where people expect her to complain about old injuries, and not create new ones.

The bond between himself and his mother was a strange one. He never met his father. She reluctantly began to reveal the facts of that day and his father to him, when he turned twelve. Telling him about his father leaving them, and later, other truths were revealed in time. In eighth grade she disclosed how he left her while she was pregnant. Finally, when Jim entered high school, to prevent him from trying to track him down, she told him about the beatings. But that wasn't the whole truth.

She's blamed herself for Jim's sexual orientation, for making him grow up without a father. His mother thought it was a factor in his sexuality, but Jim never attributed his lifestyle to that. In reality, he is attracted to men, and always has been. He never put that on her, and had finally reached the point where he was comfortable with it himself. It was not a choice for him. He was gay.

What he did attribute to his mother, if only to himself, was his inability to be close to anyone, male or female. He had never been truly intimate with another person, although some days he felt he was getting closer. They have been seeing each other for almost a half year now, yet Gordon's never seen his house. Three months passed before he saw the inside of his place, and most of his relationships never lasted past the ninety-day review period. Jim had his hang ups. Fully aware of the deficiencies in his relationship skills, and the irony of how stark in contrast it is to his natural ability with people in general.

He eluded trust in his voice and manner, a skill he clearly inherited from his mother. Even the most justifiably timid of the ladies at the shelter talked to him, and they were often surprised to learn he's gay. A few even tried to accuse him of faking being homosexual, so the girls at the facility wouldn't hit on him. He appreciated those odd compliments, regardless of them being a bit skewed.

Jim sowed some few wild oats in college and right after, but then he settled down into a series of short-lived monogamous relationships. He didn't want to say anything out loud, because things are going well with Gordon. His experiences overlapped somewhat with those of Jim's, and he had an endless well of patience and understanding in his soul. That is one of the things he loved about him.

He stopped himself on the way to the porch. Did he just say he loved him? Where did that come from? I am not in love with Gordon. Am I? Shaking his head to clear the thought, he started up the steps.

But you are thinking about him on the way to your mother's house. Okay psych major, enough self-analyzing for now.

Jim knocked on the door, and waited, expecting the door to be locked. Locking doors was something she drove into him when he was small. Knowing she always bolted them, removed some of the worry he kept about his mom's safety.

Elizabeth Whistler answered the door in her usual way; first peeking out the small window in the center of the door, followed by a smile when she recognized you, and then open the door. He stooped down so she could reach his face.

"Jimmy," giving him a small kiss on the cheek.

"Hi Mom," kissing her on top of her head, which caused a short look of annoyance and acceptance.

She was a little older now. Jim thought to himself how she's finally starting to look like a librarian. Some men have a hard time admitting their mother is beautiful, and Elizabeth was a beauty. Now in her fifties, most casual viewers thought her to be in her late thirties, and often mistook her for Jim's sister.

The years etched lines on her face, small, and centered around her eyes, they multiplied exponentially the past few years. She had him very young, barely out of high school. Her parents were greatly disturbed about the whole situation. They argued about it until he entered school, and they moved into this house. Only then did her mother and her finally put aside their differences over her having him so young. Granny loved Jim after the fact, but her and grandpa Pete were dead set against her keeping a baby at such a young age, without a husband and all. He adored his grandmother, but lost her to cancer when he was four. Sadly, he didn't remember much more of his grandfather as he died from a broken heart when he was six. It seemed like circumstances and fate kept any significant male role models out of his life.

"I see almost all the leaves have fallen." He said stepping into the kitchen. Throwing his coat over a chair, and instinctively gravitating to the stove to see what's cooking.

"Did you want me to rake those up for you?" He asked, lifting the lid off a large stockpot.

"New England clam chowder." She offered, knowing full well it was his favorite. They learned to live without saying they cared about each other, but they always found a way to show their appreciation for one other. "Well, I know how much you like it, and said, who says it's only for when it's colder?"

"Thank you, Momma. They never make it as thick and rich as you do. At the last restaurant I ate at it was so thin that I told them, if I wanted soup I would order the soup, not chowder."

"Oh, you didn't," taking the cover from him, and stirring the pot. Jim always got a kick out of watching her cook on the stove. It was a huge old gas range, and she had such an affinity for making soups and stews, but could barely reach into the bigger pots when they were on the back burners.

"Momma, why don't you let me buy you a new oven. They make them lower to the ground now. It'll be a lot simpler, and safer to use."

"Are you trying to say I'm shrinking, or getting too old to stir?" Thick with that motherly tone that has just enough humor to mask the seriousness behind it.

"I want to make it easier for you Momma. Is that so wrong?"

"I could never get rid of this old range. Do you have any idea how much history is in this stove? All the meals I created are only half the memories." She protested. "How about the time when you were seven and decided to dry your new sneakers in the oven, and nearly burned the house down."

"The house smelled like smoke for weeks."

"Or how about when you were twelve, and tried to make me a cake. I'm still not sure what you put in that to made it explode."

"To tell you the truth, I don't remember either," he admitted laughing.

"It took me two hours to clean out the oven, but I didn't want to say anything because you had your heart set on making me a cake for my birthday. It was so sweet of you."

"I still can't bake a decent cake." Jim giggled. "I always buy them. Which reminds me, your birthday is coming up, and happens to fall on a special day. One you might be interested in celebrating in a very specific way."

"And what special way would that be?"

"Oh, perhaps you've heard of a little show they're putting on at The Beakman Theater called Riverdance."

"Oh no, is that on as my birthday?"

"What's wrong Momma?"

"I already agreed to go to Riverdance with a friend of mine. I never realized it was the same day."

"So, is this someone I know? I probably shouldn't get my hopes up if doesn't even know your birthday yet."

"His name is Walt, and don't you worry none about it now. He's a nice man. Retired Air Force, and lives right here in Gales Ferry."

"How long have you two been hanging out?"

"Oh, not long, but he's polite and treats me well."

"So how did you meet this guy?"

"Just a fluke really, we started talking at the grocery store. He's a sheriff's deputy for the county."

"You're dating a cop?" trying not to be surprised.

"I wouldn't call it dating, yet. We only been out a few times, and he asked me to Riverdance last week, and I said yes. Maybe you could go somewhere with Gordon on Friday night, and we'll celebrate together on Saturday?"

"You mean, please don't bring Gordon, and force me to explain that my son's gay? You haven't told him, have you?"

"He knows all about you being a psychiatrist, and the type of work you do, and he was very impressed."

"Let me guess, you left out the part about me being gay?"

"It's too early, Jimmy. I want to wait until I'm a little more sure I want to keep him around."

"You know Momma, being gay is not contagious for God's sake."

"He's a little old-fashioned, that's all, and I'm not sure how well he'd accept it."

"There's nothing for him to accept. Everything is settled. I can't believe I'm going to be 37 and my mother is still making excuses for me."

She stops stirring the chowder, replaced the cover, and puts the ladle down in a slow deliberate way, before turning her gaze directly at Jim.

"I have never, and will never make any excuse on your behalf. Never. But I do not tell you how to progress in your relationships, or what and when to tell them about me, so please don't lecture me about not telling a man I've only known for six weeks that you're gay. If and when he becomes important to me, I will tell him."

"What about what's important to me, Momma? Don't you think it's important to me not to hide who and what I am? How sad it would be if my own mother was still doing that?"

"You have to let me deal with this thing in my own way. I have not lied or denied anything, I'm just delaying the truth for now."

Jim bit his lip, again hold back his voice. There were so many other things he wanted to say, but they would all lead to an argument, so he refrained. But just once he wished she'd prove the acceptance of him she keeps claiming to possess.

Taking a deep breath, he sat down at the table deflated. She moved to the cupboard and removed some bowls.

"So, this Walt. What's he do for the sheriff's department?" Changing the subject.

"Well, he's a deputy," setting the table for two. "He does whatever type work the deputies do for a police office, I guess. He did say, he would be surprised if the police didn't come to ask you about the murder in Waterford yesterday."

"What murder Momma?"

"You didn't hear about that man they found dead on the riverbank? They left the body at the policemen's picnic area. You'll have to tell me what that says about whoever did this."

"No, I didn't hear anything about it, but I was busy. Why does Walt think they would talk to me?"

"He said they'd probably want you to help establish a profile on the killer since the victim was a convicted abuser of women."

"All this happened today?"

"They found the man's body this morning, and released his name on the early news at five, because he didn't have any family in this area."

"And the man was an abuser?" Jim wondered if they might ask his opinion.

"Yes. He had seven or eight offenses on his record for assaulting an ex-wife in Massachusetts, and three different girls here in Connecticut, including one a few weeks ago in Westlake."

"Oh my God, Momma. We had a girl come in from Westlake last month, and she's still with us. You don't think it could be the same girl he beat up?"

Before she could answer, his cellphone rang in his coat pocket, still draped over the back of the chair as if he had just come home from school. He reached inside and answered it.

"Jim Whistler," in his calm professional voice. He looked at her with a strange look saved for weird occurrences. "Don't let them talk to anyone until I get there. I'm leaving my mothers in Gales Ferry right now, and will be there in twenty minutes... I'm serious unless they show you a warrant, don't let them talk to anybody... I'm on my way."

He hung up the phone and slipped it back into his jacket.

"I'm sorry Momma, I have to go." A concerned look came over on his face. "That woman from Westlake, it was her."

SIX

Jim ran around the back of the shelter to the porch, and slipped into the office through the side door. Karen was inside pacing. Sitting patiently was Frank and Hanson, looking like they had all the time in the world. If they were upset about the time him took to get there, they did a stellar job of not letting on. He rushed into the room, and immediately put on "the composure," his nickname for his professional mode.

"I'm sorry for making you gentlemen wait, but I am legally responsible for all the women who end up living here. I'm Jim Whistler."

"We're well aware of you and this sanctuary. You do outstanding work here, Whistler." Getting to his feet. "We didn't mind waiting. Frank Carmine, detective with the New London police and my partner detective Dave Hanson."

"I assume you've met my chief counselor, Karen Alexander." Jim passed on while shaking hands.

"Oh, yes sir." Hanson smiling widely, "We were at the courthouse about a year ago when she laid out that piece of shit who was stalking one of your girls. Frankie and I were the senior cops on duty, and refused to arrest you."

"I guess I owe you both thanks." While completing her own round of handshakes. "Sprained my damn wrist on that a-hole."

"I wanted to smack him myself. He was a punk who deserved it." Frank countered. "Like this victim we found, Wilson. The guy's a five-time loser, wife abuse, beating up girlfriends, it's a miracle it didn't happen sooner. We don't think this girl..."

"Boatwright, Ellen Boatwright." Hanson filled in the details.

"Right. We don't believe Miss Boatwright actually killed this guy," Frank continued to explain. "But we need to rule her out completely, and she is going to be our best starting point for information."

"Oh, I agree and hopefully she'll be able to help." Jim turned to Karen. "Is she already down here?"

"She's waiting in the conference room."

"Then I guess we should get this over with. Follow me gentlemen."

Jim opened the door to the other room, and Karen led the way into the meeting room, where Ellen was sitting at the end of a table for eight. The whole room was meant to be warm and the chairs comfortable, because the experiences shared here are not.

She was sketching a rough picture of a sailboat and a lighthouse on a rocky shore. It was not a great work of art, but showed some talent. In her right hand was a lit cigarette. She quit smoking when she left Jeff Wilson, but she liked to keep one burning, especially when she was drawing.

She kept one aflame most of the day now, even though she didn't actually smoke anymore. It was the cigarette that gave her a few extra steps on the final day she spent with Jeff. She was sure she would not have escaped from him, if she didn't break his grip on her throat by searing his arm with the business end's glowing embers.

When he let go, she kicked him in the balls and ran for her life.

All the women that live here usually come running.
Ellen was no different, late twenty's, thin, frail, and quiet. It
had been a month or so since the last beating, but the memories
of it will not disappear overnight. She continued to doodle on a
sheet of paper as they enter the room, then she stood
respectfully as they all came in. Karen and Jim sat down next
to her, as they all took spots at the table.

Jim handled the introductions.

"Ellen. This is Detectives Carmine and Hanson from
the New London police. They're investigating Jeff's death."

The two investigators nodded politely, but didn't try to
shake Ellen's hand, they knew better. You do not touch an
abused woman, ever.

"Hello, Ellen." Frank began gingerly. "We have a few
questions to ask about Jeff."

"Like if I killed him, right?"

"No." He stated bluntly, shaking his head. "I'm already
positive that you didn't do this. You may be glad, but you didn't
do this."

"I wish I did." She murmured.

"And you had good reason to want to," Hanson
stepping in, "But, who else might have wanted to kill Jeff?"

"Can you think of anyone else who might have hated
him enough to do this?" Frank inquired. "Any kind of enemies,
bad debts, anything like that?"

"Not really. He didn't owe anybody anything I knew
about. All he owns is the that shitty trailer he lives in. He buys
drugs from a guy in New London he calls "Doogie Houser"

because he's young, but I never met him. Mostly weed, but sometimes coke, but he doesn't ever buy enough to get him killed."

"So, no one comes to mind, anyone with any sort of motive at all?" Hanson interjected.

"I guess not, not here anyways, but I wouldn't count out the women he beat up in Massachusetts. Maybe one of them has more balls than me."

"We are checking on that too, but you can't think of anything locally, any arguments with anyone?"

"You don't have any trust funds you could pay a hitman with, do you?" Hanson added jokingly. Jim recognized the tactic, using humor to mask a serious question. He wondered if he learned that from his mother.

Ellen spoke in a depressed tone, "Don't I wish. I wouldn't be here if I had money, that's for sure."

She looks at Jim and Karen for a moment.

"I don't mean you haven't been... I mean, I wouldn't if..."

"We understand, Ellen." Jim stopped her. "We wish you didn't have to live here either."

"We're just glad we were here for you when you needed us." Karen added, putting a reassuring hand on hers.

"Well, I no other questions right now." Frank announced. "Dave?"

"Nothing else from me, you can go if you'd like. Thank you for your time, Ms. Boatwright" Hanson replied.

"Is that it?" standing up timidly.

"I guess so Ellen, thank you." Jim assured her.

As soon as he stopped speaking, she whisked her drawing and cigarettes off the table and bee-lined for the door back into the shelter. She opened it and turned back to the others.

"Is it true?" She paused. "That whoever did this to Jeff, they did him... um, in the butt first?"

"Yes, it's true." Frank confirmed.

"Good." She spit out firmly, and disappeared out the door.

"Can't blame her myself. How'd you know it wasn't her so fast, Frankie?"

"Wait, so you didn't know why he thought it couldn't be her," Karen asked. "But never stopped him to ask why? Interesting teamwork, you guys must have been partners for a while."

"Shit Dave, she was drawing with her left hand for Christ's sake."

"Left-handed." Hanson blurted out, like he'd just lost a race. "I can't believe I missed something so obvious."

"I guess you're buying lunch today." Frank said standing up. "Plus, she's not big enough."

"I figured you were going by her size, shame she couldn't give us anything."

"Yeah, that definitely a bad sign."

"Why is that bad, Detective Carmine?" Jim re-entering the conversation.

"It means whoever killed him probably didn't know him personally, and was trying to punish him, or because he enjoyed it."

"So, we have a serial killer here?" Karen queried.

"It's a significant possibility." Hanson fielding the question. "They say there's one born every day."

"Then, what are we looking for?" She followed up.

"Probably a man," Frank started. "One who thinks he's championing women, by killing these abusers."

"And doesn't appear to be turned off to the thought of anal sex." Hanson clarified.

Karen looked at Jim, and back to the detectives. The emotion left her face.

"You don't think the Doc is..."

Frank cut her off quickly.

"No, absolutely no, not at all. We've already seen the police report from last night. The Doc here was busy with his own asshole at the time. Nice job with the punk ass intruder you had, but yes, otherwise, technically, he would fit the bill."

"I've heard the details of this killing." Jim standing up to see them out. "I could never kill a man like that, no matter how much I felt he deserved it. I couldn't kill an animal like that."

58

"We never thought it was you Doc. Period." Hanson explained. "But you should keep an eye out for any friends or family who wants to be a hero."

Jim stared at them both for a long moment before he spoke.

"So, was I a suspect because I'm gay, and as detective Hanson put it, wouldn't be turned off by anal sex, or because I'm right-handed?"

Frank glanced at his partner for a second, then back to Jim.

"Honestly, we didn't know you were right-handed."

SEVEN

Jim always thought straight people were under the impression that gay sex was different from hetero sex, but it was the same. It's about caring, loving and touching, and when life's treating you well, true intimacy, and occasionally some hot passionate coupling.

The night had been a stellar one by Jim's estimate, and he needed one. Maybe that's what finally convinced him to invite Gordon over for dinner. Which led to drinks, which left them here, lying in his bed sharing each other's warmth. Jim watched the candle burn on the stand in front of the book, with Gordon's arm around his waist sleeping. It felt amazing to be together, but the ability to feel at ease around someone again elevated the whole event.

The night transpired in nearly flawless fashion. He couldn't script a better evening than the one he just had with Gordon, but as he stared at the giant book in the candlelight, he knew something was wrong somewhere. An uneasiness was swirling and gnawing inside him, giving him a bad inclination that the trouble would soon affect him personally as well.

He slipped out from under Gordon's warm appendage and out of bed. Jim's stirring woke his partner. Gordon watched him as he slid out of the bed and crossed over to a burning candle.

"You've got a great ass for a guy in his thirties."

Jim turned and struck a pose with his hands on his hips naked, showing off his toned figure. He played baseball in high school, and college before he officially came out. That ended his sporting career his senior year, when a few assholes on the team with better batting averages decided they wouldn't play with "the fag".

"I'm going to take that as a compliment. Young man. For your sake..."

"So, what type of book is this monster?"

Gordon's question stopped Jim in his tracks, not knowing how it once saved him from a real-life monster.

"Well, umm," He stammered, getting his bearings and trying to decide how much to reveal about the tome. "It's actually a dictionary from around 1860, but reads more like an encyclopedia. The entries are quite long."

"Have you read it?"

"Not much really, it's so old I'm afraid of damaging it."

"I'm guessing it was a present from your mother, the librarian?"

"Yes, some time ago." Not elaborating on the origin of how it now resides in his room now.

"What was the occasion?" The question was innocent enough.

Jim looked at him lovingly for a moment, then bent down and blew out the yellow flame. He moved back to the bed, sat down on the edge, and placed a hand on Gordon's chest.

"Gordon, it feels so good having you here that I'm sorry we didn't do this sooner. But there are several stories about this book that you're just going to have to wait for me tell them to you. They're very personal, but I will someday. I promise."

"I like your faith in our longevity. I can't even say with any sort of surety, how long it has been since I've been truly comfortable with someone. I thank God, we found each other."

Jim didn't know what to say. He was in unfamiliar waters of both emotional and sexual desire at the same time. His growing feelings for him were true, and that scared the hell out of him.

Gordon didn't let him dwell on his thoughts. He pulled him towards for a kiss and a little more of the best cure for anything keeping you awake at three in the morning, hot sex.

EIGHT

Frank experienced a near psychic phenomenon occasionally, where he would wake up in the middle of the night, and know to get dressed. It has occurred several times since becoming a cop, and used to scare the shit out of Sarah, because the news was never good. Plus, his instinct was never wrong.

Sitting at his kitchen table he waited, fully clothed with his coat over the back of the chair. Along with his phone, his badge and pistol were laying on the table waiting to be drafted into service. He always called it a gun, because that's exactly what it is, a gun. All that weapon bullshit they drilled into people's heads in the military was a crock of shit. A helicopter is a weapon. Bombs and grenades are weapons. He owned a semi-automatic 9 mm Glock with a 15-round magazine. The handgun was fairly lightweight, which Frank liked. This is not a weapon. It is a gun, pure and simple.

His eyes went back and forth between the pistol and the phone, expecting one to ring. He didn't like killing, only psychopaths did. A fact of life for a cop is you may have to shoot someone someday, and he wounded five people over the years, and three of them died. It got easier to rationalize over time, and that bothered him. He's never been questioned about his shootings beyond the perfunctory requirements of the department, mostly because he never shot an unarmed man. But, three men are no longer on this planet because of Frank and his gun, and their refusal to live without violence. Guns have a strange yet simple dynamic. They kill. They protect. Like beauty, it lies in the hand of the beholder.

There's a dark realization when you draw your gun you can't escape. An active acknowledgment of the possibility of your own death. You never overcome the anxiety, but you learn to ignore it. Frank would think about the people he's trying to safeguard, the ones you hope to save, and the terror they must be feeling. It lets you think past your own safety, because if you let the fear in, it's over for you.

The scariest moment in Frank's memory is also the only time he gave up his weapon. It happened during a hostage situation. Some madman with a gun was holding his own daughter at gunpoint. He already shot the wife dead right out in the street, and now had the fourteen-year-old girl, one arm around her neck, the other kept the barrel nuzzled to her head. The killer backed up into a doorway alcove to shield his flank. SWAT had taken control, setting up a perimeter, and keeping the press from getting too close, as they jockeyed for the best camera angle. The situation reached the boiling point and became a complete media circus, with film crews all around the event.

They would learn later that the guy was hopped-up on crack and heroin, and kept speeding through mood swings like a roller coaster. Frank made a decision to try and trade places with the daughter. In a moment of compassion, the lunatic agreed to swap the teen for a police captive. He trusted his fellow officers to back him up. He laid his gun out on the ground for him to see, and stepped out from behind the cruiser, only thirty feet from the man and his daughter. The man realized having a cop for as a captive would have the equivalent leverage as holding a teenage girl.

The mere seconds dragged on like an hour, as he walked slowly with his hands up to trade situations with a young girl, whose life would never be the same. He tried to ignore his fear by concentrating on what she might be thinking. This poor girl was being held hostage by her own father. The man she always thought would love and protect her from evil, killed her mother while she watched, and was one muscle spasm away from taking the life he gave her.

Frank could see the pure terror in her eyes as he approached them. He knelt down on the sidewalk, but just outside of the doorway, forcing the maniac to come to him to facilitate the exchange. At least that was their plan. However, knowing the plan and being ready for the results are two different things.

The man stepped forward not realizing he had given up the safety of the small alcove. The outcome would depend on one thing, the position of his gun. The split-second between letting go of his daughter and putting the revolver on him would be crucial. It all came down to the angle of the barrel at that exact moment in time. If it was not pointed at him or the girl, a sniper would end it. He knew how SWAT would handle this guy, since he already killed one person, taking him alive was no longer a priority. The SWAT guys worried Frank sometimes, as they were only a step away from being hired killers. They only call them when things are well past talking, and when they arrive, they know they are, in all likelihood, there to kill someone. That was the difference between regular cops and SWAT. Most policemen spend their whole careers avoiding gun play. SWAT lives for that shit. They're a necessary evil, like having an army. He respected the SWAT team. He had complete faith in their skills, but it didn't keep him from worrying about their judgment as he kowtowed unarmed in front of a killer. Would they wait for the right angle or just take any shot the perp gave them immediately?

Again, he focused on the girl's plight. After watching her mother gunned down in broad daylight for no reason at all, she was trying to make sense of this cop kneeling down beside her. A man who didn't know her from Adam. Why would anyone do such a thing? Frank's thoughts were identical at that moment.

The man edged forward with the girl. Her eyes were so enlarged with horror it seemed like they might burst right out of her head. She was beyond tears, in shock, and nearly catatonic as he pulled her up close to Frank.

"Everything's gonna be okay now, honey. Your dad's going to take me hostage instead now."

Although he was extremely fucked up on drugs, the killer kept some wits about him. He understood he was a target. Holding the teen tight against his chest, he squatted down by Frank, and swiftly slid the gun from her head to Frank's. The stilted exchange never allowed the angle, and left Frank as the new hostage. Then another poor development occurred, the girl never moved.

She sat there after he let go of her, too scared to move, to cry, to talk, or even take a breath. Completely immobilized by her dread, she stood fast like a stone. He prompted her quietly, but firmly.

"Go on girl. Go to the police. They'll help you. Go on, go home, you can leave now."

Maybe it was the "Go Home" comment since the home she knew was gone forever, but she didn't move a muscle. Frank hesitated himself, unsure what to do. He needed her out of there as fast as possible. All he could think of was being a parent, and prayed somewhere inside this "dad" there was one last act of compassion. He prodded the man cautiously.

"Tell her to leave."

The silence was frightening. The man looked at her with anything but parental caring for a long moment. Frank thought this could be over for one of them, and he prayed it would be him. Then the man spoke up.

"Get out of here, you fucking brat!" He screamed at her in a burst that caught them both by surprise, and then he pushed her. That was the moment.

When he shoved her, the angle appeared.

As the shot rang out, Frank was staring at the teenager. She turned to run as her father coaxed her into action, and had just turned her head when the bullet hit. He was glad she didn't see it happen. Frightened by the sound, she tripped and fell face down on the pavement, where she laid motionless until the other officers picked her up and led her away.

Frank never saw the projectile strike the man either. It left one clean hole through the center of his forehead. SWAT guys don't miss. But, knowing and being ready are two different things. He had never been so close to someone who got shot before, even though he had killed three men before, but never at this range. He was watching the girl when the round struck its mark. The man never said a word. The scene turned into a surreal slow-motion event as the sun's rays turned maroon from the cloud of blood bursting into the air. Aerosol hemoglobin assaulted him like the spray from a speedboat on the water. The red mass engulfed him, and felt heavy on his skin. This was not river water. Even the shitty water of the Thames River would have been better than the crimson mist that now covered Frank. It wasn't a cooling spray either, but the sickeningly warm splatter of a forfeited life. The hemoglobin clung to him like syrup. In an instant his whole body turned red from the splatter. Turning in time to witness the man fall down, his eyes transfixed as he fell. His vision partially obscured by the droplets of crimson in his eyelashes, as the man crumpled to the ground in a lifeless heap. He could already feel the smallest of the drops drying in the afternoon sun, and immediately, the smell. Blood has a putrid odor when it is outside the body, and it is not pleasant.

They whisked the girl away quickly to what would probably be a lifetime of therapy. Then they turned their attention to Frank. Hanson got there first. He still hadn't moved, as if the plasma had paralyzed him as well.

"Frank!? Frank?! Are you hit?" Holding everyone else back until he got an answer.

"Don't touch me." He murmured, and went to clean off his face, but as he raised his hands, he found that they too were coated in blood. How could he remove the blood off his face with blood on his hands? He dejectedly wiped them on his pants and stood up slowly.

"Can I have something to wipe my face with?" He stammered almost robotically showing his detachment with those around him.

"Sure Frank." Hanson snatched the blanket off the gurney the paramedics had wheeled up to retrieve the dead assailant. "Use this."

"Hey, that's for the victim." The paramedic protested.

"He's not the victim!" Blasted Hanson. "Were you watching the same thing I was?! He's a fucking murderer, and he's dead!"

He grabbed the medic and pushed him towards the body still yelling at him.

"He's missing the fucking top of his head! You think he's gonna miss a fucking blanket?!"

The volume of Dave's voice, and proximity snapped Frank out of his stupor.

"It's okay Dave. Give me the blanket."

Hanson gives the blanket to his partner and turns back to the EMT.

"Carmine just saved that girl's life and you're worried about a fucking blanket."

"Dave, forget it." Gravitating back to reality.

"Do you fucking believe this guy?!"

"DAVE!" Frank's eye contact with Hanson finally calmed him down. "I need shower..."

Frank would not get the chance to wash the scent of blood out of his nose until several hours later, but he was never able to scrub the stench out of his mind. He carries that day with him always. The sensation of being covered in blood, is part of why he stays out of the morgue. The essence was the same, that odor of blood outside the body. It reminds him of the fear, and Frank hated the fear, every cop did.

Then the cell rang and danced on the table, as he expected. He picked up the gun and put it in his shoulder holster, and slipped the badge onto his belt. Then, he answered the phone.

"Carmine?" His voice solemn, but firm.

"I'll be right there."

NINE

Hanson was already waiting by the time Frank got to the warehouse. For years the building was a small fish cannery. They processed fish here for years from what was left of the area's fishing fleet. Now the large ships do their own processing right on board, so as the need dried up, the place closed down. Then it became a nightclub, which had a good run for a few years. They didn't have enough business to keep them afloat, and they shut their doors over a year ago. Now it sits by the river's edge waiting for the next great idea to revive it to former glory.

The deck they built for the club was still attached to the rear of the complex. They used to put some tables and chairs out during the summer months. The dancing fools would come outside in the winter to cool down, steam floating off their bodies under the subdued glow of the dock lights. The hall to the back deck also led to the bathrooms, where his partner stood surveying the crime scene.

"The woman's room" Frank noted as he walked past the uniformed officer at the door. "How poetic."

Dave was looking over the body, stripped naked and slumped over a toilet with his hands handcuffed around the base. The floor was covered in blood, but the majority was in the nearly full bowl containing a putrid mixture of vomit and hemoglobin. When he stood up and turned around, he was holding a wet paper towel to his nose and mouth.

"Man, this place stinks like shit." Groaning and shaking his head, hoping the motion will cause enough of a draft to remove the smell from his nostrils.

"Dave, it's a fucking bathroom. Shit was the baseline."

Hanson rolled his eyes at the comment. Frank moved past him and squatted by the bowl for a quick inspection of the body. As he suspected, his throat was cut deeply. Bruises covered nearly the entire surface from the struggle. Not surprising since most men aren't going to let you strip them naked and tie them to a commode. He definitely went down fighting. The skin around his wrists had torn away to where you could see the bone of the left wrist. It was apparent that this fight had two parts, before and after he tied the victim to the toilet. Judging from the blood on both his head and rectum, he didn't enjoy either half.

"So, he didn't appreciate being the life of the party." Frank deadpanned. "Blunt trauma to the head to knock him out, waited for him to wake up, gives him the pony ride against his will, and takes him out to boot."

"That's pretty much my theory." Hanson agreed. "He put up a hell of a fight, most of which was after a blow to the head that made it a lost cause."

"Same guy?"

"Same guy."

"Shit. What's up with this one? Does he like men, but can't deal? He likes to fuck them in the ass, but can't look himself in the mirror..."

He stopped dead in mid-sentence as he turned to find Carrie Mckenna standing in the bathroom with them.

"Oh, yeah. Carrie's here."

"Don't stop on my account." Using a tone that eased the situation. "I'd like to hear what your theory is."

"Hi Carrie." He said, as he clandestinely managed to shoot a few visual daggers at Hanson, who smiled widely. "My best guess, at this point, is the guy is most likely homosexual, or with hidden gay tendencies-"

"Not so hidden anymore." Dave added.

"Fair enough, and, uh, I'm guessing some sort of chip on his shoulder against men, feelings of inadequacy or jealously maybe."

"I like the basis," Hanson theorized out loud. "But here's a relevant fact. The deceased is one Jay Lockhart, age thirty-two, and recently arrested at the Gildersleeve woman's shelter after getting his ass kicked by one Doctor Jim Whistler, who was out on bail."

"He's the douchebag from the shelter? Why the fuck didn't you say..."

He quickly looks at Carrie who is following his train of thought with an expression bordering on dedication.

"I'm sorry, Car..."

"Frank." Placing a hand gently on his arm reassuringly. "We are standing next to a dead guy with the better half of his trachea hanging into a toilet. I don't think you saying, "fuck" in front of me is an issue you should concern yourself with."

Trying not to look like a chastised child, he nodded in agreement sheepishly. She cuts him to the core so easily it scared him. Even trying to be a gentleman felt like a mistake. For some reason he couldn't seem to get comfortable around her. He hadn't been like that around a woman since he first met Theresa, and he's known Carrie over two years now.

"Here's what I got so far," She started. "White male, thirty-two years old as Hanson said. No detective work there, he found his wallet."

"Don't I get credit for finding the wallet, at least?"

"Not when you found it in the pants around his ankles." She fired back casually. "Anyways, you can judge most of this by looking at him. There are lots of bruises, but almost all of them occurred after an obvious blunt trauma to the head. While he is mostly likely unconscious, the murderer strips him down. Handcuffs him to the john, gives him the, what was that, oh yeah, the pony ride. This is when the lion's share of the bruises happens. It appears that he had to beat him into submission to accomplish his task. The torn skin on the wrists shows him pulling away from the toilet causing the handcuffs to pull towards the hands. Evidently, he's not a big fan of pony rides when he's the pony. And then came the coup-de-grâce, one straight deep throat cut, definitely from a right-hander. No apparent semen, but there may be on the inside. I'll let you know."

She smiled slightly in her calm confident way. He caught himself staring at her wrapped up in her voice as it slipped past her pouty lips, completely washing away the memory of a dead body only a few feet from his own shoes. Even the putrid odors surrounding him faded as he watched her talk. Damn he was in deep.

When she finished, he just stood there, waiting, in case she had more. Or he simply wanted her to have more.

"That's all."

"Oh, alright, thanks Carrie." Snapping out of a daze, feeling more dim-witted than he normally did in her presence. "We'll start with that. You'll have more later though, right?"

"Of course. Be in my office at five o'clock, "Spoken without a shred of doubt he would be. "I'll have more on this guy, and the final on our friend from the pig pen."

She walked out without waiting for an acknowledgment. Leaving Frank standing dumbfounded like a teenager who just finished a discussion with a college student.

Dave laughs quietly. "Frankie, she makes you swoon in the middle of a fucking crime scene, imagine what she'd do to you in candlelight. Ask her out for Christ's sake."

"I wouldn't be able to talk if I saw her in candlelight. I can't focus around her, like..."

"Don't try to fucking explain it. Just accept it. You want her, and she wants you. Lord knows why? But everyone knows, I'm surprised somebody hasn't started a pool on when you're gonna ask her out."

"Whatta ya mean, everybody knows?"

"Everybody knows Frankie, *everybody.*"

Frank looked out over the river from the deck behind the warehouse. He was running motivations through his head, while Dave stood beside him doing the same. They did this joint thinking thing occasionally where they both ran theories through their heads a few times, until one of them would develop an idea and break the silence. Hopefully with something insightful.

This time, it was Hanson who snapped the lull.

"I can buy the homosexual angle, but why kill men? Is he jealous? Does he enjoy it? What is his motivation?"

"He's enjoying it. He has to be. Why else would he wait for him to recover before giving him the pony ride? He's clearly punishing them with the sex. I bet he talks to them while he's doing it."

"So, is he enjoying the sex or the fact that he's punishing them? And, is he actually punishing them, or are they substitutes for someone else?"

"Good question. They could be a representation of someone, his father who beat his mother, or for abusing women, by treating them like women, in his perspective, especially if he's aware of their history."

"Or both. What if it's both?"

"Okay, let's put the motive aside for a minute. I've got another question. Who's next?"

Dave hesitated briefly. "It'll be male, and an abuser of some sort, probably of women."

"I agree. So, let's track some most recent high-profile assholes, who either walked or is free on bond, and we might figure out who the next target might be."

"That could be a long list." Hanson explained in a tone almost embarrassed to be a man. "With the men around here, shit. We don't know what criteria he is using to judge by, does he have to see it happen for himself, or just read about it somewhere?"

"Let's cross-reference the two losers we got. See if anyone knew both of them."

"You mean other than Doctor Jim?"

"Yeah. Other than Doctor Jim. If this guy's not getting his info first hand, I want to know how he is collecting his stats."

"He either knows these people or is well-read. Great, we have an intelligent psycho on our hands."

"So, what else is new? Why is it that although the average crook is getting dumber, the average murderer seems to be smarter?"

"Maybe we're getting dumber, Frank."

"Speak for yourself, Dave."

"Hey I'm not the one who won't go out with the most beautiful coroner in the world, even though she's made it obvious that she wants you."

"Carrie makes me feel like a moron around her."

"She's a fucking Yale grad in forensic science and medicine. Next to her, you are a moron."

"Gee, thanks Dave."

"Think about if Frankie, she's practically a genius for Christ's sake, but she doesn't care. She likes you the way you are."

"Stupid and unrefined?"

"Street smart and unrefined. Heavy on the unrefined."

"And how would you describe Carrie?"

"Oh, now we're getting into a danger zone."

"What's that supposed to mean?"

"Don't make me describe her, Frankie. She's hot as shit, but she never gave me the time of day, 'cuz she don't like us pasty guys. She prefers you olive-skinned Latin lover types, with Mediterranean blood."

"What the hell could she want with me? I'm ten years older than her."

"So, what, Frankie. She likes you. Go for it."

"She's just infatuated for some reason."

"Hello, Frankie Carmine" Hanson said waving his hand in front of Frank's face. "Are you in there? What ever happened to the love'em and leave'em, happily divorced, never want another relationship, Frankie? If I didn't know better, I'd swear you're worried about whether or not this could work long term."

"Well, shit, Dave. Would you want to start something with Carrie only to have it fall apart in six months?"

"Are you gonna live your life based on bad things that might happen, or good shit that might happen?"

"It's not that simple Dave."

"Yes, it is. I'll tell you want. I'm going to the shelter and talk to Karen Alexander, and you go check what Carrie has, and if I get a date before you do, I'm kicking your ass."

Frank chuckled to himself as he started to walk away. "You better bring a friend."

TEN

Dave Hanson pulled up to the woman's shelter. Jim Whistler was in private practice on Tuesday's, so he wouldn't be there except for emergencies. Besides, he wasn't there to visit him, he wanted to talk to Karen, but he had to be careful. He was clearly trying to mix business with pleasure, and knew it was a slippery road at best. Taking a deep breath as he stood on the porch, he raised his hand to knock on the newly repaired door. When it opened, she appeared in front of him in all her subdued glory. His smile was involuntary and genuine.

"Detective Hanson, to what do we owe the honor of your presence today?"

"Well, I wish I could say it was solely that quiet allure of yours, but I'm afraid there's a little more to my visit."

"So, I do have more than a quiet allure?" Driving it home with a coy smile.

"Hmm," he stalled, but recovered quickly. "I thought that much was obvious to everyone."

"Come on in Detective. We can talk in the office."

One of the best things about having a woman lead you to another room is the ability to completely check her out without her seeing you do it, providing you stop before you arrive at the destination. Karen liked her clothes a little on the loose side. She was not heavy, but she wore her outfits in such a way as to hide the curves of her true outline. This left the exact details to Dave's mind, and he was painting them in with a positive light. He was sure that beneath her mildly tapered sundress was an exquisite form of a woman who took care of her body. After all, we are talking about a woman he'd seen cold cock a guy with one punch. Unlike Frank, he liked women with an independent streak. They never get attached too soon.

She led him into the office, closed the door behind them, and pointed to a large comfortable chair. It looked like it belonged in a living room instead of a place of business. It was practically a recliner, giving the room the feel of a small apartment.

"Nice Wingback," as he settled in. "Not exactly typical office furniture."

"That's our soft chair. The last thing one of our guests' needs is to sit at an uncomfortable desk and fill out paperwork, so we have a comfy one."

"Interesting, does it work?"

"I think so. It makes them more comfortable, and we do strive for that here."

Dave looked at her for a long moment, thinking about pleasure because the business part was going to be unpleasant. She did have a way of drawing you in slowly until you weren't sure if you were paying attention. He leaned in closer to her.

"Can I ask you something?"

"Sure, you're the detective. You ask questions. We give answers. Isn't that how this works?"

Her smile encouraged him.

"This one's kind of, unrelated." Treading carefully.

She pitched towards him, mocking his body language in a way that only drew him in further.

"Can we have dinner sometime? You and me?"

"Can I pick the restaurant?"

"Sure. Absolutely"

"I have expensive tastes." Giving him fair warning with a smile.

"No problem. I stashed away a little nest egg away for just such an occasion."

"Fine, then. There's this new place on the water I've been meaning to try, they even have 5.9% financing."

Unable to decipher her looks yet, Dave was caught off guard and it showed. Karen laughed out loud at his reaction.

"I'm kidding." Savoring her joke. "I know a great little place, but not too fancy."

"How's Friday night, sound?"

"I am on duty here Friday. Would Thursday work for you?"

"Sure, Thursday's good. Seven-ish"

"Sure, touch base with me here Wednesday afternoon to confirm."

"Excellent, I'll call you then."

"Okay, so now the pleasure area is settled." Adopting a more formal tone, preparing her for more bad news. "Let's do the business thing."

"Yes, well, I'm not going to beat around the bush on this," slipping back into the chair. "We found another body."

"I figured as much for you to come here. Same details?"

"Oh, yeah. Jay Lockhart, the name ring a bell?"

"Wait, isn't he the guy Jim fought with last week?"

"Same jerk, only now there isn't much fight left in him."

"You don't think..."

"No. Not at all." He cut her off. "We don't think Dr. Jim is involved. But there is the possibility that the killer knows him, or agrees with his work. He might be trying to impress him, or just punish these men."

"Not that they wouldn't deserve to be punished."

"Hey, I've got no problem with this guy's choice of victims. In all honesty, we're going to be better off without them. My concern is they may be a substitute for who he really wants to hurt."

"He? So, you think the murderer is a guy?"

"We're about ninety percent sure, but we haven't confirmed it yet."

"So, you think the killer is acting out against someone or some ones in his life. If true, the person responsible for turning them to murder could be just as deserving as the victims, only he can't bring himself to kill them for some reason."

"Very good point, but we can't be sure. We need to find this guy, so we can be certain. I'm afraid of what might happen when he can't find any guys who do not merit his attention as much as the current casualties."

"What if he starts lowering the requirements?"

"Exactly. What if beating women, suddenly becomes only yelling at a woman in public? You can't kill people for lack of manners or upbringing."

"Okay, what's the profile so far? How can we help?" Showing genuine concern.

"Well, the obvious thing, as of now, is he's taking down abusers of women."

"His one redeeming quality to date."

"Agreed, but he's also sodomizing them first, and making sure they're awake for it, then killing them brutally."

"So, you think he's gay and identifying with females being beaten?"

"That is one theory for right now. We probably won't know for sure until we catch him."

"If you catch him?"

"No, it's a matter of when. Killers leave clues, and we're already working out his profile. The first two victims had highly visible cases of abuse. They were both in the papers. But we also want to see if they had any mutual friends, or enemies."

"Did you ask Dr. Jim?"

"About Dr. Jim," He proceeded gingerly. "I have the feeling if this killer isn't personally involved with his targets, or their victims, and isn't punishing them directly, one of the next logical possibilities is that they might be trying to impress the doctor."

"Why would they want do that? Do they want him to validate them somehow?"

"They could be sympathizing with both his sexuality and accomplishments championing women."

"I wouldn't exactly call it championing them, as much as it's more like picking up pieces and rebuilding their confidence."

"That may be closer to the truth unfortunately, but a lot of people consider you and him heroes for the work you do. Granted this theory is a little far-fetched, but we don't know for sure what's motivating this guy, and we need to examine any possibility we can fathom."

"Wait, you want me to spy on Dr. Jim's friends?"

"NO. No. Not at all. In my experience, quite often people are oblivious to others around them who may hold them in high esteem, and sometimes do things they normally wouldn't to sway them or win their favor."

"So, you're saying I would be more aware of a person who's trying to impress the doc."

"Exactly. Distance lends enchantment, and occasionally clarity of vision. This is not my favorite theory, but in this regard, I think you would be able to see it before Dr. Jim would."

Karen just nodded for a moment considering his words. She didn't like the implication the killer could be trying to faze Jim in some way, but at the same time she had to acknowledge the outside possibility of his theory.

"Okay." Reluctantly agreeing in principle. "I'll keep my eyes open, and I run some references checks between the women involved with the two victims and see if anyone shows up on both lists."

"Excellent. The more angles we cover the more likely we are to finding this scumbag."

"You're sure you can catch this guy?"

"We'll get him." Again, with conviction.

"Before his next victim?"

"I hope so," Knowing their chances were slim to none. "I hope so."

ELEVEN

Frank stood in the hall outside the medical examiner's office. He always collects himself before he goes in, but knowing Carrie was expecting him made him even more nervous than normal. You never knew what or who might be laid out on a gurney when he came through the door. Shaking off the willies, he took a deep breath and entered the morgue.

He breathed a sigh of relief when he didn't find anybody halfway through an autopsy when he invaded the room, but she was nowhere in sight. Crossing the exam room he peaked into the office, but she was not there either.

"Looking for someone, Frank?" He heard in a sly low tone, so close to his ear her warm breath swirled around his lobe.

"Jesus!" He exclaimed, focusing all his energy on not jumping out of his skin. Trying to remain cool, he slowly turned around to find Carrie's beautiful face mere inches from his, smiling like the cat that ate the canary.

"You're not afraid of little ole me are you now?" She purred seductively playing with the lapel of his jacket.

"I bet you enjoyed the hell out of that didn't you?" Hiding his exasperation.

"I do believe, Mr. Carmine," Whispering as she moved in close enough for him to smell her perfume. Its clean, crisp scent raising his blood pressure a few more notches. "That was the first time I've ever seen you excited."

"You've never seen my face when you call me then." The words slipped out before he could stop them. He didn't mean to say that out loud, although they were true.

"So, my voice excites you?" Relishing the revelation, while moving in closer to him.

"I'm not saying it does, and I'm not saying it doesn't." While he looked around in the manor he used when looking for clues, and not a brief break in a promising conversation.

A small chill ran down Frank's spine as he realized he was still standing in the morgue. He scanned the room quickly, and it hit him. Everything suddenly caught his attention, the autopsy table, the cabinets full of dead people, the medicinal odor. Forcibly he snapped himself out of it, then stepped back to look at her and smiled almost feebly.

"You just remembered you're in the morgue, didn't you? Oh well, come on in the office."

She didn't wait for an answer as she walked into the room expecting him to follow. Frank gave her a head start, so he could watch her walk across the room with that confident strut of hers that drove him crazy. He was fully entranced with her stride when she stopped in the doorway and turned to him quickly. It took some effort not to run right into her and even more so to hide his embarrassment at being caught in the act.

"You do realize..." Using her sultry voice while playing with his collar again. "This would be far less stressful if you'd simply admit you like me, Frank."

"Everyone likes you, Carrie. Every male over the age of 13, and probably a few early bloomers too. Oh, and lesbians, well the ones whose vision works."

"Hmm, you might need to work on your compliments," She bemoaned, then turned and headed into the office in a defeated posture.

He followed her into the small room. She grabbed a file off the desk, sat down with the folder, and pushed the other chair towards him with her leg. Frank tried not to gawk at the tone of her outstretched limb.

"Sit," She commanded in her firm but inoffensive way.

"Yes ma'am." He obeyed albeit sarcastically.

"Now you're learning." Smiling widely, she crossed her legs. "I have the final reports on your two ponies?"

"My what?" Completely missing the reference.

"You know, the pony rides. The ones on the bottom. White males, deep throat wounds..."

"Oh, oh, the ponies. I get it. What's the scoop?"

"Apparently, I owe you dinner. We're definitely looking for a man. The sodomy was evidently unprotected sex. We were able to catch a few skin cells, but not enough to run a gene trace, but they're absolutely male, type "0" blood, and Caucasian. Where have you been the past few nights, Frank?"

"Don't worry they weren't my type."

"I'm beginning to think you don't like females either."

"Ha, ha, ha." He deadpanned. "Anything else new?" Picking up a small toy off the desk to fidget with.

"Not really. Right-hander, around six foot tall. This knife is not only sharp, but strong to make these kinds of deep cuts. It is definitely a straight edge, as there is no evidence of a serrated blade."

"Like a shaving razor?"

"Maybe, but it could be any large well-made, precision knife. Offhand, I'd say about seven or eight inches in length, like a good man."

Frank dropped the toy on the floor as the words unfolded in his head. Damn she loves doing that, he thought. After three attempts, he actually retrieves the novelty from the cold tiles. When he finally picked up the knickknack, and looked up she was just staring at him smiling.

"What's the matter, Frank?" She cooed mischievously. "Jealous?"

"Wouldn't you like to know?" Standing up and placing the gadget back on the table. "You got anything else or did you want to see how long you can keep me off guard."

"Oh, but it's so much fun to see you squirm."

"I'm sure it is. I'm known worldwide for my squirming ability."

She smiled at his comical rebound.

"One last thing; dinner, my house, tomorrow 7pm. A bet's a bet."

"You wouldn't rather a nice restaurant where you don't have to do dishes?"

"I prefer the home court advantage." As she scribbled on a pad. "Seven o'clock Frank, if you don't show, remember; I do know how to make a death look like an accident."

"Are you threatening a police officer?" Playing along jokingly, knowing full well he wound be at her place a half hour early, only to wait until five minutes to the hour before he'll knock on the door. It would take a team of wild horses to make him late. He was finally going to be alone with her. It both excited and scared him.

"Frank, let's be honest, shall we?" She rose gracefully and she glided over to him. Her hypnotic eyes peering directly into his sole, as she tucked the little piece of paper in his shirt pocket. "You've been threatened by me since the day we met."

"Ouch." Defensively slipping away hopefully his sense of honor intact. "Ouch"

"Seven o'clock, Frank. Don't be late." She called after him as he exited the office.

"I'll be there. I can't wait to see what you whip up for dinner."

As he walked out leaving Carrie leaning against her desk, trying to decide whether he'd actually show up. Of course, he would, she thought to herself, smiling.

"And wear something that comes off easy." She mumbled, with a devilish smirk.

TWELVE

He watched them for some fifteen minutes, the two young lovers on the bench next to his. They had obviously chosen this spot for the same reason as him. Except for the other matching one offset beside it, they were nearly invisible to the rest of the waterfront park. They faced out looking over the river. The young adults carried on oblivious to the older man reading a magazine mere yards from them on the other loveseat. Secluded from prying eyes by the riverfront foliage, and feeling secure in the man's attention being paid to his periodical, they kissed passionately.

Out of the corner of his eye, he reveled in the prospect of young love. All is right in the world when sweethearts meet. Events only ten feet away do not exist when you're in the arms of a lover, and he smirked to himself as he peeked into their world. They caressed openly, in the shade of the large oak tree that darkened both benches. Fully, unaware of him cautiously spying on them as they embraced and fondled each other, becoming bolder and more daring in the sanctuary of their love. On and off he found himself secretly watching them, as he began to kiss her neck and rub her back. Hiding his clandestine nosiness, he witnessed her returned his affections in kind. It reminded him of his youth, which brought a frown to his face.

It was so long ago when he was the age of these lovers, when his heart was so full of love for a woman, he thought his chest would explode. All day his thoughts would be filled of her until the very moment he would see her again. The plans he made. The dreams he had. It was all so far away now. For a second, he could almost feel the good times, the walks in the fresh snow longing for summer, the cool evenings on the porch in fall talking about possible names for children, the promise of a future together. The good feelings of those moments came flooding back, but those days are over.

She took it all away.

He was so lost in his memories that he almost hadn't noticed the couple's rising voices. Their playful loving had evolved into an escalating argument. They separated on the bench. Their words became louder as they moved away from each other, placing a space barrier between them to match the sudden rift in their relationship. What happened he thought? They were just kissing.

Their ire rose until he could distinguish every word they were saying, no longer trying to hide themselves from the world.

"You called me Kathy!" Jumping up anger.

"I'm sorry. It just slipped out."

"You still want her! I bet you're still sleeping her, aren't you!?" Letting out her rage.

"I'm not seeing her anymore," His voice starting to rise. "I haven't seen her in weeks."

"Weeks!? Weeks!? You said it was over months ago. Now you're saying it's only been a few weeks?"

"It has been over for months." He explained. "I saw her a few weeks ago, and we only talked a little bit, nothing happened."

"I don't believe you."

"That's your fucking problem." Getting unexpectedly loud. "You never trusted me."

"You cheated on me. I had good reason not to trust you. Even after you said it was over with her, my girlfriends kept seeing you together."

"Fuck those bitches. They never liked me. They're trying to break us up!"

"Don't call my friends, bitches. They had every right to tell me what you were doing. If you had been faithful, then they wouldn't have had anything to tell me to begin with."

"We're not married. What do you fucking own me now, or something?"

His words stopped her dead in her tracks, as her face became a stern scowl, and her voice dropped to a slow steady pace.

"You're right. We're not married, and from now on we're not anything you lying sack of shit." She turned to leave. He grabbed her hand and pulled her back.

"Don't you walk away from me, bitch!"

When she yanked her arm away from him violently, and he backhanded her roughly. She was more shocked than hurt as the fire flared up in her eyes.

"Nobody hits me mister."

"Oh, yeah." Raising his hand to strike her a second time.

At the top of his back swing the man snatched his wrist. He spun the young man around and punched him in the face. The blow sent the young man sprawling backwards over the bench and into the grass. The older man moved in quickly and placed his foot on man's throat, as he lay dazed on the ground, while the girl stared in amazement at the stranger defending her honor.

"I'm going to give you one chance to apologize to this woman for hitting her." The man said in a calm, but deliberate manner, with pure fire in his eyes.

"Fuck you, old man." He spewed out defiantly.

The man shifted his weight to his one leg, cutting off the young man's breathing. Leaning over him, and squatted down close so only his captive heard him speak.

"You will apologize to this woman," He whispered firmly. "Then learn some manners, because if I ever hear about you striking another woman, I will snap your neck, and they'll find you floating in the river. Do you understand me?"

The young man couldn't talk with the man's heft on his voice box, but he nodded yes. The man took his foot off his throat and addressed the girl.

"Ma'am, I think he wants to apologize now."

She approached slowly, as her former paramour rubbed his neck to soothe it.

"I'm sorry I hit you." Mumbling, and barely audible.

"I'm afraid to think how far you might have gone if this man wasn't here?" Still shaken as she spoke. "Would you have beat me up, or worse? I don't want to think about that, but I can tell you this; we are done as any sort of couple." She turned to man. "I don't know who you are, but thank you."

"It's a shame I was even necessary ma'am." Showing compassion. "Some men don't know how to treat a woman properly anymore."

"Maybe you could give lessons." She suggested.

He leaned in to her, "I think I just did."

She smiled and touched the man on the arm, and walked away without another word.

The younger man was still rubbing his throat, as he looked up at his elder standing over him with a menacing look.

"Who the hell are you, man?"

"I am a man who knows the consequences of men who beat women, and I'm trying to ensure it doesn't happen again."

Without warning the older man kicked the young man in the side of the head knocking him unconscious. He looked down at the youngster sprawled out in the morning dew.

"You've been warned."

THIRTEEN

Frank and Dave strolled out the front door of the police station. The late afternoon sun angled down on them harshly, as they made way for their vehicles. They had run out of clues for the day and needed to rejuvenate. Tomorrow, they would tackle it anew, but they were no longer thinking solely of the case. Not today.

"No way," Dave said as they walked down the stone steps. "She just ordered you to be at her house tonight? Oh, that is fucking priceless."

"The whole thing was a setup." Frank explained. "I bet she knew it was a guy right from the start, and made the bet knowing I couldn't discount her instincts. Either way she gets what she wanted; this is one smart woman."

"She's too smart for you, Frankie. She ordered you to show up. Freaking classic. I love it."

"And without a shred of doubt in her mind I would be there too. If it was anyone other than Carrie, I wouldn't show up to spite her."

"You are the only person alive who gets upset over a beautiful chick throwing herself at her." Laughing out loud. "I guess you're just going to have to fuck her."

"Fuck who?" A female voice interrupted their conversation.

Looking up, they are both stopped in their tracks by Sarah wielding a microphone with a cameraman in tow.

"The Statue of Liberty." Frank joked flatly. "I figure someone owes her a good fuck."

"So why are they letting you do it?" She shot back.

"Nice talking to you anchor lady." He walked around her without stopping, focused on the future, and the rest of his evening. She was his past. All he was thinking about now is Carrie.

"Okay. Okay. Truce. I only want to do a few questions on the murders."

"Ask Dave." Barely even acknowledging her as he opened the door to his IROC, parked directly in front of the station. "You haven't insulted him yet."

Frank gets into his Trans-am and drives off. He never notices the man in his early fifties sitting at the bus stop, observing the whole scene. Who turns clandestinely from the car to the remaining participants of the conversation.

"One of these days, you two are gonna get over each other."

"Fuck you, Dave." Spit out of her mouth without missing a beat.

"If that's a proposition, sure. If that's an insult, no interview for you."

"Jesus Christ, Sarah." Her cameraman jumped in. "Just once can we come to the police station without you pissing off someone?"

"I like this guy. Who'd you piss off to end up shooting for this one?"

"If I knew I wouldn't be here." Mumbling loud enough to be heard.

Hansen laughed heartily, as she shot a dirty look at her sidekick.

"Okay, Dave." Sarah refocusing on her task at hand. "How about a couple of questions for the news?"

"Okay, but only if this guy gets a raise. Keep them general, there's not much to report, and let's try to make it seem promising?"

"Sure, sure." She agreed.

"How's my hair look?" Pantomiming comically while coiffing his hair.

"Actually, not bad today, Dave."

"Good answer. Alright, shoot."

"I'm rolling." The cameraman starting the videotape. "Whenever you're ready."

"We're here with Detective Dave Hansen, one of the detectives working on the recent murders of two men. Detective, is it true both men had a history of beating woman?"

"Yes, they did." He answered calmly knowing damn well they hadn't released that yet, but he'd be damned if he let her take credit for scooping anything new. "We've been using that information in our profiling of the killer."

"So, is there an established profile for the killer?"

"At this point the profile is not complete, however we are sure of the details we have, and the investigation is moving forward."

"Are there any suspects currently, Detective?"

"We are following several leads at this time, but it would be premature and possibly damaging to the case to reveal any further specifics at this time. We are looking for a white male, over six feet tall, but the rest of the profile is incomplete at this time."

"Can we expect an arrest anytime soon?"

"We'll make an arrest as soon as humanly possible." Nodding in the positive to drive his point home.

"Thank you, Detective." Turning to the camera to close the interview. "As you can see, the investigation is continuing in hopes of bringing this killer to justice as Detective Hansen said "as soon as possible". This is Sarah Gennaro reporting for channel five."

"We're clear." The lens man reported. "Tapes fine."

The photographer immediately headed back to their van.

"Sarah Gennaro?" Dave asked. "Does Frankie know you went back to using your maiden name?"

"He does if he's watched the news this week." She replied. "You guys don't have squat, do you?"

"We have some definitive leads, but nothing solid. Did you tell him, or figure he'd see it on the evening news?"

"My name's been Gennaro on paper ever since the divorce. Now it's Gennaro on the air."

"Fine. Say hi to Joey for me. He's a good kid." As he began to back-peddle out of the conversation. "Oh, and say hi to Michael too."

"Michael who?" Acting innocent in regard to the statement.

"Please, Sarah. We're detectives. Did you think he wouldn't find out you're dating someone?"

"So, what's the big deal?"

He stopped for a moment, and walked back to her.

"You know what? It's not a big deal. Which means you don't have to hide it like you're doing something wrong. You're not dating in high school anymore, you're divorced. I freely acknowledge that Frank needs to grow up, but so do you. And, you should have told him you went back to your maiden name. It's not like it wasn't expected. I'm surprised you didn't do it sooner, but to make him learn about this on the air is childish. You two, you never get tired of taking shots at each other instead of going on with your lives."

She absorbed his words for a long moment, but nodded somberly in agreement.

"For a jerk, Dave. You have your moments."

"Yeah, me and Frank take turns. This is Frank's week to be the jerk, in case you couldn't tell."

He turns and walks away to a side lot where his car is parked. She heads back to the van where the cameraman is already loaded up and in the driver's seat ready to go.

As she reaches the vehicle, the man on the bench speaks up.

"I've seen you on the news. You're a good reporter."

"Thank you." Invoking her '*do I know you*' tone.

"You we're married to a cop? That must help in your profession."

"Not after you divorce him." Not sure why she was volunteering information to a stranger.

"I'm sorry to hear that, Ma'am." With an inflection of compassion that made her believe him. "You're a beautiful, talented woman. I'm sure there is a long list of men who would be honored to be part of your life."

"I'd better go. I need to file this report so you can see on the news tonight" Grabbing the handle to the van's door. "Thank you for the compliments, but I'm afraid If I stay here much longer, I don't think my ego won't fit in the van."

"Continued success to you, Miss Gennaro." Giving a slight wave and supportive smile.

She nodded politely and got in the vehicle. As they drove away, he had mixed feelings about his little outing today.

He came to the police station with the hopes of finding out who the detectives are that were assigned to catch him. Of course, he was not planning any action against them, to the best of his knowledge they are just men doing an honorable job with little thanks. And, he had no plans to harm the cops put in charge of hunting him, unless it became absolutely necessary. It was important that he determine their identities. They wouldn't understand his mission, but it would be very beneficial to know who they are, and now he did.

Surprisingly, he learned more than he planned. Who was this one named, Frank? How could he leave a beautiful woman like Sarah? There was something about him he didn't like already. He couldn't say for sure if he was an abuser, but he obviously doesn't know how to treat a woman. What man in his right mind would let someone like her get away from him? Or did she send him away?

What disturbed him the most was that they had a child together, a boy. Detective Hansen said his name was Joey. Was he really a good kid, or was he being polite?

The questions circled around his head. He only wanted to glean who to be wary of, but now he perceived so much more. Perhaps too much. It was clear some research is required. There are reasons a strong beautiful woman like that is single, and most of them aren't encouraging. A few of them are downright punishable. For the sake of the boy, he hoped that was not the case.

But deep down inside, part of him hoped they were.

FOURTEEN

Frank Carmine stood outside Carrie's apartment, working up his courage. A man who's faced down drug addicts with semi-automatic weapons, is now pacing himself silly in the hallway of an alluring woman. What made his indecision worse, is that he's always wanted her. From the moment he first saw her, he was swept away by her beauty. The quiet confidence and intelligence she projected mystified him. So beautiful and smart it scared him, which he had never admitted to himself until this very moment. Why did she scare him? Was he afraid of having her and losing her, like he did with Sarah? Did he really lose Sarah or did he let her go when she stopped believing in him? What did go wrong with his marriage? It might have been both of their careers being so successful, or did they stop working at being a couple? And why the hell was he trying to figure this out right now, standing in the hall in front of his dream woman's apartment?

He tightened his grip on the two bottles of wine, and started to give himself a pep talk. Jesus! Pull yourself together. She's just a woman he tried to tell himself. Yeah, and a Rolls Royce is just a car. For emotional support he leaned up against the wall across from her door, and took a deep breath. Inside he finally conceded how much he wanted her, and that she scares him, now to face down the fear.

He was shaking the bugs out of his head by jumping up and down wriggling his limbs like he used to do before stepping into the batter's box in softball, when the door swung open to reveal Carrie smirking widely like the cat that ate the canary. She fought back the urge to laugh.

"You coming in champ, or you gonna wait for the trainer?" In a seductive tone that hid her amusement.

"I'm already trained." He managed fighting off the embarrassment. "I'm even house broken."

"That good. I just had the carpets cleaned."

She propped herself up against the door in a shortcut, black, spaghetti strap dress that clung to her body like it was hand made for her by Versace himself. It took a concerted force of will to not to drool on her as he eased by her into the apartment. As he entered, she felt like a heat source as their bodies passed in close proximity to each other, and the heat was on full blast. Her perfume woke up his senses, feminine with a hint of strength, but not overpowering, the perfect scent for her.

The residence was well cared for, decorated in a sharp mix of old-world charm and new age flair, and medicinally clean. A new and delicious bouquet now dominated his nostrils, as it slowly overpowered the faint fumes of her scent. He couldn't quite identify it, but it smelled fantastic.

"I don't know which smells better." Holding out the bottles of vino. "That fragrance of yours, or whatever that aroma is coming from the kitchen."

"Do you need a little help making up your mind?"

Carrie took the bubbly and put them on the table, already set with dinner candles. Then, she slithered right up to him, tilting her head and positioning her neck mere inches from his waiting sniffer.

"First, take a full whiff of the perfume." She whispered in his ear, as she moved in closer to him, placing her hands on his chest.

Instinctively Frank gripped her hips with a firm but tender hold. He could feel her palms involuntarily massaging his bosom as he inhaled deeply, his nose savoring her cologne now wafting through his ole factory senses. His breath flowed across her neck, making her tingle and the tiny hairs straighten fully in the balmy breeze. The body heat was scintillating and comforting.

"Mmmm," He murmured as he pulled her a little closer. "That's nice."

Sliding her hands down to his side, and lightly pressing herself to him, she felt her breasts press-up against him, and basked in the strength of his sturdy frame. He tightened his hold on her, until her warmth and sweet odors were making his faculties swirl. Frank moved forward and gently pressed his lips against the smooth skin of hiding her pulsating jugular vein. She didn't say anything as he began to place small kisses on her nape, she wanted him to continue. Ever so slowly she pulled him in, until she had her arms all the way around him.

"I hope the food tastes this good." Kissing her between the words. His right arm slipped around her to feeling the contour of her spine down to the small of the back. Without thinking, his left hand came up to hold her head, as his neck kisses got more passionate.

He tilted her head back to gaze at her. She left him speechless. Not knowing what to say, as he wanted to say something clever or romantic or profound. But, like always, she read his mind. She placed a finger on his lips.

"Ssssssssh." She teased, never letting her eyes stray from his. "We're done talking."

He stared into the emerald depths of her eyes and everything else vanished from his consciousness. The killings, the job, his family, his partner, they all became distant memories pushed aside by the captivating patterns of her eyes. They were entrancing, then she smiled. Her white teeth added to the glow of her already radiant face that made his heart melt. What kind of asshole was he to have kept himself away from such beauty? That is never going to happen again.

He traced the outline of her face with his hands. Her skin, soft to his touch, sent electricity through his fingers. She leaned her head in, increasing the friction of his caress. His hands held her face as he moved in slowly, staring into her eyes until their lips met, so delicate and gentle at first. Just enjoying every light touch of their mouths and tongues, with growing strength and passion until they were locked in a steamy kiss that would make cupid blush.

Frank ran his hands up and down her back. He loved the small of a woman's back, and hers had a well-defined dip that drove him crazy. Working his fingertips up her back, they found her smooth inviting shoulders. It became all too apparent now that she was not wearing a bra, and that knowledge pushed his blood pressure to new heights, in all the right places.

She hugged him tightly as she kissed him back with two years of deferred desire. All of her waiting led her to this moment, and he wasn't getting away. His arousal became obvious as she compressed herself against him, her breasts flattening against his chest. The warmth and the security of his arms around her was intoxicating. Every possibility was planned for, even the meal she prepared was chosen for its ability to survive if made to simmer for a long period of time, should it be unexpectedly postponed. It was clear their supper would be delayed. She now had every intention of making sure that transpired.

His hands were inside what little fabric made up the back of her dress. She pulled back ever so slightly using his fingers to catch the minuscule straps and slipped her out of the apparel on both sides.

She looked at him with a devilish smile. Frank was smitten. This woman owned him now.

Suddenly aware that the only reason her frock hadn't dropped to the floor yet was his fingers holding the diminutive strands, he arched back to enjoy the view and let go. The fabric rippled down the curves of her body outlining every curve as it slid down to her ankles in a heap. He swallowed hard standing in front of a woman he had fantasized about for two years now, only this time she was truly in the flesh.

He couldn't help himself from taking a long lustful look at her tantalizing form. Her face was touched by heaven, and her body shimmered like silk. Still wearing her stiletto pumps, she was tall for a woman. She stood eye to eye with him in her slinky high heels. Her skin was meticulously, and her breasts fit her body perfectly, full but not big. They highlighted the remaining contours of her figure to perfection. Frank almost stopped breathing as he let his eyes run down the full length of her figure. He salivated over her beautiful bust and rosy red nipples. His eyes lingered surveying her inviting body, down across her flat stomach to the patch of bright crimson hair, now beckoning at him like a soft fire in need of stoking. Even her legs seemed more exquisite fully exposed, save her high heels that accented the definition of her toned calves and thighs.

She let him stare for an extended moment, after all, she yearned for him to look all along. Her long-stifled desire for him to run his hands over her skin like this finally coming to fruition. She had him where she wanted. Oh, she knew she had him now, body and soul. Her smiled widened.

"I am so going to kick my ass for waiting so long." He stammered almost inaudibly.

Casually she reached over and turned down the oven to the warm setting.

"Dinner can wait."

Carrie eased back, so he could bask in the full view of her body from head to toe, and stepped out of the dress. Her face lit up at his reaction, then turning to the bedroom, she put out one hand to Frank.

Without a word he placed his hand in hers, and she walked him into the back room. A large wrought iron canopy bed dominated the center and focal points of the boudoir. It was piled high with pillows. When she led him to the edge of the bed, he reached up to undo his collar, but she stopped him.

"Please, let me."

She slowly unbuttoned Frank's shirt kissing each new inch of skin as it was revealed to her. Then peeled it off his shoulders, she threw it on an overstuffed chair nearby.

"Frankie, Frankie, Frankie." Her hands running all over his chest. "Why did it take you so long to come around?"

"I got hit in the head a lot when I was a kid."

She sat back down on the mattress as she peeled his pants off, and was nearly struck in the face as he sprung out of his trousers.

"Hmm." She cooed. "That would explain the swelling."

He had dozens of comebacks for that, but he couldn't speak. He finally knew when to keep his mouth shut.

Carrie was sure she could have managed any number of great tag lines of her own, but like she had said earlier, she was done talking.

FIFTEEN

"Where was it written that gay men have to be experts on food?" Gordon asked as he and Jim walked down the street after dining out together. "The waiter, who was so obviously over the top gay, acted like I disgraced the entire homosexual nation because I didn't know what Crème Brûlée is made of."

"I'm so glad you asked," Jim said laughing out loud. "Because to tell you the truth, I still have no idea what they put in it."

"Oh, so that explains the, *'hey, Gordon how about some Crème Brûlée'* when he asked about desert. You set me up."

"I'm sorry. I've eaten it for years, but I've been dying to know what is in that stuff." Between laughs. "I can't believe the guy went postal because you didn't know."

"Freeze, gay police," Pulling an imaginary gun. "Name three songs by Judy Garland, and the ingredients to Crème Brûlée."

They both laughed leaning on each other for a moment.

"Aside from the gay Mafia waiter the food was damn good," Jim looking around. "Although, not the best part of town anymore."

Most of the storefronts on this end of the street bore closed signs. There still remained an eclectic mix of second-hand stores, head shops, and corner boutiques. Still, the area held a slight semblance of what the neighborhood had once been. It covered a few blocks along the river, in what was once the cultural center of the city. All that existed before the mall opened, and ran them out of business. The block now stood like a skeleton of a once proud village still clinging to some essence of importance.

"This neighborhood used to be the place to be," Gordon recalled. "Look at these old buildings. They have so much more character than the crap they design now."

"Hey, be careful. My boyfriend is an architect. Don't make me kick your ass."

"I don't mean my work, I meant other architect-" Stopping mid-sentence and staring at Jim, smirking. "Boyfriend? Have I met him?"

"I don't think so. You would definitely remember him. Tall, dark, handsome," Moving in close and whispering. "And, hung like a horse."

"Flattery will get you anything."

"What do I have to say to get you to come back to my place?"

"On a weeknight, hmm. I suppose, a heartfelt please would be enough."

Jim placed a hand on each of his shoulders. "Gordon, please come stay at my house tonight."

"I was hoping you'd ask me. It would be the proper way to finish a great night out."

They embraced for a moment, enjoying the feeling of closeness deepening between the two of them. Jim had been looking for this exact sensation his whole life, and although everything felt so right, it scared him. What if it goes away? What if it falls apart because of him? What if he can't keep him happy?

Before he could answer, a woman's scream broke up their embrace. They turned to find a young woman in her early twenties being followed by a man roughly the same age. They both dressed in a Gothic punk, mostly black and leather fashion.

"I said, fuck off, Carl. You piece of shit!" The girl screamed at him and walked away.

"So now I'm shit, huh?" He replied. "You didn't think I was shit last week while you were sucking my dick."

"I was fucking drunk you idiot." She fired back him. "I would have blown your father if he kept buying me drinks."

The words carried down the empty street. They looked at each other and shook their heads almost in unison.

"Dungeon Lounge crowd." Gordon explained. "It's right around the corner."

"That old punk place is still open? Go figure. Every other bar on the block is gone."

"Well, some of that is in part due to the Dungeon Lounge. People who hung out at the other bars got tired of crossing paths with the Dungeon's crowd. They finally stopped coming down here."

They turned to watch the couple across the street. Gordon stared at Jim with intensity waiting to see if they should get involved. The encounter had already flared up his hackles. Jim dedicating his life to defending women and others in need, is one of the things he loved about him. He watched his eyes as he studied the situation debating whether or not to step in, having complete faith in Jim's decisions in this matter.

It felt like watching your hero do what made him famous, but on a smaller scale.

"What do you think, Jim?"

"I'm not sure yet. So hard to tell with the way some people talk to each other nowadays."

The man pulled the girls arm turning her around to face him.

"I got twice the dick my old man has." Thinking this would help his position.

"Couldn't have been very big or I'd remember." Trying to pull away from him.

"Well, maybe I need to refresh your memory, bitch." Pulling her close to him. "I should give it to you right here."

"That's it." Jim began to cross the road toward them.

"I got your back." Gordon fell in lock step with him.

"Let go, Carl ya fuck." Her agitation ramping up. "You weren't even worth fucking for drinks."

He grabbed her in close and starts to try to kiss her. They speed up to a quick trot.

The woman frees herself from his grip by stomping on Carl's boot.

"You fucking bitch!" Hopping on one foot in hopes of mitigating the pain, until he saw red.

Carl reared back and punched her square in the face. Not a slap like most men might use first in a fight with a woman, but a straight punch in the face that sent her sprawling on the walkway.

Jim reached him first; grabbing him firmly and pushing him back several feet before saying a word. He stood taller than the man, and outweighed him by twenty or thirty pounds.

"That's all for you. Say goodnight to the lady."

"Fuck you, man." Carl stumbling backwards thanks to his intoxication, finally losing his balance and falling down.

He scrambles back to his feet quickly.

"Fucking asshole, this ain't your gig."

"I'm making it, my gig."

"Fuck you." He charged at the woman. Jim jacked him up stopping him a few feet from the girl, as Gordon helped her up.

She wiped her face, finding the fresh blood trickling out of her nose.

"You fucking punk, Carl. I'm fucking bleeding!"

Teresa breaks out of Gordon's grip, and steps into a solid punch striking her abuser in the face. She might have knocked him down except for Jim holding him. The blow clearly stuns him.

"Okay. Okay." Gordon pulling her back gently. "You got him back. Damn good shot too. Let's call it even. Come on, I'll get you a taxi home. What do you say?"

"You paying for the cab?"

"Yes, I'm paying. This one's on me."

"She ain't going nowhere," Carl protested, shaking himself away from Jim's grip. "Cause I'm kicking her ass."

"I don't think so," Jim stepped to one side to keep himself between him and the girl. "It's over. Go home."

"What are you sticking up for that cunt for? I thought you fags hated women."

"That is the dumbest thing I heard all week. We love women. It's misogynists and homophobes, that we hate."

"Get the fuck out of my way, dick smoker." Carl made a break towards the woman.

Jim leaned in with his weight and flat palmed him square in the center of his chest. His feet went out from under him and he landed on his rear, more embarrassed than hurt. He jumped back up as fast as he could.

"I'm gonna beat your faggot ass all up and down this street!"

"I don't think you have the skill level for that." Stepping one step towards him, but remaining calm. "Think of how popular you'll be in jail if you come at me again, and I kick your ass, when they find out in the joint some fag beat you down. You're about to have a full dance card. Your call, Carl."

Caught off guard by Jim using his name, he stared at him for a long moment sizing him up, and realizing the size advantage he is giving up in this match-up.

"Fuck you faggot. But, you'd probably like that."

"Not my type. I like them with manners and respect."

"This ain't over Theresa, you bitch. I'll see you around."

"I better not hear about it." Jim interjected.

"Fuck you. If I were you; I wouldn't hang around here for long."

He ran off in the direction of the bar. With the threat gone, he turned back to Gordon and the girl.

"You, okay? Theresa, right?"

"Yeah. Yeah. I'm cool. He hits like a girl."

"Fair enough." Jim said smiling. "Come on. The cabs cruise South Main Street up one block."

"Hey, I appreciate you backing off Carl and all, but I can hail a taxi on my own, man. Just come through with the cab fare you promised."

"We'd feel a lot better if we saw you to the taxi ourselves." Using a tone that hid the fact that he knew cash would send her right back to the lounge. "Wouldn't we, Gordon?"

"Sure, would. We are going in that direction anyway."

"Fine. Suit yourself." Giving up sensing the quiet resolve behind Jim's statement.

They all started walking down to the end of the block.

"Honestly, I don't even remember fucking him at all." She confided.

"You might need to consider that you could be drinking too much, if you can't remember something as important as sex." Jim pressed politely.

"Sex ain't important," She surprised them. "Only men think it is."

Neither of them knew what to say to that and decided to let it ride.

"So, is it important to you guys?" She asked as they stood at the corner waiting. "I mean, gay men. Is sex important to you guys?"

The question clearly caught them off guard. Gordon tried not to laugh as he smiled at the thought. Jim smirked as he thought of what to say.

"Sure. Sex is important for gay couples as a way to show the emotions they share for each other, just like regular couples."

"Nobody ever wants to show me emotion. They just want to fuck me, or have me suck their dick. TAXI!" She screamed as one came into sight from around a corner.

"I think you're going about it wrong." Gordon interjected, a little worried about talking out of place. "It should be about caring first, and showing physically should come later."

"Sure, that sounds good on paper." The taxi pulled up to a stop and she opened the door. "But it don't work in real life."

She got in the taxi and closed the door. Jim leaned through the open window and handed her a card. Gordon gave the driver a twenty.

"It wouldn't hurt to find better people to hang out with." He said compassionately. "This is my card. You call if you feel like talking to someone. First visit's on me."

"You're a shrink too. A gay shrink? Ain't that something." Flashing a faint smiling. "Thanks doc. Who knows? Maybe I will."

"Good bye, Theresa. Best of luck to you."

She drove off in the cab.

"I didn't talk out of turn back there, did I?"

"Gordon," Jim putting his arm around his neck. "What you said was beautiful. I was impressed."

They put their arms around each other and started back up the street.

"Me? The way you handled that guy. Now, that was impressive. You could have kicked his ass so easily, but didn't. I gotta admit, part of me wanted to see you beat the shit out of that idiot."

"I know what you mean. Sometimes I don't know where I find the strength to hold back, but not tonight. Having you here gave me the resolve not to drop to his level. I'm glad you were here with me. It was like..."

"...Male bonding." He interjected laughing lightly.

"Something like that."

Jim stopped, gazing at Gordon for a long moment. It would be one of those moments you hope to look back at years from now if all goes well, as one of the early turning points of the relationship. They had shared something moving and it had brought them closer together, and they could both sense it.

Jim moved in and kissed him. Gordon's face lit up with a smile.

"Right on the street, for all the world to see?" Gordon mocked. "If I didn't know better, I'd think you cared about me."

"If I didn't know better," Jim started cautiously. "I'd swear I'm in love with you."

Without a word they began kissing on the sidewalk, not caring who still lingered in the area. The essence of what transpired moved them both. No more hiding. No more denial. Now comes the building of trust and responsibility in their relationship.

"So, just you and me now? Together, like a couple?" Unable to hide the ecstatic look on his face.

"You and me." Looking straight in his eyes. "Just like a couple."

Gordon smiled and pulled him into a hug. They held each other tightly.

"Let's head to my place." Jim whispered.

"Yeah, because now that we got the emotion out of the way, I was thinking about showing how much I care in a more tangible way."

"Alright then, where the hell, did I put that car?" Pretending to search frantically for a moment.

"Should be up one block, over one, and up one more on the street. It's probably the only car left."

"If it's still there, and not up on blocks."

They started walking up the sidewalk, and had made it only a short way when they heard the footsteps.

Racing around the corner came Carl, now with four other friends in tow.

He pointed at the two of them.

"I told you they'd still be here." He assured his buddies, all in a light trot coming towards them. "Hey fag boy. Where's your big talk now?"

"Okay, be cool. We're clearly outnumbered, so making a stand is out." Jim started planning strategically. "At the end of this building, there's an alley through to the other street. Keep walking until we reach the entrance, then we'll cut through and up to the car. It should let us beat them to it by a full block."

"Sounds like a plan. Just say when."

Jim waited until the men slowed to a walk when they realize that he and Gordon were not running away.

"You about to have five guys work your ass over, homo." Carl called out as they approached. "But not the way you wish, bitch."

"NOW." Jim said.

He and Gordon broke into a run for the alleyway only a couple yards away. The group of men started running as soon as they made a break for it. They reached the alley with a decent lead over the pursuing gang.

Dark and stinking of the garbage cans and dumpsters that lined it, they only ran about twenty yards deep before they found a parked van blocking off the exit to the street on the far side.

"Head for the dumpster. We can climb it and over the van." Jim spit out breathlessly as he angled for the metal container.

The gang entered the alleyway, and started gaining on them. Their lead had already been cut down by a third.

Jim vaulted up on the dumpster and on to the roof of the vehicle, but almost too smoothly as it left Gordon to navigate the same maneuver. He tried to follow, but as he leaped up on top the can's lid he lost his footing, slipped off backwards, and landed hard on the concrete. He lay on the ground, motionless.

"GORDON!" Jim yelled as he jumped down off the van, and scurried to Gordon's side.

He was out cold. Suddenly the odds became a little worse. The gang stopped running about fifteen feet away.

"Awww, what's a matter?" Carl taunted. "Did little fag boy's girlfriend fall down and go boom?"

Jim stood up slowly, fighting to suppress the anger, knowing he needed his wits about him to survive this. He did not know how badly Gordon was hurt, and now he had to fight for both of them. His rage flared up into a full-blown forest fire within him, as he turned to size up the men. There were five of them, none bigger than him, but five of them.

By judging their stances, or ability to stand, he did a quick threat assessment of his opponents. Two appeared to be visibly staggering. He would worry about them last. Carl stood closest, but the last two seemed to be the ones to who posed the greatest threat.

Dressed in full punk leather, they seemed lucid and apparently hadn't drunk much yet.

Just as he downplayed him as a threat in his head, Carl reached down and grabbed a bottle. He broke off the end on the brick wall and began closing in slowly.

"I'm gonna make you nice and pretty for your girlfriend, or maybe I should start with your little boyfriend first?"

It was not his words that fired Jim's anger to an uncontrollable level, but the sheer bravado of this drunk, whose only real confidence stood behind him four strong. He couldn't control himself anymore.

"You so much as point that bottle in his direction you spineless little shit, and I'll kill you with my bare hands." Jim spurted out before he could catch himself.

"You ballsy little fag, for someone about to get the ass whipping of a lifetime." One of the punks spit out.

"I'm warning you now," he said calmly. "Some of you are about to be seriously hurt. I promise you that if you continue."

With that, Carl made a charge. Jim quickly snatched a lid off one of the cans and met the bottle deflecting it to one side. It left him open for a right cross. Regardless of how dangerous it was, he could not hold back under such odds, and struck Carl with a powerful straight punch to the throat that immediately dropped him to his knees, coughing violently.

The talkative punk picked up a garbage can while the other one charged in. Jim had to deal with the one charging in first, his anger still rising. He needed to level the odds as fast as possible. As the mouthy one stepped into range, he pushed a straight kick clean through the knee of his planted front foot. The leg breaks backwards, dropping the second punk in a heap of howling pain, but two down.

He turned back to the others, just in time to duck the incoming trash can. It sailed over him and landed right on Gordon's head. The blood appeared immediately near his temple where the edge had struck him an otherwise glancing blow. Checking on him as quickly as he could, he realized he had made thee cardinal mistake of fighting; and taken his eyes off the other men.

In the movies, bad guys always waited to take their turn one at a time, only to have their ass kicked by the hero, but in real life not even drunks are that stupid.

Jim steadied himself in time to meet the first punk about to tackle him, closely followed by the last two assailants. He shifted his stance and tried to counter-balance the punks charge, staying on his feet until the other two joined the push from behind, hoping he could turn them, but instead he went over backwards.

He was in trouble now.

The weight of the three of them landing on him on the alley's concrete pavement, knocked the wind out of him. His head struck the ground, it jarred him bad enough to blur his senses. He was in serious trouble now.

With no strength left to fight back, the punk positioned himself on top of him and began to punching him repeatedly in the face. Losing consciousness fast, and all he could think about was failing Gordon. How the man he loved lies bleeding and defenseless because of his lack of concentration.

He noticed one of the drunks laid out next to him, who had apparently knocked himself out in the fall. The other one kicked him in the legs, and hip area below where the first punk sat on his stomach.

Jim tried to keep his head moving, to dampen the strikes, but it wasn't working. His strength diminished with each blow. He couldn't see out of his eyes any longer. The taste his own blood filled his mouth, as he feared that this might really be it. His worst nightmare had come to life, he was going to be beat to death in an alley by a homophobic piece of trash.

While he slipped in and out of consciousness with the punches, he would swear the one kicking him had stopped. It sounded like two fights were going on. Oh, my God, he thought, the other drunk is beating on Gordon while he's unconscious. This brought out a higher level of effort, but to no avail. His strength was gone, his vision was worthless, and his hearing had been reduced to a series of random piercing tones, but then it stopped.

Abruptly the blows ceased. The punk rocker's weight lifted off his chest. Why did he stop? He wondered if he had passed out? No, he was experiencing too much agony for that, as his head throbbed with every beat of his heart. Did he hear fighting? Was that a scream?

He couldn't fight the darkness any longer, as it swept over him like a shadow taking away the pain as it went. Then, his world turned black.

SIXTEEN

Frank sat in an overstuffed chair next to Carrie's bed. Engulfed in the silence dominating the apartment, that was full of life just a few hours earlier. Ole Frankie felt twenty years old again making love to Carrie, like some teenager whose poster model had come to life and seduced him. Every muscle in his body tingled with life. He had muscles he had forgotten he had, and they were sore now, but in a way that brought a smile to his face.

He couldn't help but stare at her sleeping in the low ambient light seeping in through the shades. She glowed like Aphrodite laid out in the center of her huge bed. He couldn't resist pulling the sheet back to admire her form, and marveled over the moonlight silently caressing her body. His mouth salivated as he absorbed her elegance. He just had coitus with a goddess, and the goddess wanted him. Not to sound cocky, but he did right by her, and didn't stop until she almost begged him to. There was a sense of triumph when her knees gave out, as she tried to stand to go for some water. He wanted to make her weak. She had made him weak for a long time now.

She looked stunning lying on her back with her hair spread out around her head, her succulent breasts pointing upwards almost begging for attention. Every part of his manhood ached to jump back in bed and seduce her again. Hell, he wished he could make love on her until he died outright from exhaustion, but he couldn't.

It was there, crawling up and down the small of his spine, and knowing something bad happened makes you dirty inside. Which is why he always got out of bed and waited. He didn't want to risk the disturbance rubbing off on someone else, and he wouldn't wish this on anyone. Sarah never understood that. She said he closed himself off to her, when he should have been opening up. She couldn't understand he was protecting her from the slimy aura of the premonitions.

Not even with the pure beauty of Carrie's naked body sprawled out in all her glory right in front of him, and he still couldn't shake the dirty perception at its core.

At least the view was better than his kitchen. Hell, the vision of her *au naturel* is superior to anything he could think of to date. Well, maybe not his son being born. That was a heartwarming, life affirming day. Which reminded him, he needed to spend more time with Joey.

Did Carrie want kids? He could imagine how beautiful her children would be. Oh, lord what if they were girls? He'd have every idiot in the state knocking down his door tying to hook up with her daughters. Hold up. Getting a little carried away he thought to himself, completely excusing the pun. However, the very second, he broke the pleasant train of thought, the sensation crept back into his vertebrae.

She moaned, as she turned gently in her slumber. He prayed she wouldn't wake up. He didn't want to explain this yet, but at the same time he wanted to tell her everything.

Her eyes opened ever so slightly, as she woke up. Moonbeams echoed through them making them sparkle in the shadowy light of the room. He leaned towards the bed staring at her.

"Carrie," He spoke softly. "You are the most beautiful woman I have ever known in my entire life."

She smiled widely and lit up the room even further. Oh, he's in deep, and fast with nothing he could do about it.

"Frank, is something wrong?"

"The truth?" He asked hoping she would ask him to sugar coat it.

"Yes." She sat up. "I want you to tell me the truth. No matter how bad. Promise me. Right here and now, you'll always be honest with me."

The tone of her voice pierced right through the core of his resistance, and shredded away what was left of the defenses he had set up to keep her at bay.

He moved over and sat on the bed beside her, caressing her hair and cheek. He couldn't lie to her if he wanted to.

"I promise. The truth, always." He leaned in to kiss her gently on the lips. Even this slight touch of her mouth made him forget the original question. He pulled back to look at her. He drifted aimlessly in her eyes.

"Frank" She whispered snapping him back to reality. "Tell me what's wrong?"

He carefully moved back into the chair.

"It can't be that bad." Holding out her hands. "Come back over here and tell me."

"I get these feelings." Ignoring her request. "I can tell when something bad has happened."

"Like a premonition?"

"They're not that specific." He continued. "I generally feel like shit until I find out I'm right, and I'm always right."

"You're not the only one in the world who's shown precognitive abilities. You managed to develop a sense most of us will never learn how to use. Fascinating, but come back to bed until they call you."

"I can't, Carrie. It's a bad… This feeling creeps up and down your spine, until you learn what happened. You don't want this, it feels like... evil inside you."

She sat up on the edge of the bed, and took his face in her hands. She smiled the most comforting grin, and kissed him on the lips.

"You're trying to protect me from it aren't you?" Already knowing the answer. "This is about this case too."

"Why didn't I meet you in high school?"

"Because I was still in elementary school?" Teasing him with a warm smile.

"Smart ass. I'd swear I could tell you anything, and you'd understand."

"I will, I promise."

"Sure, you say that now."

"No, I mean it." She swore in an inflection exuding honesty. "I'll prove it. Let's put this to rest. I want you to tell me the worst thing you have ever done."

"Oh, no. I don't think that's a good idea." He protested.

"No, right now." With her defiant look that this isn't open to debate. Her magical glow morphed into fiery determination to earn his trust. "I'll tell you mine next time. I swear, but my game. You go first. What's the worst thing you've ever done?"

"I can't tell you, Carrie. I just can't. Plus, this... event has been bothering me a lot lately too."

"Talking it over would be therapeutic. It can't be that bad. What'd you do? Kill someone? Frame someone? I'll understand. I want you to be comfortable with me. I need you to trust me with anything. I really do."

Frank stared into her eyes, but it did not help his resolve. He frowned and glanced down.

"Me and Sarah had several break-ups in High School, and right after before we moved in together and got married." He started quietly. "During one of the separations, I got with this girl I knew for some time, named Amanda. She had recently broken up with a guy I didn't like much. I was on a split from Sarah, and I talked her into going out with me. I had my first apartment back then, so I had her over for dinner. I ordered some pizza. This was before I learned to cook. I was young and dumb back then. I figured she just broke up with someone. I had broken up with Sarah, again. That if I got with her, she would probably...you know."

"Give you some?" She interjected.

"Yeah. That was the plan. So, we ate pizza, and watched TV and bitched about our recent ex.'s. We started making out and all systems were 'go'. We got naked. Things got pretty heavy. A little oral foreplay on both our parts. I throw on a condom and I'm ready to rock, but almost immediately after I put it in, the tears start."

"About what?" Ever so gently.

"She started crying about her boyfriend. Turns out he's been the only guy she'd been with so far, and she wanted him back. We'll I'm nineteen and already inside her, and I didn't think that was a reason enough excuse to not finish. So, I... continued."

"What did she say?"

"She kept begging me to stop." Frank looking down and shaking his head as he spoke with remorse in his voice. "But I was young, and stupid, and horny, thinking if she let me in, I had a right to finish."

He went silent for a moment. This time she let him collect himself on his own. He was opening up to her, and it meant so much to her. He was nearly in tears.

"She cried the whole time. Over and over, all she did was ask me to stop, but I didn't." He paused and swallowed hard. "When we finished... Well, I finished. She got dressed quietly. She said to never tell her boyfriend or anyone because she would deny everything and left."

"Have you seen her since?"

"All the time. She lives here still, married another guy from our school and has two little boys now. She's a good mom, but she never spoke to me again."

"Did you ever apologize to her?"

"What do I say to her? I'm sorry I raped you? I've never had the courage to talk to her since then. Now you know why this case bothers me so much. I could fit the criteria this guy is using to justify killing these guys. I raped a woman, Carrie."

She got out of the bed, pushed him back into the chair, and positioned herself in his lap.

"So that was the worst thing, right? A fifteen-year-old date rape?"

"What do mean, that's all? I raped that poor woman."

"I am not saying what you did was acceptable. It wasn't." In her calm reassuring manner. "A woman has the right to say no whenever, but there are a lot of mitigating circumstances here. She played along through both giving and receiving oral sex, and changed her mind only when you began to have intercourse, which she initially approved. It would be disingenuous for her to claim there was no attraction. But that doesn't justify anything, it was still wrong. But I understand why now, and in that respect, I can handle knowing what happened."

He studied at her face so full of understanding and caring, and for the first time he thought it might be a forgivable offense. Perhaps, he would be able to finally move past this.

"I can't put into words how happy this makes me that you've trusted me with this."

"Do you think it's too late for an apology now?"

"I think that is an excellent idea. You can purge this out of your system. She'll probably want to vent, so you have to be prepared. I'll even go with you for support if you want."

"Oh, that'll go over great. Hi, my girlfriend and I came to apologize for me raping you fifteen years ago. I should go alone."

"Maybe so." Then with a coy look. "So, I'm your girlfriend now. You sure move quickly, Mister Carmine."

"I'm sorry, I didn't necessarily mean...."

She put her fingers over his lips to silence him.

"Say it again."

"Girlfriend." He repeated softly.

"I like it." And kissed him passionately.

He pulled her in tight, and she snuggled up against him enjoying the moment.

"So, next we do yours, right?"

"Of course, we agreed."

As if on cue, the cellphone laying on his jacket beside them rang. He reached out to pick it up.

She stopped him from picking it up for a moment.

"I made you forget for a while, didn't I?" Smiling widely.

"Yes. You sure did."

Frank answered the phone. She studied his face for his reactions.

"Carmine. How long ago?... How many?... Aw shit.... I'll be right there."

He hung up.

"How bad?"

"Dr. Jim Whistler and his boyfriend were jumped by four punks down off South Main Street. They're both in the hospital."

"Doctor Whistler, from the women's shelter. Oh, my God. Were they hurt badly?"

"They weren't specific, but both of them are still unconscious."

"Oh, no. I like Dr. Jim. He's one of the good guys."

"Well, they didn't roll over and make it easy for them. They gave them a hell of a fight."

"What do you mean?"

"Let's put it this way. You might as well get dressed. Two of the four attackers are your newest customers."

SEVENTEEN

Frank and Carrie came rushing in to the hospital together. Hansen stood in the lobby with Karen Alexander, and the physician on duty. As soon as they were close enough, he spoke up.

"How bad is he?"

"Hey Frank. Carrie. You know Karen," Dave handled the introductions. "This is Doctor Ellison."

"Mr. Whistler is stable." The M.D. began. "He's still unconscious. He's been beat up pretty extensively, but I don't expect any permanent damage."

"How about his friend." Carrie interjected.

"Gordon Newsome, is also comatose. He has a severe concussion, and though we'll need to re-evaluate him when he wakes up, we anticipate him making a full recovery as well."

"So, they'll be alright in the long run?" She inquired.

"They should be." The doctor continued. "We're still trying to ascertain the extent of Mr. Newsome's concussion, but in general they'll both should recover with little to no rehab. Providing they both wake up in the next two to four hours maximum."

"What about the perps?"

"Check this out, Frankie." Hanson jumped in. "Go ahead Doc, give him the stats."

The Doctor and Karen look at him with concern.

"Well, there are four assailants." The physician explained. "Two of them are dead, apparently from neck fractures. One was also knocked out cold, but didn't sustain a fracture, and the last one has a severely broken leg, bent backwards at the knee."

"No shit, Doc Jim did all that?" Shot out of Frank's mouth without thinking about it, until he heard it out loud.

"The Doc can handle himself." Hanson showing a little too much excitement. "Remember, he's a black belt."

"Yeah, but Doctor Whistler hardly seems the type to use violence to that level." Carrie surmised joining the conversation.

"He would in a life-or-death battle." Karen confirmed in case there were any lingering doubts.

"It sounds like it was." Frank turning to Carrie. "Let me know the cause of death on the two perps as soon as you can. See if you confirm the doc here's preliminary assessment. Call my cell."

"I'm on it." And kissed him on the cheek before he could react. "You know where I'll be."

She slipped on down the hall, he turned back to find Dave sporting the biggest shit eating grin he'd ever seen. Frank chose to ignore him for now. Instead, he addressed the M.D.

"Where you keeping him?"

"Upstairs, room 304. You'll recognize it by the patrolman stationed at the door."

"Thank you doctor." Shaking his hand. "If you'll excuse us."

"Karen." Hanson turned to her. "I'll let you know the minute he's awake. Are you gonna wait for a while?"

"Only another hour or so." Checking her wristwatch. "One of us needs to be at the shelter."

He nodded in agreement, and touched her hand briefly before turning and catching up with Frank already half-way into the elevator. Dave slipped into the lift just as the doors were closing. As soon as they closed, he started ribbing him.

"Somebody got some, and drove here together, did we?" His face dominated by a juvenile grin.

"So, what's your point, detective?" Remaining aloof.

"Alright, tell me. How good was it?" Then waiting like a teenager getting a report from the first of his friends to ever have sex.

Frank turned to him. A smile swept across his face. He placed his hands on both of Dave's shoulders for effect.

"Dave. The way I feel right now, I could probably kick your ass twice." Smiling widely.

The doors opened on the third floor. Frank stepped out quickly. Dave followed right beside him.

"I'm starting to get concerned about you judging your well-being on whether or not you can kick my ass."

Frank stopped a few feet from the uniformed cop guarding the room, and lowered his voice.

"I'm only gonna tell you this much, because I don't want to jinx it. Carrie is incredible. Not only is she beautiful, she made me comfortable with her to the point I told her things you don't know about me."

"Come on? I know everything"

"No, not everything."

"Aww, now I feel a little hurt."

"It was scary. Everything about her is amazing. I can't believe I put this off so long. Even the meal, which had sat for two hours before we stopped and ate, was still absolutely was fantastic."

"You got laid before dinner. Oh, you are the man."

"What can I say?" Turning to the officer at the door. "Hey, Pete how's your wife?"

"Same ole ball and chain, Frankie. How'd your date with Carrie McKenna go?"

Frank turned to Dave who was giving his best *who me* impression.

"What? We had some downtime while we were waiting for you." Dave spit out in his defense.

"It went well, Pete. Thanks for asking."

He steps past him into the hospital room.

"What are you a moron?" Dave clandestinely accosts the patrolman away from Frank. "*How was your date*? No wonder you're still a flatfoot."

"Hey, fuck you Hanson." Pete shoots back firmly but quietly, mindful of the situation. "I didn't know it was a big secret."

Dave entered the room to find Frank introducing himself to Jim's mother, Elizabeth. She got up from the chair beside the bed to greet them.

"Mrs. Whistler. This is my partner, Dave Hanson."

"We've got the men who did this in custody, ma'am." Dave reassured her politely. "They're in jail already."

"Is it true?" She spoke so faintly they barely heard the question.

"Is what true, ma'am?" Frank queried.

"That Jim killed two of these... people who attacked him and Gordon?"

"Ah." Stumbling on his answer "We can't be sure of that yet."

"Well," She stated softly but firmly. "I don't blame him if he did. He was fighting for his life, and probably Gordon's as well."

"Nobody would say otherwise, ma'am." He assured her. "But until we actually talk to your son, we can't be certain."

"He's lucky he had all that training." Dave added.

"I didn't want him to take that martial arts training at first." She began speaking not looking at them. "He was only sixteen, but I figured it might be beneficial for him, with his father being gone, to have some sort of male role model. The master was such a collected person. Jim really took to him. I didn't like the violence, but the self-assurance and self-respect, I liked those aspects."

"It helps to have a quality instructor." Frank agreeing with her.

"Master Chueng was a great teacher. He turned my boy into a man. It gave him the confidence to enforce his values, and not by fighting. He gained a composure all men should envy. When he first told me he was gay I was hoping the training might cure him. It seemed so manly and all, but instead it taught both of us that there is more to being a man than being able to love women. Jim's twice the man that most men are."

"I think we would agree with you, Mrs. Whistler." Dave confirming her statement. "Your son is a truly good person, and that's more than I can say for myself, as much as I'd like to."

"I'm going to tell him that as soon as he wakes up." She spoke firmly in a way that made it seem her soliloquy was for her. "That even though he's gay, he's turned into one of the best men I've ever known."

"You just did." Came feebly from Jim's mouth alerting them all to him now being conscious.

"Jim?" She rushed to the bed quickly. "You're awake?"

"I am." His weak voice focusing the room on him instantly. "And, I can't tell you how much it meant to me to hear you say that."

"I mean it, Jim. I'm sorry I didn't say so sooner."

"Mom? Who else is here? In the room? I can't see too clearly yet, although the voices sound familiar."

137

She looked at Frank and he nods yes.

"It's Detectives Carmine and Hanson. They're both here. They said they already caught the men who did this to you."

"Excellent. I would smile, but I can't open my eyes."

"The doctor said you'll be fine," In that tone of motherly worry. "There shouldn't be any lasting damage at all."

"Physically." He murmured. "How's Gordon?"

Again, she turned to the detectives hoping they would fill in the details on Gordon's condition.

"He has a concussion," Frank answered for her. "They're still evaluating him, but for now, he's unconscious but stable."

"I let him down." Jim mumbled dejected.

"Mrs. Whistler." Frank said compassionately. "We need to talk to your son alone for a few minutes, then you can come back in and stay with him if you'd like."

"I could use a drink of water or something. I'll be right outside, Jim."

"I'll be okay, mom. You go ahead."

"Fifteen minutes." Speaking firmly as she stopped in front of Frank before leaving the room, in a way that seemed more like a warning than informational.

She exited the room with the refined elegance that dominated her personality.

"Well." Frank started. "I see where you get your determination. What happened to your father?"

"He never married my mother. He was killed in Vietnam. She never talks about him. I don't think she truly cared for him."

"I'm sorry to hear that." Hanson agreed. "Well looks like you had a hell of a night. How much do you remember?"

"You can give us the short version for now, Doc."

"Well." He swallowed and spoke softly. "After Gordon and I finished dinner, we stopped a guy named Carl from harassing this girl, Theresa. We put her in a cab and sent her home."

"Take your time, Jim." Frank cajoled. "We only need the basics for now. You can flush out all the details when you're stronger."

"Okay." Steadying himself against the pain. "So, this Carl show's back up with four friends."

"Four?" Hanson noticing the discrepancy immediately. Frank quickly held up a hand for Dave not to let on.

"Yeah. There were five altogether. They chased us down an alley, but there was a van blocking it. We tried to jump on the dumpster to the van, but Gordon slipped off and hit his head hard enough to knock himself out. I jumped down to protect him."

"So, Gordon was injured falling off the dumpster?"

"At first. I, ah, squared off with them, and warned them they were about to get hurt if they continued. So, Carl breaks a bottle and comes at me, but I blocked it with a trash can lid, and throat punch him. He drops like a rock. Then one charged me while another picked up a full garbage can. When the first one got close, and planted his leg I snapped his knee backwards with a quick kick."

Jim started to cough, wincing badly with each spasm. He took a beat to settle down.

"So, you had the upper hand." Frank summarizing to get him back on track. "You took the first two out of the fight quickly. When did you lose the edge?"

"After the one guy threw the can. I ducked under it, but I turned and watched it hit Gordon in the head. He started bleeding immediately."

"He took seven stitches right above the hairline." Hanson filling him in. "You probably won't be able to see the scar."

"Go on, you turned your head." Frank pulling him back to his story.

"And they all rushed me. I tried to twist out from under them on the way down, but the two of them landed on me. They crushed the wind out of me. One of them was knocked out by the fall because he stopped fighting. One sat up on my chest and started to pummel me. The other one kept kicking me until just before I went out."

"So, the other guy stopped kicking you first?"

"Yeah, he just stopped kicking me. I think he talked the other one into leaving, because he let up punching me before I passed out."

"Did he say anything to that effect? Let's get out of here? Anything like that?"

"I don't recall clearly. The ringing in my head made it all cloudy at best. I couldn't see after the first five or six punches. All I remember is getting hit a lot, and that it stopped just before I lost consciousness."

"That's enough for now. We only needed enough to help question these punks. We'll let you rest."

"You've already got them?" He asked, not sure if he was ready for the answer. "All of them?"

"Shit, Doc." Hanson tossed out playfully. "You left most of them lying on the ground yourself. All we had to do is pick them up."

"Good." Jim to himself.

"We'll be in touch, Doc." Frank as they excused themselves out of the room.

Outside, Elizabeth Whistler stood waiting in the hallway clutching bottle of water. She looked at her watch when Frank and Dave stepped into the hall. He checked his defensively.

"You can go back in ma'am," nodding politely. "And, to answer your question, no, your son did not kill the two men who attacked him and Mr. Newsome."

She headed for the door without a word.

"Mrs. Whistler." Frank stopped her in the doorway. "You raised a hell of son there."

"Thank you." She replied humbly, and went back inside the room.

EIGHTEEN

"Okay." Frank said turning back to Dave the moment the door closed behind Mrs. Whistler. "Make with the perp list."

His partner whipped out a small notebook, and quickly went over his notes.

"No Carl."

"Shit. One's missing."

"Who's missing?" Pete interjected trying to be involved.

"I smell a shakedown coming on." Dave said.

"Who do we have left that's here in the hospital still?"

"Well, either the one that knocked himself out tackling the doc, or busted knee guy behind door number two."

"What are you guys talking about?" The patrolman inquired in earnest. "The perps?"

They were both absorbed in thought and oblivious to Pete's attempts to join the discussion.

"Leg guy?"

Dave nodded. "I agree. Definitely."

They head down the hall without ever acknowledging the junior officer.

They moved past another officer into the room of "Leg guy." A nurse was quietly checking his chart. It was still just before sunrise. The room was quite dark. Frank flipped on the lights as they entered. The R.N. quickly shut them back off.

"What do you think you're doing?" She whispered with authority. "This patient needs his rest. Don't disturb him. Who do you two think you are?"

"I am Detective Carmine." Flipping the switch on again. "This is my partner Detective Hanson. We're going to question this witness."

"Not right now you're not." She said reaching for the light switch, still holding the clipboard.

He stepped in front of her, and broke out his *authority* voice.

"Lady, this asshole was involved in a hate crime that led to a double homicide. The only reason he's in the hospital, and not a prison cell is because I have not given permission for them to move him yet. His injuries are not life threatening. Now he can talk to us here and now, or I'll make the call, and he can answer questions while his painkillers are wearing off behind bars down at the station."

"Well, I never...." She started.

"Look, lady. I'm sure you're a good nurse, and I'm not mad at you and I don't mean to take it out on you. But, this piece of shit's gonna tell us every damn thing he knows about how two people ended up dead tonight. Now, get out."

"We'll take that." Hanson added, grabbing the clipboard from her.

"I'm going tell Doctor Wilson about this immediately." She declared on her way out.

"You do that." Dave shot back as he opened up the chart. "We have one Donovan Morrison. Obviously, his parents were rock and roll fans. Age twenty-three, awww, compound fracture of the knee, with severe ligament and tendon damage. Sounds painful."

Hanson put the chart back on the hook near the foot of the bed, then picks the end of the frame up about two feet and dropped it. The patient bounced about six inches off the mattress and awoke rather abruptly.

"What the fuck?" He stammered disorientated, while looking around trying to recall where he was. "Where am I?"

"County Hospital. Dipshit." Frank skipping any formal introduction. "You don't remember how you got here?"

Dave took over as his partner leaned over the bed menacingly.

"Let me refresh your memory. You and your punk ass friends jumped two men in an alley, but because you can't fight for shit, you got your leg broken. Any of this coming back to you now?"

"That fag broke my fucking leg!" Excited and sitting up quickly.

"You attacked them!" Frank pointed out while pushing him back down. "And do not say fag again, or I'll break your other leg."

"Who the hell are you guys?"

"Detective Carmine." He holds his badge right up to his face almost belligerently.

"Detective Hanson. Now, who's Carl?"

"Why what happened to him?" He asked, now fully invested in the conversation.

"You're not getting the concept here." Frank said. "We are the detectives. We ask the questions. You answer them. Who is Carl?"

"How do I know you two are real cops? You could be friends of those fags..."

Frank grabbed him up by his hospital gown and pulled him up into his face.

"We are friends with those fags, and the only reason I haven't kicked your sorry ass out the fucking window is because I'm a cop. If I was a civilian friend of those two, I'd be kicking your one-legged ass all over this room, until the cops did show up. Who the fuck is Carl? And if I have to ask you one more fucking time, I will take you straight to jail now, and put you in a cell with the biggest motherfucker you've ever seen who hasn't been laid since Carter was president, who doesn't care whose ass he gets a shot at as long as it's tight. Do you understand the fucking question?"

Donovan's eyes lit up with fear. Dave had to bite his tongue not to laugh out loud, `since Carter was president' that was fucking priceless he thought.

"Okay, man." Donovan said finally convinced of Frank seriousness, even if Hanson knew otherwise. "Carl Prescott. He hangs out at the Dungeon man. Fuck."

"Describe him."

"Shit, I don't know. He's about five ten, eleven at the most. Brown hair. Maybe 170 pounds. He lives over in Groton somewhere."

"Was he the ringleader for all this?" Dave asked.

"Yeah, he came running into the bar saying, these two fa- homos were giving him shit because they had him out numbered. So, a couple of us jumped up and ran out with him."

"That would be you, Mike, Calvin and Ted?" Consulting his notebook.

"Yeah, we all followed him down the street." He continued. "We chased them into the alley. They tried to climb over this van by jumping on the dumpster, but one of them fell off and busts his ass. We never touched him."

"What happened with the other one?" Frank probed with intensity.

"Fucking Carl breaks off a bottle and goes for him. The fag trashes him with one punch to the throat. So, Ted picks up a garbage can, while I run in to try to smack him, and he fucking stomps out my knee, man. My fucking leg bent out backwards. I hit the ground man, and blacked out."

"You were unconscious the whole time?" Dave followed up.

"It fucking hurt, man. I ain't never felt nothing like that man. When I saw my leg was sticking straight up, and I passed out."

"I don't believe you." Frank said menacing. "I think you were in pain, but remember what else happened."

"I swear man. I don't remember anything after that. The paramedic woke me up in the ambulance with the smelly shit."

Frank looked over at Dave who nodded in agreement clandestinely.

"If I find out you lied to me," Slowly and deliberately. "I will quit the police force and beat you into a coma myself."

They started for the door. The patient sat up quickly.

"Hey what happened to the other guys?" Hiding the fear in his voice.

Frank stopped in the doorway.

"Calvin's upstairs, but Ted and Mike are dead. Apparently, they don't know how to fight worth a shit either."

"You're lying man, right?" Donovan pleaded. "You're just saying that to scare me. Hey, come on man. Tell me the truth, now. Come on, man, they're not really dead."

Without acknowledging his question, they stepped out into the hallway. They say `Hi' to the patrolman as they walked on down the hall.

"I guess we'll need an APB on this idiot Carl Prescott." Dave said scribbling in his notebook.

"Don't get your hopes up. I have a pretty good feeling we're going to find Mr. Prescott tied up somewhere with a gaping throat wound."

NINETEEN

Frank and Dave entered the hall leading to the medical examiner's office. It was in the hospital's basement which seemed to make the footsteps echo more, adding to the already ominous feeling of going to the morgue.

"I'm telling you right now." Frank warned. "If you say one stupid comment about me and Carrie, I swear I will leave you here as a corpse."

"My, aren't we touchy about our new girlfriend. You forget I've known her for over two years now."

"Just don't embarrass me. I still feel off balance around her as it is."

"Yeah, that's true, sex effects your equilibrium."

He smacked him in the shoulder with a backhand, points at him and giving him one of those `don't even start' looks.

"Okay, Okay. I get it, jeez." He relented and led them into the office.

Carrie was doing the preliminary inspections of the two bodies still. Frank was glad she hadn't gotten to the cutting part of the examinations yet. The two men lay on separate tables. They both had obvious dark purple and black bruises on their necks.

"Hey beautiful." Dave said. "What did you get, so far?"

She looked up from the corpse to find Dave standing there smiling, but when she sees Frank with him, she smiles widely.

"Hi guys. How's Doctor Whistler?"

"He regained consciousness a few minutes ago." Frank said trying not to stare at her. "We were able to talk to him. He put up a helluva fight, but was out manned. His partner Gordon slipped and fell off a dumpster knocking himself out when they first tried to escape, hence the standoff."

"He took out the first two guys by himself?" Sounding impressed.

"Three, one is missing." Hanson said.

"There were five of them? The Doc did himself proud. What's his prognosis?"

"He's messed up, but he'll recover." Frank added. "We got an APB out on the missing perp. Turns out he's the one who started the whole thing."

"What about these guys?" Dave interjected. "How'd they die?"

"Quick and clean. Whoever killed these two knew what he was doing. Look at this."

The detectives moved over to the tables, as Carrie uses her pen to point out small round marks on the face and chin of one of the two men.

"You see these small bruises?" As she pointed out the dark bruises on the skin. "They're finger spots. Thumb here, the slightly bigger one. The others on the other side of the face. Got a solid grip fast, and wham, broke their necks in one swift motion."

"Professional, or military?" Dave mused.

"Sure, maybe. I don't think either of them saw whoever did this. This guy was behind him, judging from the bruise pattern."

"That matches what the doc said happened," Frank started. "Just before he passed out. The last two stopped beating on him for some reason. So, they were probably taken out from behind while they were still working him."

"It would explain why they didn't see it coming." Dave theorized. "Too busy getting in easy shots on him while he was down."

"Sure, that fits what I've seen so far." Carrie continued. "I'll have toxicology reports this afternoon, and we'll find out if they had anything other than alcohol in them. You said one got away?"

"Yeah, the scumbag that started the whole deal." Frank explained. "Evidently Jim and his friend stopped him from harassing some woman before this all went down. They sent her home in a cab."

"I have to ask this out loud, but who would bail out doctor Jim like this and not want to take credit for saving him?"

"Frank thinks he's our killer?" Dave answered. "Helping the doctor who was defending a woman would fit right into the killer's manner of thinking."

"Keep another gurney ready. I don't think we're going to find this Carl guy alive."

"Sure." Carrie went on. "It would make sense that if he was there to save the doc and his partner, he might have witnessed the original confrontation with the girl."

"You should become a detective, Carrie." Dave said. "You're a quick thinker."

"True." She agreed with a smile. "However, nobody ever shoots at the coroner."

"She's got a point." Frank said smiling. "We've got some field work to do today. I'll touch base with you this afternoon. Call me if you need anything."

"Oh." She reminded him. "Don't forget to pick me up later. Anytime between five and six is fine."

"Oh, same car, eh?" Dave antagonized slyly.

Before Frank could say anything, Carrie kicked him in the shin playfully, but still firm enough to sting.

"Grow up, Dave." She said flatly.

"Oh, shit." Frank' eyes lighting up.
"What? What's wrong?" Carrie suddenly a bit worried.

"Joey's little league game is at six tonight. I don't have to take him there, Sarah's bringing him. But I missed his last one, I can't miss two in a row."

"So, we'll go to the game." She said nonchalantly.

"What about Sarah?" Frank asked not meaning for it to be out loud.

"Uh, Frankie." Dave interrupted. "This is your chance to be up front about you and Carrie, unlike Sarah's been with that Michael guy."

"Dave's right. She'd find out anyway, and it will be better if she hears it straight from you. She'll probably come clean about, who was it, Michael. Besides Joey loves me. He even helped with an autopsy one day. Hell, he actually held..."

"...I know. Some guy's liver. I can't believe you let him do that. Thank God he's never told his mother."

"No shit." Dave exclaimed. "Little Joey held some dude's liver. Fucking kid's got more balls than his dad."

"Oh, I wouldn't say that," Carrie cooed brushing up against Frank seductively. "His dad's got pretty big balls."

It is a rare day when something makes Frank Carmine blush, but today is that day.

"Holy shit, Frankie." Dave pestered. "Are you blushing?

"Thanks, Carrie." He said as his face turned red. "I'll be here by five-thirty. Come on Dave. Let's go before I get rated on any of my other body parts."

"Hey you two." Carrie blurted out stopping them near the door. "All kidding aside. Granted this guy got the drop on these drunks, but whoever this man is, he is strong and knows how to use his hands, so don't take any unnecessary chances. You know what I mean?"

They nodded in agreement. She crossed over to Frank and kissed him on the cheek, returning the color to his face.

"Now beat it, so I can get some work done." Shooing them out of the morgue.

"You know Frankie." Dave began once they entered the hallway. "You and her will make a good couple, honest."

"We've only been a couple for a day, and I'm already afraid of screwing things up and losing her."

They continued down the hall oblivious to Carrie holding the door open an inch, so she could hear their exiting comments. She smiled widely at Frank's statement and let the door close quietly. Leaning up against the wall, she allowed herself a moment to delight in the sentiments of what Frank said, relishing her thoughts, before turning back to her work.

TWENTY

Frank and Dave had spent the last two hours talking to every person in the neighborhood where Jim Whistler and Gordon had been attacked. The other perp at the hospital turned out to be fruitless, as he remembered nothing other than trying to rush Doc and knocking himself out. They couldn't tell which embarrassed him more, being caught ganging up on a homosexual, or being knocked out without even getting in a shot. Either way he proved worthless to their quest to piece together the events of the previous evening.

They had run into only a few scattered tenants left in the area, most of who had heard nothing, saw nothing, and knew nothing. A picture of the `see no evil, hear no evil, speak no evil monkeys in the back of their minds as they talked to some of them. People were afraid to share the few meager details they might know.

The bartender from the Dungeon confirmed that all five of them had been drinking fairly heavy all night. None of the club's patrons were any help, as they were still in the bar when the fight went down, which left only a local homeless man who they found near the scene. The man reeked of booze from the night before, when he was so drunk that when he couldn't make a phone call, so he pulled a fire alarm for help.

Proud in his staggering stupor, the man had refused to let the cops or firemen take him to a shelter. They interviewed him as he sat on the steps of an empty building. He tried to be helpful, as he showed them where he was resting when it happened. His spot involved him lying under a piece of cardboard in the alcove of a boarded-up store, about a half a block from the passageway between the buildings.

The man was tall and thin, a wiry man in his fifties, wearing clothes that were tattered and worn. His beard was full of dirt and bits of paper presumably from his makeshift bed. His voice was hoarse, with a whiskey-soaked quality, and spoke with broken, uneven metering.

"I was trying to sleep." The man explained. "When all these guys ran by me, and into the alley over there."

"So, what did you do after they disappeared around the corner?" Frank asked.

"Laid back down, it wasn't none of my business. So, I didn't do nothing. I didn't want them to come after me."

"I understand that considering there were five of them. Then what happened?"

"After a minute or so, one dude came running back out carrying his friend."

"Somebody carried one of the men out of the alley?" Frank tried not to sound too excited. "What did he look like?"

"I couldn't see his face." The man went on. "The guy he had on his shoulder blocked my view."

"Did the other officers ask you about this man?" Hanson interjected.

"No, they were busy helping the ambulance guys. They told me to hang out in the neighborhood, and you two would come ask me questions this morning."

"Thank you for talking to us." Frank let the patrolmen's slip up go, and got back to the first solid lead in the case. "Can you tell us about his features other than his face, like height and weight?"

The drunk staggered to his feet and compared himself to the two of them physically.

"Well, he had dark hair, brown, I think. He looked taller than me, but not as tall as you." Pointing at Frank. "But he had bigger muscles."

"So not as tall as Detective Carmine, but wider and stockier." Dave trying to clarify his comments.

"Yeah, he was pretty strong, 'cause he ran down the street to his car carrying the hurt guy on his shoulder. He put him in the car and took him with him."

"He took the other man with him?" Hanson spelling out the man's answer.

The detectives gave each other worried glances of impending doom over this revelation.

"Yeah, but he must of been drinking cuz he couldn't remember which car was his."

"What do you mean by that?" Frank continued.

"He tried to open two or three cars before he found his, threw the guy in the backseat and got in."

"So, he tried other cars first." Dave jumped in. "Did he start his car right away?"

"No. No, he didn't. He couldn't find his keys, or something cuz he didn't start the car for a while."

"So, he got it started and drove off?" Frank plied him for more details. "Did he drive past you?"

"Man, he shot right by here squealing his tires. He was in a hurry to help his hurt friend. I don't know why he left all them other guys in the alley, probably didn't like none of them."

"Something like that." Dave added. "What kind of car was it?"

"A big ole Buick Electra 225. I used to have one when I was younger. Mine was sky blue metallic and could outrun everything in the county."

"This Buick." Frank interrupted him reminiscing. "What color was it?"

"Black, like a damn hearse. That's an ugly color for a car, man."

"Did you see the license plate?"

"A little bit, but I don't remember none of it."

"Was it a Connecticut plate?"

"One of those ones with the lighthouse on it."

"The 'save the sound' plates." Frank pressed. "One of those?"

"Yeah, with the lighthouse." The man repeated.

"You've been very helpful. We need you stay around here until this afternoon okay. I'm gonna have a patrolman come write down everything you told us."

"Ain't got no place to go anyway. Can I at least get a dollar for something to eat?"

158

At the edge of his peripheral vision, he noticed the open deli on the corner. An idea was born.

"What's your name again?" Frank questioned the older man.

"Alvin, but everybody calls me Al."

"Alright, Al. Come with me."

He led the man down the street to the store. Dave followed along, not sure what he had in mind.

They entered the small shop; Frank approached the middle-aged Korean man at the counter.

"Are you the owner?"

"I own this delicatessen, yes." The man replied.

"My name is Frank Carmine." As he showed him his badge. "I'm a detective. What's your name sir?"

"Tom Jeong, how can I help you officer?"

"Tom, I want you to meet Al."

The men nodded at each other, while he retrieved a twenty-dollar bill from his pocket.

"Are you an honorable man, Tom?"

"Yes, sir. Very honorable."

"Well Tom. This twenty dollars is for Al here to spend in your store. You're to make a list for me of what he buys, but he can only have food. He can't buy any alcohol or cigarettes with this money, understood?"

"Yes, sir. No booze or smokes, only food."

"You okay with that, Al? You have a twenty-dollar tab with Mister Jeong here, but you can only buy food. I don't want you to give him a hard time about booze. Is it a deal?"

"Man, I can't even have one beer?" He protested.

"After you sign the statement with the patrolman this afternoon." Frank laid out his plan. I'll bring you a one myself, but not until then. I'll make it a forty. Deal?"

He thought about it for a moment. "Okay, deal."

He held out his hand and Frank shook hands with him in agreement.

"Is that alright with you Mister Chang?" Wrapping up the negotiations.

"Yes, sir. That is fine. Twenty dollars. No booze."

"Thank you, both of you." The detectives slipped out of the store.

"Slick move there, Frankie. Not only did you keep him where we can find him, you probably sobered him up for his statement later."

"I have my moments. We need to call in and find out who's missing a black deuce and a quarter, ASAP."

They started down the street, but before they reached the car, Frank's cellphone rang.

"Carmine." Answering his phone. "Hi, Carrie what do you got for me? Good news and bad news... I'll take the good first... Gordon Newsome came to and seems to be all right, for the most part. They put him in the same room as Doc Jim."

"What's the bad news?" Dave's anticipation was clear in his voice.

"What's the bad news then?" Frank felt an uncomfortable twitch inching up his spine. "When?... Shit, I knew it... Where?... Tell them to look for a black Buick Electra 225 with a '*save the sound*' license plate... It's right there?... Part of the crime scene? We're on our way."

He hung of the phone and snapped it back on his belt.

"They found our boy."

TWENTY-ONE

Jim and Gordon lay side by side resting in a semi-private room. They put them in a recovery room together as they requested. The evening news is on their television. He can't see through his swollen eyes, so Gordon explains anything requiring sight to understand fully. They are watching a story about what happened to them. Sarah is reporting from the alley where they were attacked.

"Great news this morning as both Doctor Whistler and Mister Newsome are up and talking to the medical staff, and out of danger. The police have yet to comment on the search for the attacker, and the possible identity of the mysterious savior who apparently killed two of the assailants. This is Sarah Gennaro for channel five news."

Gordon muted the sound.

"I get the willies when I think that the man who saved us, might be the same guy who killed those men." He said solemnly.

"Whoever he is, I'm starting to believe the detectives. Maybe this... person does know me somehow."

"And evidently likes you. Thank God."

"I guess Hitler was busy." He deadpanned as he hears the door open.

"Um, Jim, we have visitors."

He did not recognize either Elizabeth Whistler or Walter as they entered the room. The fact that he was in uniform kept him from worrying if they shouldn't be there.

"May I help you?"

"My name is Elizabeth. I'm Jim's mother." She crossed over to Gordon. "You must be Gordon. I'm so relieved that you are alright."

She put out her hand, and they shook hands, which caught him off guard.

"Jim, Gordon this is my close personal friend, Walter." He stepped up to shake hands with him as well.

"Hello, Gordon." He said shaking his hand. "Pleasure to meet you. I'm glad you're going to be okay."

"Walter, the sheriff's deputy?" Jim queried holding out a hand anxiously.

"Yes, sir. In the flesh."

"What's he look like, Gordon?" He asks, holding on to his hand for a moment.

"Well." He started, still a little off kilter from the unexpected visitors. "He's about six two, and about two, ah ten, Walt?"

"Two twenty thanks to Elizabeth's cooking." Still clasping Jim's hand.

"Brown hair, with a stately touch of gray." Continuing with his assessment.

"Thank you." He said smiling.

"A little rugged looking, his uniform's well-kept, but an attractive man all in all." He summarized.

"That's quite a compliment, Walter." Elizabeth interjected. "From a man with the exquisite taste to choose my son."

"He's got a firm, calm grip." Finally letting go of Walt's hand.

"I was a bomber back in the Air Force. You need a steady hand for that."

"You never said how handsome Gordon is." She said politely.

"I didn't want to brag." Jim managing a slight smile. There was something very important going on here, and only he and his mother could acknowledge it.

"I wanted to fill you in on the latest on your attackers." Walt spoke up. "They found the last punk, Carl Prescott about a half an hour ago. It was on my radio on the way down."

"Is he dead? Like the other ones?"

"I'm afraid so." Speaking in a sullen tone. Jim appreciated his attempt to soften the news. "They tracked him in an abandoned warehouse, with the same wounds as the other victims. Looks like your admirer is not all there."

"I don't know how to feel, Walter, owing my life to a murderer."

"It must be an uncomfortable feeling." Walt replied. "We'll find him though. I'm sure all of these punks deserved a good old-fashioned ass whooping, but they didn't deserve to go out like that."

"I don't know about that." Gordon said. "At least with the one who started it all."

"I can understand that." Walt said. "I guess I might think the same if I were in your shoes about now."

"I'm just pleased the two of you will be okay." Elizabeth running a hand gingerly through Jim's hair, and touching the non-bruised areas of his face gently. "That is the important thing to me."

"How long have you two been dating, Mrs. Whistler?" Gordon asked, following her cue to change the subject.

"Now you are too old to call me Mrs. Whistler. You are to call me Elizabeth. Walt and I started seeing each other about two months ago."

"If you don't count the three months it took me to convince her to go out with me. I thought she'd never say yes."

"Mother needs a lot of persuading sometimes, Walt."

"I'm learning that." Walter laughed.

"You two act as if I was unreachable." Elizabeth finding herself on the defensive.

"You're quite an attractive woman, Elizabeth." Gordon stated. "I'm sure some men might be afraid to approach you."

"Well, thank you, Gordon. It's nice of you to say, but men are hardly ever intimidated by me."

"No, he's right." Walt agreed. "I watched you for a couple of weeks, before I even tried to talk to you."

"That can't be true?" She quipped.

"It is the God's honest truth. I thought you were the most beautiful woman I'd ever seen, and it took me a full month to work up the courage to speak to you."

"A man who flew bombers into combat, afraid of talking to a woman." Stating her disbelief. "Now who's going to believe that?"

"I would." Jim spoke up. "Several men asked me about you, because they were too scared to talk to you directly. Some of them never did."

"Well, I'm sure glad I did." Walt continued. "Best damn thing I've ever done in my life."

"Do you have any children, Walter?" Gordon inquired.

"No unfortunately. My wife left me the first time she couldn't follow me to a duty station. I never found a woman I wanted to have kids with since. Too bad Elizabeth isn't really only thirty instead of just looking like it. She's obviously a hell of a mother."

"Oh, you are such a flatterer." She smacks him playfully on the arm.

"Thank you, Walt." Jim acknowledging the part of the compliment belonged to him.

"You've done a great job with the shelter, Jim." Walter commended him. "I hear it is the model for others now."

"We do the best we can for the women who need us, although I wish none of them needed us."

"I think we all wish that was true." Walter said. "Well, I guess we're all getting together for Riverdance on your mother's birthday."

"We are?" Jim wondering if the surprise showed on his battered face.

"I told Walter how we usually spend time with each other on my birthday, so he got two more tickets so all four of us can go together."

"There is this awesome new Asian-fusion place in New Haven right near the theater." Gordon said jumping in. "My treat for your birthday, Elizabeth."

"You're welcome to pay next year, because I already promised to pick up the tab this time."

"Fair enough, but let us pick the restaurant, because Gordon always finds the best ones." Jim said.

"It's a deal then." Walt nodded in agreement. "I can't wait to see which restaurant you choose."

It was probably a good thing that Jim's eyes are swollen shut, because he was sure otherwise, he'd be rolling tears down his cheeks right about now. His mother had finally introduced him, and his lover to a boyfriend, proudly. Not even Gordon knew how much that moment meant to Jim. Yeah, it was a small blessing he couldn't open his eyes, because seeing this moment could not make it any better, and it was a long, long time coming.

TWENTY-TWO

"Think this guy has a thing for water or what?" Dave wondered aloud as he and Frank screeched to a halt in front of the waterfront warehouse where Carl Prescott's body had been found.

"I hadn't noticed that yet, but you may be right."

"Then again most of the empty buildings around here are on the water." Deflating his own theory.

"You're right, he's left every victim near the river or the coast, even the one he didn't kill there."

The building was another old riverfront factory long past its heyday. It had been unoccupied for so long they couldn't remember what it housed last.

"Didn't this used to be a foundry, or something."

"Wasn't it some sort of printing place."

A patrolman out front directed them to a side door. As they went down between the buildings, they spotted the Buick Electra.

"One deuce and a quarter." Dave looked inside giving interior a quick once over. "No sign of a struggle in here. I'd say the guy was out for the entire ride."

"I think we can give the doc credit for knowing how to throw a punch."

They entered the aging edifice to find a uniformed officer who pointed them to the back room, where the crime scene was located. The smell the death found them long before they reached the room. The putrid stench of blood separated from the body invaded their ole factory senses. A lab technician was examining the corpse as they approached the door.

"Holy shit." Frank exclaimed looking inside the room.

They expected a dead man with his throat slit, but this far exceeded their expectations. This was extreme. The room was trashed in a way that you could tell the room had been recently ransacked on top of the years of garbage collected on the broken tiles. Then, there was the blood.

It was everywhere. He glanced up at an old light fixture hanging from the ceiling and spotted a few drops on the torn faded shade. Blood splatter covered nearly every area of the room, but the bulk pooled around the victim.

The victim's body slumped over what appeared to be an old printing press, with his hands tied to the frame with electrical cords. The body was completely naked and sported bruises on almost every inch of visible flesh.

They tiptoed over to the deceased not to step in the hemoglobin covered sections of the deck. The technicians wore their full white suits, a clear sign of a messy crime scene.

They watched as one lab tech worked to identify the extensive damage to the body. They inched forward carefully trying not to disturb any of the work in progress still.

"Jesus Christ." Dave declared involuntarily as he surveyed the damage. "The fucking guy really went ape-shit this time."

"You can say that again." The technician working on the cadaver said standing up to talk to them. The lab tech stood up and removed their hood, and only then did they recognize Carrie. "It looks like he had a field day."

"Hey Carrie." Frank managing a smile despite the circumstances.

His instinct was to lean in and kiss her, but he remembered where he was. Instead, he reached out and squeezed her arm gently to acknowledge her. She understood and smiled briefly. Frank studied the room taking in the full extent of the carnage.

"This is not good. This is beyond his normal punishment. I can't tell if he was pissed off or enjoyed himself this time."

"It might be both." Carrie said. "But, it's gonna cost him."

"How's that?" Dave queried, still looking at the various bloodstains and pattern around the room.

"He forgot to wear a condom." She explained. "I found a semen sample in his rectum."

"So, he got off?" Frank asked.

"At least this time he did." Carrie replied. "I can't say for sure with the other ones, but this time the pony ride had a climactic finish."

"He really worked this guy over." Dave said. "This place is a freaking a war zone. He beat his ass all over the room before he did him. He was angry this time. Why else would he go to this level of brutality?"

"That would reinforce your theory about him knowing Doc Whistler." Carrie theorized. "And explain why he went the extra mile this time."

"What makes you say that?" Frank knew half of the answer just looking around the room.

"First there are the clothes; before, he pulled down their pants, or stripped them when they were unconscious. This time they're in pieces. He ripped them off him a little at a time while beating him all over the room. Check out his ankles."

They looked down to find the last three or four inches of his pants legs still around his ankles even though his pants and underwear were completely off his body.

"He's got bruises and was bleeding from a number of places." She continued. "Look at this."

She walked them around to the other side of the press and carefully lifted the head with her gloved hand to let them view his battered face. It was so swollen you could barely distinguish the nose.

"Jesus-fucking-Christ." Dave exclaimed. "He probably broke every fucking bone in his face."

"Worse than that. Look closely and you'll see the varying color of the facial contusions, or all them for that matter."

"This was long and drawn out." Frank interjected somberly.

"Yes, it was. He beat this man on and off for as long as three hours. My guess is every time he went out, he waited until he regained consciousness to start over."

She carefully reached over and tilted his head back. The throat was a shredded mass of flesh.

"Not one clean cut like the others, but more like eight or nine. All deep. All vicious, and all with a very, very sharp blade."

"This was personal." Frank said. "He's must be pissed off that this guy went after the doc. It's the only reasonable explanation."

"What if he's just starting to enjoy himself." Dave speculated. "Maybe his true homicidal tendencies are now paired up with his latent homosexual tendencies, and Voilà, one messy crime scene."

"I don't know, Dave. All these guys are woman beaters first. Why not do the other ones the same way?"

"It takes time to do something like this. Why not reserve the special treatment for the catalyst of the whole fiasco?"

"Okay." Carrie began. "I'm not the detective but it seems like his actions say something like: You can be a drunk homophobe, but not a woman beater, and definitely not an attacker of the protector of women, in this case Doc Whistler."

"I like it." Dave said. "She's getting better at this. The others get a quick death, because he doesn't know if they fit his criteria for a full pony ride."

"The perps that were already down, weren't a threat anymore." Frank added. "This guy's got a strange value system, but there are some threads of twisted honor or rules to it."

"He had to have seen the first confrontation to be able to ID the ringleader. Why not take him right after it happened?"

"He probably didn't have time? He ran right back to the bar for the reinforcements, because Doc Whistler and his friend were still on the scene."

"They would have seen him grab him. He's crazy, but he's been careful too."

"Well, he screwed up by leaving a semen sample in this guy." Carrie retorted. "I'll tell you his eye color by this time tomorrow. How'd you guys know about the car? You find a witness?"

"A homeless man in the neighborhood." Dave answered. "He saw some of it, but nothing inside the alley, and he was drunk."

"He did watch him carry the body off." Frank clarified. "We got an approximate size and shape of the killer, along with black or brown hair, but that's all. He identified the car too."

"Well, the good news for today is, thanks to him forgetting to wrap his Johnson," Carrie informed them, "I'll be able to tell you his physical traits, eyes, hair, skin color."

"He's a white guy." Frank said. "Who appears to idolize doc Jim, and he's had some sort of fight training, probably military."

"Jesus, this place is a mess, Frankie. This was definitely personal. Absolutely, no question about it."

Frank nodded his head for a moment surveying the gruesome scene.

"I think you're right, Dave. We may want to stick close to Doc Jim, and we might find this guy."

"Do we want to do a back ground check on the boyfriend, Newsome?"

"It couldn't hurt, but keep it low key. I've got a feeling this is more about the Doc than him. What that link is, is our hundred-thousand-dollar question, but we're close."

"Well, since he stole the car." Dave went on. "Then he walked away from the crime scene, unless he left a car near here."

"How would he have known Doc Jim would lead him to another abuser. I don't think he's psychic, but I'm convinced he knows who Whistler is and either likes him, and/or the work he does."

"Oh, no doubt he reveres him in some way." Dave said. "This victim was flat out tortured before he offed him. We should keep an eye on the other two survivors. If he thought Jim had already finished them, it could have been the reason he didn't bother with them."

"The other two guys were out cold and lifeless when the paramedics got there." Carrie stated.

"He might have thought the Doc had killed them. The other two had more severe injuries. The compound knee fracture and a concussion. This guy may have been the only one still moving of the three that he didn't kill on the spot."

"That matches the ringleader theory." Frank said. "If he saw the first confrontation with the girl."

"No matter what this guy's getting more violent." Dave said. "And he's enjoying it now, sexually. He could have a thing for the Doc, but can't express it for some reason?"

"You think he's gay?" Carrie's eyes expressing her sincerity to help.

"Maybe he is, but he's in denial over something to be this angry." Frank said. "Might be part of his identification with battered women, if he sees himself as a woman who can't be a woman. He wouldn't want to see other women being punished for being female."

"I can agree with that." Dave agreed. "But there's no denying the personal enjoyment in it this time. This guy's probably sitting in a room somewhere right now nursing an erection."

They all just let Dave's words hang out there for a minute as they surveyed the room for a moment.

"Let's get a tail on Doc Whistler, leg guy, and the other idiot that got knocked out at the scene." Frank said.

"I agree." Dave said. "The sooner, the better."

TWENTY-THREE

"Are you going to be okay with this?" Carrie asked, as she and Frank pulled up to the baseball park where Joey's little league team was playing.

"As long as I let Sarah's snotty comments slide, I'm cool. How about you?"

"I'll be fine. I already know everybody."

"Not Michael."

"Who's Michael?" Taking his hand for the walk to the field from the parking lot. "Her new guy?"

"Yeah. Dave had to tell me. She's never admitted it to me in person."

"Then we do get to be the adults today, don't we?" Spoken so reassuringly that he believed her.

"Hey dad!" Joey yelled, running off the sidelines towards the two of them.

Like any normal ten-year-old kid, he was energetic and inquisitive, and a spitting image of his father with curly black hair and brown eyes. His build was thinner than his dad's, and he would probably end up taller than him, but there was no mistaking him as Frank's son. He even had some of his father's cockiness.

"Hey, Miss Carrie." Nearly out of breath from running over to meet them. "Are you staying to watch the game?"

"Sure am. Your father says you're a pretty good player."

"Yeah, I'm fast too. They're moving me to third base from shortstop, because I can throw better than Danny. So, you're hanging out with my dad now? Are you like, his girlfriend or something?"

"Yes, I am. Is that alright with you?" Squatting down to talk to him directly.

"Sure, as long as I get to come visit the morgue some more."

"Well actually, I got in a little trouble for that." Smiling and standing up. "Your dad thought you shouldn't be handling body parts. I don't know why?"

"Cause he's a wuss." Joey shot out without hesitation. "He's afraid of dead people. They can't hurt you Dad they're already dead. Right, Carrie?"

"Well, there is still the possibility of disease." Trying to back up Frank's position in some way.

"I was wearing gloves."

"Who you calling a wuss, little man?" He threatened playfully. "You keep talking about your own father like that, and I'll make you spend the night in the morgue."

"That would be so cool. Can I bring a friend?"

Carrie couldn't help but laugh. He tried to muster up some sort of resolve, but between her smirk and Joey's laughter, it faded before he could find it.

"Don't look at me." She protested between chuckles. "You're the one who suggested it."

"Don't you have a game to play?" Attempting to regain control of the conversation.

"Yup, and we're gonna win too." Lowered his voice to a whisper. "This team stinks."

"So modest, like his father," Carrie laughed. "Good luck, Joey."

"Thanks. Oh, yeah." Turning back to face them. "Mom brought her new boyfriend, Michael."

The fact he rolled his eyes while making this statement made Frank smile on the inside.

"So, what's he like?" Slipping into detective mode.

"He's so boring." Joey exclaimed. "And he doesn't know anything about sports at all?"

"Well, as long as your mother likes him, and he's straight with you. You be fair with him. Is he nice to you?"

"Yeah, I guess he tries to be, but he's such a dork. He's so stiff, like he has a stick in his butt all the time."

"Well, your mom must like him, so try to cut him some slack." Not knowing why, he was sticking up for a guy he hadn't even met yet. "Maybe you can teach him how to loosen up enough so the stick will fall out."

Joey laughs loudly.

"Eww, gross." Joey winced.

"Give me a hug and go play your game." Kneeling down for the embrace. He liked hugs, and he tried not to be stingy with them like his father had been. It was important to

178

him that his son knew and felt loved by him, and a hug is easier than saying it aloud. Sometimes you understood two arms wrapped around you more clearly.

He sprinted back to his squad warming up on the diamond. Frank turned to find Carrie staring lovingly at him.

"Uh oh, what did I do?" Wondering if he had screwed up somehow.

"You're a great daddy, Frank." Her face sporting a supportive smile as she slipped her arms around him.

Carrie gave him that "woman in love" stare. It is part love, part trust, and part faith, and when it comes from a woman you're also in love with, it permeates your whole body making you feel warm and full. Like all your organs in your chest just doubled in size, and there's not enough room in your rib cage for them. It is the best feeling in the world.

Frank enjoyed the way her gaze swept him into her soul. His feelings for this woman grew every moment. They had played a cat and mouse for months, and now Tom and Jerry were on the same page, together, as one.

He reached up, stroked her cheek and kissed her. They began to kiss passionately oblivious to everyone and everything around them. The thrill of a new love drives all other problems right out of your mind. Unless of course, they walk right up to you.

"I take it you two are an item now?" Sarah's voice piercing the moment like an icicle.

They only separated a few inches.

"Be the adult." She whispered to him having every faith in him doing so.

Smiling at Carrie, he turned to face Sarah. She had her new beau, Michael, beside her, but it was clear from her stance, a half step in front of him, who was running the show. Wearing a stylish suit that appeared too hip for him, he was waiting for her to handle any introductions. She had found a man she could control he thought to himself. Poor sap.

"Ah, that would be yes." Frank extolled. "You remember Carrie, don't you?"

"Hello Sarah." Carrie said politely.

"So, you two are finally an official couple? No surprise there." Sarah in her casually snide voice. "You've been drooling over her for a year."

"Well, that's understandable." Michael quipped trying to be part of the discussion.

Only Frank saw the subtle glare in Sarah's eye when he complimented Carrie. Oh, is he ever going to pay for that later he thought to himself.

"Why thank you kind stranger?" Carrie basking in the acclaim.

"I take it you're Michael?" Holding out his hand. "Frank Carmine, nice to meet you finally."

"Michael Littleton." Shaking Frank's hand, he could tell Michael was putting more into his handshake than normal to make a strong impression. "My pleasure."

"So, you work with Sarah?"

"I'm the news director."

"So, you like organize the whole thing from behind the scenes?" Carrie asked.

"Yes, I do." He stated proudly. "I let the beautiful people like Sarah, do all the on-air work."

"Thank you, Michael." Sarah's tone still reeked of condescension acknowledging his feeble attempt to dig himself out of the doghouse by throwing her a compliment.

"Listen, Frank." She continued. "We just got word of a shootout between drug gangs over in New Haven."

"I can take Joey back to my place tonight." Frank said. "Go score the scoop."

"Um..." She started awkwardly. "Is Carrie going to be there? Overnight?"

"Does Michael stay overnight at the house, yet?" Frank trying to be diplomatic, and careful of his tone.

Sarah paused, glancing at Michael for a moment before answering.

"Not all night. He leaves before Joey gets up."

"Well, I don't believe Joey's that easily fooled." Absolutely loving having the upper hand. "So, yes, Carrie will be staying the night, and I would rather be straight with him about it."

"Fine. Whatever." Forced to agree by not having a basis for a defense.

There was an awkward silence that Frank let hang enjoying the moment.

"You don't have anything more on the guy who's killing the abusers by any chance?" Michael jumping at the opportunity to change the subject.

"We are making progress." Frank instinctively using his authority voice. "We've gotten a lot more information on his profile now. We'll catch him."

"Some people want to give him a medal." Michael said. "Not only is he only eliminating wife beaters, but he apparently saved Doctor Whistler and his friend's life."

"If he was just taking these guys out back, and kicking their ass, I'd agree with them. But this man is very unstable, and he's getting more violent each time. We will bring him in, and soon."

"Excellent. Well, we probably should go grab our seats." He said gingerly to Sarah.

"I want a scoop when it goes down, Frank." Sarah added flatly.

"If I have time, I'll do that."

"Nice meeting you, Michael." Carrie chimed-in.

"Same here," he said, shaking her hand.

As they walked off Frank started to giggle out loud.

"What's so funny?" Carrie asked.

"That guy is dead meat. The last thing you want to do around Sarah is compliment another woman. He is *never* going to hear the end of that. I hope he's not driving to New Haven with her, because she'll make it forty-five minutes of pure hell."

"Not one sarcastic comment. I'm so proud of you."

"Do I win a cookie?"

"Oh, I think that might even entitle you to dessert later." While slipping her arms back around his waist.

"Mmm, desert, and what's for desert tonight?

She leans in close and whispered in his ear in a voice that could melt steel.

"Irish crème."

"My favorite." He kissed her.

Nobody noticed the man sitting nearby, looking like any other grandparent watching his kid playing baseball. The man had stately good looks for a man in his late fifties, a little shorter than Frank, but stockier.

They walked over to the stands on the far side behind Joey's team, they were unaware of the man on the bleachers who had done such an excellent job of pretending not to be listening. Especially when he heard every word.

TWENTY-FOUR

It had been a good night, Frank thought as he tucked his son into bed. Joey had already whipped both he and Carrie in gin rummy by a sizable margin, but what really pleased him was how well the two of them got along together. Sure, they had previously known each other, but they seemed to click tonight in a way that made him feel like he was finally doing the right thing as far as she is concerned. He even demanded that she come tuck him in with Frank.

He sat on the end of his bed watching this woman who was beginning to mean so much, so fast that it scared him, put his son's fears to rest as well.

"I'm glad you're gonna be my dad's girlfriend, Carrie." Joey said with ten-year-old honesty that squeaks out without a filter now and then. "Are you two gonna get married?"

"Hmm, I don't know," With an ease Frank would have never mustered for that question. "Do you think we should?"

"I think so. Dad needs someone to take care of him." Lowering his voice to a whisper. "He can't cook very well."

"What? I heard that. What about my world-famous hamburgers, or my legendary fourth of July grilled lobster?"

"What about your meatloaf?" Prodding his father, laughing hysterically.

"So, tell me about this meatloaf, Mr. Carmine," Carrie mused. "Should I be concerned?"

"It's not that-, I only burned it *one* time."

"Dad, you dropped it on the floor and it broke the tile."

"It did not. Where are these stories from? Are you trying to make me look bad in front of my woman? Say goodnight, Ms. McKenna, and then wait for me in the kitchen, because I don't want any witnesses when I kill my son."

"Yeah, he's gonna make me eat his meatloaf." Joey now hysterical with laughter.

Carrie gave him a hug goodnight between laughs, and was caught off guard when he kissed her on the cheek.

"Goodnight, Miss Carrie."

"Goodnight, Joey. We'll see each other soon."

As she got up and Frank slid forward on the bed, she placed a hand on his shoulder and raised her eyebrows in such a way as to let him know she was pleasantly surprised. She stepped outside the door, but couldn't help herself as she stopped just out of sight hoping to eavesdrop the rest of the conversation.

"I like Carrie, dad. You should marry her." Making it sound so simple. "She's real pretty."

"She sure is, isn't she?"

Frank noticed her shadow giving away her hiding place on the other side of the door jamb. So, he stood up, and put a finger over his lips asking for Joey's silence, and smiling, backed up to the doorway quietly.

"Carrie likes you too." Now pointing out her shadow on the floor near the door frame.

Joey had to cover his mouth with both hands to prevent himself from laughing out loud.

"Do you know how I can tell she thinks you're important?"

"No, dad?" Then quickly then putting his hands back over his mouth not to give away the ruse.

"You are so important to Carrie." Inching silently towards the open doorway. "She's standing right outside the door to hear what you say about her."

Before she could react, Frank reached around the door, grabbed her by the arm and pulled her back into the room.

The expression on her face was priceless, mostly embarrassment, but with a hint of joy at being included in the family shenanigans.

Joey broke out laughing, no longer hiding.

"Busted." He exclaimed between guffaws.

"Okay." Carrie giggled. "You got me, Mister Detective."

"Yes, I did. Joey, tell her who the best detective in the world is."

"You are Dad." Without a moments' hesitation.

"Damn right. Maybe I should punish her for spying?"

"Yeah. You should spank her." He added trying not to laugh again.

"Spank me?" Carrie whispered breathlessly. "I might like that."

"You think I should use the belt?" He asked Joey, prompting a wide-eyed reaction from her.

"No." Joey said playing along. "Use the wooden spoon like grandma does."

"Wooden spoon?!" She protested playfully.

"Ooh, Good idea. Okay, Carrie, I'm going to need you to go fetch the wooden spoon out of the drawer in the kitchen and wait for me by the table. You're getting a spanking young lady." Dropping into a whisper," And lose the pants."

"Yes sir. Goodnight Joey. Thanks a lot." Teasing him as she exited.

"Anytime." Calling after her as she headed out of the room.

Frank sat back on the edge of the bed, and began tucking in his son.

"I probably should go easy on her, first offense and all."

"Dad, you're not actually gonna spank her."

"I'm not? What am I going do with her?"

"You're gonna kiss her." Which, he barely managed to get out between snorts.

Frank leaned in and kissed Joey on the forehead.

"You're getting too smart there, young man."

"Because you like girls, and you're never mean to them."

"That is correct, always treat girls with respect."

"So that bad guy, he won't come after you right?"

Frank felt a chill in his spine from Joey's question. It was fanned by the guilt he was carrying about raping Amanda. He had to apologize for that, and do the right thing. How else would he continue to look his son in the face when he tells him to treat women well?

"You don't have to worry about me, Joey. If that guy comes anywhere near me, or you, or Carrie, or even your mom and Michael, I'll kill him with my bare hands, before he'll have a chance to hurt anyone of you."

"I bet you could too." Greatly relieved by Frank's statement.

"Hell, yeah I could, now go to sleep before I knock you out."

"Sure, Dad. You can go kiss Carrie, now."

Frank shook his head, and moved over to the switch by the door.

"What am I going to do with you? Growing up so damn fast."

He turned off the light.

"Goodnight Dad." From within the darkness. "I love you."

"I love you too, Joey. Goodnight." And he closed the door behind him.

He strolled out to the kitchen. Waiting for him, Carrie stood bent over the table obediently with her pants pulled down to her knees. Resting on her perfect ass, balancing precariously, was a wooden spoon. Frank's heart skipped a beat.

"I've been a bad girl." She purred.

"You are so, so bad." Trying not to let his racing heartbeat throw off his timing.

"You're just going to have to punish me." She said in a low throaty tone that would have convinced him to kill.

"Hmm." Kneeling down right behind her. "I guess so."

Lifting the spoon from its perch below the small of her back, he used it to trace the outline of her superior derriere slowly while enjoying the view. Wisps of her curly red pubic hairs peeked out from between her tightly closed leg. Running his other hand over a smooth curvature, admiring the subtle combination of softness and firmness, he couldn't help himself. Raising the utensil with a devilish smile, he gave her a light smack on the cheek with the spoon.

"Frank?!" She chirped involuntarily. She tried to straighten up, but he held her in place with his free hand, using only enough force to make it clear she didn't need to move.

"I'm sorry." Murmuring directly in her ear seductively. "Let me kiss it and make it better."

Placing the utensil on the table beside her, he caressed her rear with both hands. Leaning in close to the light red mark from the strike, he drew his tongue across the spot lightly. Then he moved a few inches back, and blew a cool stream of breath on to the moist skin. This made her coo ever so faintly. Moving in again, he followed it up with a breath of hot air across the bruise for contrast. She moaned softly.

He smacked her on the other cheek with his hand. She spun around quickly to protest, but he threw her over his shoulder. Standing up, he started for the bedroom, but stopped long enough to pick up the wooden spoon.

"We might need this," And carried her into the bedroom.

TWENTY-FIVE

The week had been an eventful one for Elizabeth Whistler. She nearly lost her son in a horrible beating in a dark alley, only to have it give her the courage to truly accept who he is. The shameful part was, she had to face the possibility of losing him to appreciate the man he has become, who happens to be gay.

She raised a good man. For years, she thought her choice to not take another lover after his father left had something to do with him being homosexual. It is clear to her now, she was wrong. He simply is gay, and the time had come to say so. The whole event turned out to be more cathartic than she thought to introduce him to Walter, and proudly for who he is. The fact that Walt was genuinely impressed with Jim for who he is, and not what he is.

Somewhere in letting Walt share in her acceptance of Jim, and his honest approval of the man he's become, led to an unexpected level of bonding with him. He is a top-quality man, and is never anything but respectful to her, treats her like a lady, and never pushes her to be closer. His patience clearly one of his strong points. He tries to be just there and support her, and looking back he has done that these past several months.

The revelation if her son is truly a man now, she can let herself tend to her own life and needs. They had been there all along, kept down, hidden as if they weren't important. As she opened up to him and in turn Walter, it let her remember the pleasure of trust, and the comfort of another's confidence. The sharing of your life with someone who cares, and the physical expression of that is something she denied herself for too long.

Jim and Gordon's relationship was developing in front of her eyes. The growing faith and affection they hold for each other, as well as their commitment to one another as a couple. The joy of two people facing the world as a team. It was embarrassing her son's gay liaison reminded her of why she deserved one, and to let someone in. To share their lives together as one, beating down the challenges of life together. She decided she is ready for that again, and that's why Walter is still in her boudoir.

There is still a lot of work ahead for her and Jim, but they were off to a solid start. There were so many things she needed to tell him, apologize for, and left unsaid. She owed him that much. He deserved to know the truth about his father, and that day at the library. Tomorrow, she is going to put all their history on the table, so they could all move forward.

The candle's shadows and light flickered against the darkness, as she snuggled in tight to Walter's warm body beside her. He made love to her so passionately. Slow, and deliberate, kind and gentle, she forgot how nice it was to be loved by a man with passion in his soul. It warmed her soul that she still could arouse such passions from a man. Maybe she wasn't so old after all, or too late to start living *her* life again. And even if Walt turned out not to be the one, she was reassured to learn she could begin over now again at her age.

Walter's thick, muscled arm wrapped around her from behind, and held her hand in front of her chest. He is a big man, and she felt safe in his arms. It had been some time since she experienced this peace of mind, and she liked it. This is going to be a godsend, and she promised herself to give Walter a fair chance. Not to hide things from him, and do her best to communicate how she is feeling, and understand his feelings as well.

Yes, Elizabeth Whistler is ready to live her life again, after only taking fifty-four years to finally realize it is hers for the living. She smiled watching the candle flicker, and the shadows on the wall, enjoying a beautiful peaceful moment, in a life barren of them of late. Inside she chided herself for not trying sooner, but at least she understood now that she could, and she isn't going to let the chance slip away.

When the phone rang the first time, she thought the ringing was part of a dream, but when it rang again, she checked the clock. Whenever a phone rings after midnight a mother can't help but have one thought, "my child's in trouble."

As she snatched up the receiver, it roused Walt from his slumber as well.

"Hello?" Hoping for some sort of positive news at 2 A.M. in the morning.

Putting the receiver to her ear she wanted to believe it all a nightmare, but she recognized the voice as soon as she heard it. The years flew away.

"Elizabeth." The man said. "You've done a good job raising *our* son."

The voice shocked her into silence, not knowing what to say. She didn't want Walter to know who she was with on the line. Everything she had just promised herself about sharing honestly with this man vanished the moment the words registered in her brain. The years of self-denial and the quiet strength she developed pushed to the forefront of her psyche reaching down deep, and she spoke up.

"I don't appreciate you calling this late, young man." With an authority built out of fear. "For the record, I have a policeman lying right beside me right now. Perhaps you'd like to talk to him?"

He hung up and a wave of relief washed over her.

"Humph." Continuing the act for his benefit. "I didn't think so

She put the handset back in the cradle ever so slightly, so as not to give away how upset she truly was to hear the utterance from her past.

"Who was it? What did they say?" Walt asked concern in his voice and a desire to protect her in his eyes.

"Some idiot." Lying to him only seconds after promises herself she wouldn't. "He wanted to know what I was wearing. I swear, some people."

Walter reached over her and picked up the phone.

"What are you doing?" She asked nervously.

"Star sixty-nine. It'll say what the number called you."

"I don't think I have that feature Walter." Almost praying she was right.

"Alright, we can get around that." He said putting the receiver down only long enough to hang up, and began dialing again. "I'll call dispatch and get a trace."

"Can't that wait until morning?" Gently resting her hand on his holding the land line.

"Sure. You're right." He agreed, but took a moment to lift the clock and make note of the time. "I'll do it tomorrow."

"Thank you, Walter. Now lay back down. I was just starting to fall asleep. I always feel safe when you're here."

"Good. That's what I was going for." Hoping to put her fears to rest.

Walter laid back beside her and curled around her again, like before the phone call interrupted their slumber. Nuzzling up against him brought back the comforting warmth, but her impression of safety was gone. The candle's glow is no longer magical, and the shadows on the wall seem like her own dark secrets swirling around inside her head.

Yes, Elizabeth Whistler is having an eventful week.

TWENTY-SIX

Frank was still smiling and trying to catch his breath as he studied Carrie coming out of the bathroom naked. Lit from behind her radiance seemed magnified. She turned off the light, seductively stalked her way back to bed, and slid right up beside him in one long fluid motion.

She laid her head on Frank's chest and put her arm around him. He took a deep breath in and out.

"Um, young lady." He began gingerly. "If I do recall you have something you're supposed to tell me about tonight."

"Yes, it's my turn," she said softly, but not hedging at all. "Okay, here we go."

She nuzzled up against him tightly, and wrapped her leg around his torso as if to steady herself. In a strange way, he was hoping for something almost evil. He wanted to bring his feeling for her back to a manageable level. He had her on a pedestal from the moment he first saw her, and having her fuck his lights out passionately didn't exactly lower her down to earth in his eyes. She made love to him with passion and conviction. He hated himself for looking for a flaw, but if he didn't find one soon, he could see himself dropping the "L" word by the end of the week.

"The worst thing I ever did." She started slowly, her voice exuding a feebleness. An odd tone tinged with a fear of rejection that led Frank to hold her tighter.

"When I was in my last year of residency, at Yale-New Haven hospital. My grandmother became ill. She had been in remission from cancer for about six months, so it was only a matter of time before the symptoms flared up again. My grandfather died a few years earlier from a heart attack. He was a longshoreman who worked hard all his life, and his heart quit on him right after he turned sixty."

He debated if he should interrupt her to express condolences or not, but decided to be silently supportive and let her tell her story. Instead, he stroked her hair as she went. His desire to comfort her in anyway caused him pain.

"My heart broke when they brought her in the second time. I would stop by her room several times a day to say 'hi'. After we got her test results, it became apparent she simply wasn't going to survive this time. Her doctor asked me if I wanted to tell her. He said if I managed to do this, I'd never be afraid of telling anyone what's ailing them ever again. He didn't tell me to, he gave me the option to say "no", but part of me knew he was right. It would make me stronger and might make things easier for Gram."

"Wow, that's a tough call. Did you, do it?"

"I couldn't make up my mind. So, I slipped into her room late one night. I planned on reading her chart and slipping out to make a final decision, hoping something in the information would give me strength. Instead, the stats were terrifying. The cancer had spread to every major organ. At best, she might last two or three months with aggressive treatment. I sat down in a chair beside her bed, and cried. I remember being in the kitchen of the little house they had by the docks, watching her make crab cakes, and I started crying like a baby. I could smell them."

The tears ran down her face on to his chest as she told her tale. It was almost too much for him. He didn't want to make her finish.

"You don't have to tell me tonight. It can wait to another time."

"No." Stopping to collect herself, and wiping her eyes. "I promised you, and you told me yours."

She wiped the droplets off Frank's bosom with the sheet, and rested her head on him again, as if to conserve energy to tell the story.

"So, I'm sitting there next to her bawling like an infant, when I hear her sweet little voice say 'Carrie, honey, don't cry. I know I'm not gonna make it.' That just made it worse, the fact that she acknowledged what was wrong before I couldn't even tell her. She spoke up again. 'My time is over. I want you to do one last thing for me. You've grown into such a pretty woman' she said so sweetly. So, I said sure Gram, anything you want."

She stopped and took a deep breath, which made Frank do the same.

"I want you to send me home' she said, and I thought she meant that she wanted to die at home. I told her; I can arrange that if she would rather be there. But instead, she said 'You know all about medicines now, so you can make it painless, and they won't be able to tell you did it'. She wanted me to euthanize her."

She adjusted her grip on him and went on.

"She was fed up with the constant pain, wanted to end it all, and pleaded her case so calmly I was unnerved. She said 'Carrie, I'm done living. I have raised a family, seen a lot of places, and now I'm finished. I have a good man waiting for me on the other side and I don't want to keep him waiting any longer.' I said I don't have the strength to do this, but she held my hand. `Honey, imagine you're me. You are wasting away. Everyday takes more drugs to block the pain away. Is that how you want to die?' I couldn't answer. All I could do was shake my head no. `Then don't let me go like this. Send me home, Carrie. Please. I'm ready.' I nodded my head and slipped out of the room. I got a syringe of a drug that would stop her heart, but they'd never find it because the one she was taking, had a similar derivative with a different active ingredient. I don't know how I found my way back to her room."

"I'm right here." Frank whispered. She was determined to get this all out, and he encouraged her to continue.

"When I came back in her room, she smiled so widely you'd think she'd won the lottery. `I knew you could do it, Carrie. God bless you child' she said. I asked her a few more times if, you know, she was really sure. I told her what would happen. She was more worried about me getting in trouble than actually dying. I asked her if she needed me to tell anyone anything. She said `Tell them I love them, and I'll leave a light on for them'. I added the injection to her I.V. in her wrist, and within seconds her heart stopped, and her breathing followed. I held her hand the whole time. Her monitor alarm went off, but otherwise she passed quietly. I quickly capped the needle and put it in my sock. The physician on duty came rushing in with a nurse, and turned on the lights. I just sat there crying. He looked at me compassionately. I said, 'She just said goodbye, and to tell them to please let her go.' The doctor crossed over to me. He never doubted me for a moment. He gave me a big hug and said he was sorry. So did the nurse. They gave me the rest of the day off. I went home and climbed into my shower with my scrubs on holding the syringe and crying for nearly two hours, before I turned off the water. I know it was what she wanted, but I still felt so dirty. I still do."

When she looked up at Frank, tears were running down his face.

"That is the most beautiful thing I've ever heard someone do for somebody." He held her tightly. "Promise if I get to that point someday, you'll send me home."

"Only if you swear to do the same for me." She proposed.

"I swear to God I will if I have to, if you want me to."

"At the time I didn't think so, but now, I think I want that too."

She stared in his eyes, and yet his emotions continued to swell within him. Maybe the teardrops rinsed his eyes for a clearer view, or maybe it was the tears in her beautiful eyes as she kissed him gently on the lips. His heart tried to burst through his chest. He couldn't hold her tight enough. He couldn't feel any closer, but couldn't get close enough to still his desire. This woman owns him body and soul now, in every measurable way.

And as he wrapped himself around her and closed his eyes, he watched her pedestal rise even higher than before.

TWENTY-SEVEN

It had been some time since his surveillance techniques were used last. Though never what they should be, but with all the use they had been getting of late, they were improving. Still, they would never match his instincts.

He had managed to follow the detective for most of the morning after he left the station without his knowing. Even when he circled the block three times in a row, he never lost him, or gave himself away. What was he doing? Did he make him? Is he staking out a suspect? The thought alone made him smile, but something is askew with this detective he could not identify. His hackles tingled, like when you can smell something bad, before you find the rotten apple core that somehow ended up under the couch.

After the third time around, Frank finally pulled up to the apartment complex.

They were upscale apartments, fairly new, somewhat stylish. The neighborhood was rather nice. Modest, single-family homes surrounded the two-story buildings. It was one of the few rental complexes in the area, but well-kept. The lawn appeared to be well manicured, and the sidewalks and walkways clean. What was this investigator hoping to find here on the edge of the upper middle class?

Frank parked in front of the stone and metal edifice, turned off the car, and put his hands on the wheel. His stomach became a twist of knots. What did he expect to achieve? What's the worst-case scenario? The variations in his mind, playing out the endless scenes in his head. Shaking them off, he took a deep breath.

"Okay, Frank," he said out loud trying to muster his courage. "Let's get this over with before you lose your nerve."

He followed the walk around and up to the second story apartment that faced the street, and stared at the door. The wooden number "5" mocking him, daring him to knock. He raised his hand slowly and knocked. Although not his firmest, most convincing blow, he was sure it was heard.

"In a minute." A woman's voice said.

His heart moved into his throat as he listened to her move towards the peephole and identify him. Every second passed like hours as he waited for her initial reaction after opening the door. If, she opens the door.

"What do you want, Frank?" Amanda asked from behind the closed door.

"I, uh, wanted to speak to you for a minute, if I could please." Barely getting the words out without butchering them.

She opened the door only a few inches, and peered out. Her look was anything but promising, and she left the chain attached to the door.

"The fact that Tommy's not here right now wouldn't have anything to do with the timing of your visit, would it Frank?"

Frank's soul plummeted. After twenty years he wasn't sure what to expect, but in his worst scenarios, he never considered her thinking he'd come back for more. He dropped his head in shame.

"No, Amanda." Mumbling weakly. "Not really."

"So, you got something to say you couldn't say in front of my husband?"

"I just wanted to talk to you alone." Frank stammered, defensively while doing his best not to sound defensive. "It didn't concern Tommy directly."

"You don't think so huh-" She was about to go off. Her tone was rising, when her youngest boy came to the door.

"Who's here, mommy?" The young boy questioned her innocently.

"Nobody, honey. Go finish watching your movie." She deftly re-directed the boy back into the apartment.

She stepped out on the balcony to face him, closing the door behind her.

"Say what you gotta say, and make it quick."

"I came to apologize." He managed. "For, back in high school, for..."

"Still can't say it can you, Frank?" She shot back sharply. "Raping me? Is that what you're talking about Frank?"

"Yes." He said, drawing a deep breath, and imbuing his tone with all the sincerity he could muster. "I came to apologize for raping you back in high school."

"Well, holy shit. Frank Carmine fucking apologizes. A little late Frank don't you think?"

"You're absolutely right. I should have apologized years ago. It was wrong. I was wrong."

"Damn right it was wrong," getting a little louder. "I said no. I said no like, fifty fucking times while you were still slamming away because you wanted to finish. You didn't apologize then. Why the change of heart, Frank? Why all of a sudden, with this phony apology scene."

"I thought I should at least try to apologize for what I did."

"Well, I hope you can sleep nights now, Frank. Did you think apologizing would erase the months I felt like used goods while I tried to make things right with Pat Jensen? Now, I love Tommy. Don't get me wrong. He's a good husband and a good father, but you know damn well he works for Pat."

"Every time Tommy comes home and says '*fucking Pat don't know shit about putting up a house*', I think I should be sitting in that big million-dollar house of Pat's on the river, listening to him bitch about what a know-it-all Tommy thinks he is, while I tell the maid what to make for dinner."

"Every time he comes home bitching about his boss, don't you think a little part me still wonders what might've happened if you hadn't raped me. What if Pat didn't tell me, it was over between us, because I slept with you? Oh, don't worry, I didn't tell him you raped me. I didn't have the balls then either, but I'd sure like to tell him now."

"You changed my whole fucking life. My whole fucking life, Frank. I'm sure glad you came to say you're sorry now. I feel so much better now. It's almost like my life and my feelings matter more than you getting that nut. Fuck you, Frank. Fuck you, for raping me. Fuck you for waiting twenty years to apologize, and fuck you for apologizing."

"I don't think this apology has jack shit to do with me, does it Frank? It wouldn't have anything to do with this case you're working on. The guy who's killing all these guys that beat up woman. What's the matter, Frank? Afraid you might be on his list? I'm sure rape qualifies on his list of *shitty things* men do to women that they should be killed for. Fuck you, Frank. I hope your next."

She slammed the door behind her, leaving him alone on the balcony, in a silence that he was all too aware of. What did he expect? At least he tried, but she was dead right. He would have never apologized if not for this case and Carrie. Things would have been left as they were unless she forced it on him in some other way, shape, or form. The whole affair seemed more insidious than when he had confessed it all to Carrie. But then again, when he explained it to her, he didn't know all the details of the aftermath, from the perspective of the victim.

Frank dropped his head and walked back to the stairs at the end of the balcony.

He needed to take a bath. A shower would not erase the stink on him right now. One belligerent narcissistic asinine move by him made a seismic difference in her life, that he'll never be able to change or take back. All the criminals and even murderers he's taken off the street, it will never alter what he did to her personally. Not from her point of view. Not ever.

As Frank's footsteps approached the stairwell, he turned and glided towards the other end of the apartments. With his back to him, he was just another tenant making his way home to an apartment somewhere in the complex. Frank didn't even look, his soul heavy and sullen. He watched the detective get into his car from the corner of the building, sure that he never noticed him at all. The detective's body language was that of a man who had just buried his dog after he personally had to put him down. The fight had been taken out of him.

Frank sat in his car in silence, looking at himself in the mirror, unable to make eye contact with himself, he lowered his head again. Then, out of nowhere, he started to cry.

He smiled watching Frank try to purge himself. This depression would make the upcoming task all the easier. So, the man who was tracking him is a rapist. And as the woman said, it probably qualifies on the list of things men do to woman to warrant his attention. It most certainly does.

TWENTY-EIGHT

Frank turned the water on in the bathtub. Closing the lid to the toilet, he sat down, still in a deep fog of heavy emotions. Watching the flow stream down into the bath, neither sound or visuals registered with him. He checked the temperature by reflex, although far too hot, still held his hand under for as long as he could stand, removed it calmly, and used the other hand to adjust the heat to a more tolerable level.

He couldn't tell his partner why he was blowing off the afternoon, especially when they were scheduled to do the legwork on Doc Jim's relatives. But Dave had enough of a sense about his colleague to know when he wanted some time alone. There was something off in his voice, the disassociation in his tone was palpable. He also knew not to pry too hard. He had his own process for working things out, and then tell him the results later. Ole Frankie could work out anything with some heat, water, no interruptions, and a little time. Several of these short-term sabbaticals led directly to him solving a case, or removing a major stumbling block. If he needed some quiet time, he gave it to him, knowing they'd both benefit eventually, even if that meant doing all the family research by himself today.

As the sound of the tub filling with water echoed in the mostly tile room, he stood naked in front of the bathroom's mirror, staring at his reflection in the glass. What was he looking at? A rapist? He thought the apology to Amanda might not go well, but he never anticipated the devastated feeling he was carrying now. How do solve a crime you committed? What is the appropriate punishment?

It clung to him like fifty extra pounds of wet clothes, and stared back at him from his own eyes as he looked into the mirror. He was not a bad guy. He had done countless good things in his life, from saving lives, to the many criminals he put away who wreaked havoc on others. There were so many things that were positive, and yet still the weight bore down on him.

How did that one event change so much? Did he destroy her chances to live a better life? Would her and Pat have stayed together otherwise, or lasted as long as she and Tommy have so far? If things happen for a reason, a stiff dick seemed like a shitty one with painful clarity now. Hell, it didn't seem very good five minutes afterwards, but he couldn't bring himself to admit that back then.

Leaning over the sink, staring directly into a reflection mere inches away, what did he hope to find in the deep brown depths of his eyes? Or in the pitch black of their center? He wanted to see *the good*. It was in there. Dedicating his life to the most difficult and least appreciated job in the world, being a cop, his whole existence had become a battle against evil. Every day he tried to uphold justice, and help the public live in safety. This is who Frank Carmine is, in his heart, and to his core. But today, he couldn't find it in his eyes.

The reflection of his face appeared in his eyes, shining vapidly from inside the looking glass. The dark infinity of his pupils reflected his struggling soul. Like, everything he accomplished before this moment, is now over-shadowed by a moment of stupidity that changed the lives of two innocent people, maybe more.

Even when he had killed someone, not once did he feel this bad? However, there is something about a person attempting to kill you that releases you of any guilt about having to shoot them. There were no offsetting factors to mitigate the response here. She hadn't hurt anyone. What was he trying to prove then? What, if anything, could he truly do now?

Shook his head violently, he pulled back from the mirror, but re-established eye contact before speaking out loud.

"It was wrong. You admitted it. It's all you could do."

He collected himself, and turned off the faucet. It gurgled to a halt as he swirled his hand around to blend any uneven spots.

"Close enough," he thought as he arranged a towel on the floor in front of the bathtub, and made sure he had another larger one in reach for when he finished.

The souls of your feet are nearly impervious to heat. Fire-walkers never impressed him. Stepping into a bath, the ankles were the true test. The fluid seared his skin when first submerged, but quickly cooled to the steady warmth he desired. After living in this apartment for the past two and half years, he finally figured out how to reliably control the temperature from the spigot. He squatted down and stretched out his legs, submerging them.

He leaned back against the back of the tub, closed his eyes, and inched his way down until the water reached up to his neck. Then bending his knees allowed him to sink down enough to submerge his head and torso, until the liquid surrounded him fully. It finally began to melt the chill in his soul left by his encounter with Amanda.

Frank always connected with water, and thought of it as one of the core elements of the life. To him, we are a small piece of the world itself by way of immersion in her waters. The secret behind all hot springs isn't the heat, but the sense of connection with the soul of the planet that provided it.

He slid down further, following his normal routine, slipping all the way in until only his lips and nose remained above the waterline. Even his eyelids bathed in the tepid healing water. All his senses were now cut off from the outside world. The isolation eased the strain of his troubled mind.

Resting his arms and hands on the porcelain bottom took the weight off them, allowing him to fully relax his whole body. His left hand fidgeted with the ring on the rubber stopper in the drain, placed oddly in the center of the old tub. As the noise of society disappeared, he became one with the water. One with himself. His heartbeat and breathing, the only sounds he heard now. He drew deep balmy breaths of air off the surface, filling his lungs with warmth moist oxygen. No longer was he "on earth", but part of it. This world is fundamentally eternal, and swallows your problems with ease. A calm pushed the anger and doubt from his consciousness. The faint rhythms of his pulse slowed as he focused on them. A few years back, he learned to physically lower his heart rate by listening and concentrating, creating his own private sensory deprivation tank to help him find himself again.

After he had an epiphany, or started to prune, he would start the final "Cleansing". He would pull the plug out and concentrate on his problems going into the fluid, and down the drain until his body is completely revealed above the water line, before reopening his eyes. Re-entering reality inch-by-inch, as the cool air touched each layer of newly exposed skin. A symbolic rebirth, refreshing his thoughts and strengthening his soul. This was his private therapy, and there was nothing it could not overcome. So far.

As he lay in the bath, he would fidget with the cheap drain-plug. He would put one finger inside the metal ring, a symbol of his temporary marriage to the earth's consciousness, and drift away.

At first, he would try to think of nothing. Just enjoy the warmth surrounding him and the silence. The real world existed somewhere else, as he and the earth mother renewed their bonds. All his faith in himself and his ability to protect would return. He would renew his vows to serve with new vigor and clarity, and his indiscretion with Amanda would be put behind him, and he would continue in his sworn duties to the human race. At least that was the plan. Plans get broken.

When the fist struck his face, mercilessly destroying his peaceful sanctuary, he was unsure what or who just violated his most sacred personal space. The powerful blow instantly dragged him back to reality, as well as drove him completely under water. He didn't have time to hold his breath, so as his head hit the bottom of the cast iron tub, he choked in his first small gasp of water.

Instinctively, he pulled out the plug and reached up for some sort of grip on his attacker. Damn son of bitch was strong, and had gravity on his side. The strength of his hand clenching his head held it firmly in place. The pressure from his fingers and thumb pressing deep into the soft facial skin. Frank threw a punch at where he assumed his head might be. The strike glanced off the side of the assailant's head, but allowed him enough time to clear the waterline and catch a short breath.

His gulp of air turned out to be about one-quarter water, thanks to the splashing. His broken nose was now stinging on the inside thanks to the chlorine in public water. Anyone who didn't think they still put that in city water need only inhale some through their olfactory as a reminder. Unable to breathe, the sting somehow accelerated the sense of desperation already forming.

It would take at least fifteen to thirty seconds for the tub would drain down enough, so he couldn't be pushed under, as long as he could keep his head straight. He tried desperately to strike the man, but his lack of leverage combined with the attacker's strength seemed to be rendering his attempts futile at best. They did earn him the smallest of breaths, although now half filled with water.

Was this him? The killer he was searching for? Had he been following him? Did he know about Amanda, or is he just trying to kill the man who's hunting him? Neither prospect was encouraging.

The intruder gripped his throat with one hand. His fingers dug in like talons, adding another impediment to his breathing. If he loses consciousness before the surface level goes down, he was a dead man. Realistically, if this man knocks him out... You can't think that way right now, he told himself. Focus!

The chlorinated water in his nose and esophagus magnified the stars he started to see all around him. He'd black out soon if he didn't do something quick. With both hands pressing on Frank's thorax, he forced his head to the bottom. A faint glimmer rose inside him when he realized his nostrils were still above the water level, a fact quickly becoming irrelevant as his life was being choked out of him.

The man concentrated his weight on his two hands, attempting to crush his trachea with his palms. Then for a moment, he saw the man's face! The dark features weren't clear, but if he managed to survive, he would recognize him the next time, if there was one.

His vision began to blur, and his throat and lungs burned from the lack of oxygen. He replayed his words to Joey in his head, "if he tries to hurt you or anyone in this family, I'll kill him with my *bare hands*".

Finally, thinking one step ahead, and remembering Carrie said he was right-handed. He wrapped his mitts around the assailant's first or pointing finger and the smallest of his fingers on his right hand, and with everything he had promised his son, snapped the two of them clean backwards at the center knuckle. That hand will not be usable its fullest potential anytime soon. The man let out a yelp and let go of Frank's neck.

"I'm gonna do you slow." The man growled in a low, pained tone.

Frank tried to sit up, as the air rushed back into his lungs. He was only a few inches from laying prone when the man punched him square in the face. Son of bitch had a mean left too.

His weakened nose broke completely. With him moving upwards with all the desperation of a soul that wanted to live, as the man struck downward with all the anger of a wounded animal, the blow was devastating. Waves of stars dominated his vision, then his head smashed off the bottom of the cast iron tub again. A moment of total darkness enveloped him, before his eyesight returned. He was not going to drown, but he was in no position to stop this man.

The following punch landed with more force than the first, again driving his head back into the floor of the old bathtub. The dark now swirled around him. He couldn't tell which way was up, as a lightning bolt shot from between his eyes to the rear of his skull and back, as the second strike pummeled his already broken nose.

The third blow came crashing into Frank's face like a mule's kick being driven by a pile driver. The darkness began to encompass him just as the warm water had only moments ago. Soon, he would be unconscious in the hands of a murderer.

There may have been more blows, he would never know for sure. His body was shutting down in self-defense. The night was encroaching, and in the tattered fragments of his consciousness, the sad realization that he was leaving Joey alone in this world with a madman. Then his thoughts went black.

TWENTY-NINE

Gordon watched Jim inventory the few personal things he brought to the hospital, before finally speaking. "I can't believe they're going to release you before me."

"I know what you're thinking." Now finished packing, he turned his attention to him, and sat on the edge of the bed taking his hand. "I may look worse than you," waving his hand around his bruised face, "but concrete hits a lot harder than drunks."

He gazed at his reflection in the sterling silver machine above Gordon's bed. He still looked bad. A majority of his face still displayed fading black and blue patches, and though his image gave no indication, so did most of his rib-cage. How he managed to survive that night with only facial cuts and severely battered ribs without some much as a fracture, was a miracle itself. Anything beyond simple movements may bring about sharp discomfort the next few days, but he remained mostly functional for now.

"Not to mention garbage cans." Running a hand gingerly through his hair revealing the stitches he needed to close the wound. He's lucky the metal lid struck him above the hairline, Jim thought to himself, at least any scar would not be visible. His handsome good looks would remain intact to the viewing public, and as shallow as that may be, it was what drew him to Gordon at first. Now, he truly and humbly hoped he would be his last man.

Truthfully his exterior was faring better than his interior, as he grappled with the fact, he owed his life to a psychopath. It hollowed out its own space in the pit of his stomach. He had dedicated his life to helping people avoid anger, lessen the repercussions, and find a way back from the places violence forces far too many to visit. The irony of someone so violent and full of venom being his savior aggravated an exposed nerve in his psyche. It felt like getting a promotion for someone else's work. Sure, you deserved the acknowledgment. You worked hard all along, but someone else brought on the attention, and you reaped the rewards. A haunting sensation lingered in Jim's soul this killer knew him, and stranger, he appeared to like him.

"When we live together." Gordon started smiling, snapping him out of his gaze and daze mode. "We're getting plastic garbage cans."

"Amen to that." Jim leaned over to kiss him. It was their first real kiss since the beating. They let it linger, softer than before, deeper and more tender, and not because of the loving way they held each other's head gingerly as not to cause any pain. This was simply more of everything a kiss should be. Jim could feel what they had growing every day.

As Elizabeth Whistler and Walt entered the room unannounced, she couldn't help the impulse to turn her head in embarrassment.

"I'm sorry," She blushed. "We should have knocked."

"Must be time to kiss someone you care about." Walt took hold of Elizabeth's face and kissed her full on the lips quickly, turning her a deeper shade of red, but this time on her own behalf.

"You know, Walt." Jim paused laughing. "I'm really starting to like you."

"We brought your car down, like you asked, Jim." Playfully ribbing Elizabeth. "That car of yours has great pick up. I'm glad I followed her in my cruiser, because I don't think my old clunker could have kept up."

"Really? She never drives fast." Picking up on his mother's mild case of acting out. "Honestly, almost never. It was a point of pride to manage her time, so she never needed to rush, and we could enjoy the ride."

"I thought I might have to pull her over and give her a ticket." Trying to keep things light, knowing something heavy was about to be revealed by her. Something she would not tell only him.

"There's only two times I can remember my mother driving fast." Jim theorized aloud, crossing to his mother. "The day vandals broke into the library, and destroyed thousands of dollars in books and equipment, and when my grandfather died, but she didn't want to tell me. You waited until we got to her house, so Grandma could tell me herself. I learned, sometimes all it takes to help someone is to be there. I was there to help my grandmother, and not the other way around. Something clicked inside my head that helping people, especially women, was what I wanted to do with my life. I'm good at it now, like, knowing when someone's carrying something they want to say. What's on your mind, mom?"

Elizabeth Whistler looked at Jim with the quiet recognition that her son understood her better than she realized.

"I'm not sure if I should complement your memory or your deductive reasoning. You always make your mother proud, but I have come to a shameful realization I need to share with all of you at once, and as soon as possible."

The importance of her message, meant having to pass over the fact Jim's knowledge and insights about her proved he truly cared for her, and paid attention to the things she did and said over the years. If only she had something more rewarding to tell him for his dedication.

"Could I sit down, please," making her way to the chair nearest to her. "This isn't going to be easy. We've probably lost precious time already thanks to my indecision."

Jim turned a chair around, facing her and sat down. Walt stood behind her and put his hands on her shoulders. It was clear from his face, whatever this information was, would be news to him too.

"I need to tell you about your father, James. He's not dead." She stared at the floor, unable to bring herself to look at any of them. "His name is Robert Sheffield."

Jim wanted to say something to show his surprise, but his training took over. Keeping quiet and letting her talk.

"We dated the year before you were born. He seemed like everything a young girl wanted, tall, handsome, and strong. You look so much like him." She finally raised her head to see him, and managing a small smile.

"Robert was two years older than me, which was a lot at that age. I thought it was special for a sophomore to receive attention from a senior. He took me to his prom, and started out as a perfect gentleman, opening doors, and treating me nice, but everything changed after he graduated from high school."

Elizabeth tried to get comfortable in the chair as she continued.

"Robert kept pressing for us to have sex, but I resisted. Slowly the pressure became more consistent, until I stopped seeing him my senior year. I went out with another boy in my class, who played on the baseball team. He was a pitcher. When your father found out, he beat him up so badly, he couldn't play the rest of the season. He couldn't pitch anymore."

218

She paused to take a long breath as if the oxygen alone gave her the power to continue. Walt squeezed her shoulders lightly in support. She reached up and put a hand on one of Walt's, but only long enough to acknowledge his touch. She never looked up.

"I don't know what I was thinking. I guess I thought he must love me to be that jealous, and I agreed to let him take me to my graduation dance. Anyways, he went out of his way to be a gentleman at the prom. He even refused to get into any fights with the other baseball players who kept trying to goad him into one, after beating up one of their best pitchers. I was so proud of him. He seemed different, like a grown man with control and discipline. He told me he didn't like his job, joined the marines, and would be leaving in only a few weeks. It felt like he had direction for the first time. I should have known better."

"So, after my prom we went to three parties at different people's houses. He had at least one drink at each party. I finally drank one too; one, a martini. I'll never forget, because that was the first drink I ever had. It made my head fuzzy after only one. We visited three different houses until almost twelve o'clock.

My parents gave me a 1 a.m. curfew, and never occurred to me why he might want to leave the party before midnight. Robert said he wanted to go for a drive down along the river. I thought he meant Riverfront Street where all those large Victorian homes were, because he always used to say "I'm gonna own one these big mansions someday", but when he turned down Old Marsh Drive, I got a little worried."

"There were no houses on that road back then. It was *thee* make out spot in our town. I thought even after one drink I would know when to stop, and I did. So, when I thought we were going too far for my tastes and I told him to stop, but he didn't..."

The pause was louder than her words, as she shifted in the chair again.

"He raped me three times, once for each year I made him wait. Said I owed it to him after three years of waiting."

The tears began streaming down Elizabeth's beautiful face. Walt's grip became a little tighter on her, as Jim moved out of his chair to kneel in front of his mother, taking hold of her hands gently.

"Go ahead, mom." Urging her on tenderly. "We're listening. Everyone here loves and supports you."

"He left for the marines before I found out, and abortion was never a consideration for me. My parents didn't want that either. They decided to help me so as long as I never told him, and I agreed. I didn't want him to raise you. Against our wishes, someone let him know and I started getting letters from him, wanting to know about the pregnancy and asking me to marry him. I was clear that I most certainly would not, and I arranged to have an abortion. Your grandparents sent me out of town to live with your great Grandpa Jim in Vermont, the one you're named after. Just the sweetest man ever, but so very old. Ninety-two when, I, or we moved in with him. He required someone around to help him with nearly everything by then, and I needed to be somewhere away from town so everyone would forget about me. I ended up living in Vermont for two years."

"Grandpa Jim, I mean, my Grandpa Jim kept saying he's only staying alive long enough to see you born. True to his word, he died less than two months after you arrived in our lives. He had a heart attack at the house, and knew full well it was time, but he wouldn't let me call for help." She powered through tears welling up in her eyes again. "he said, he'd seen enough and his time was up. Such a strong man. I remember sitting on the bed beside him and placing you on his chest. He held my hands with one hand and put the other on you and slipped away quietly, smiling."

Jim had to take a moment to wipe his own tears, as did all the others in the room, almost in synchronized unison. He leaned down and touched his forehead to his mother's hands.

"I, we ended up staying almost another full year. I had started to date a young man who helped me a lot with Grandpa when he was alive, but it didn't work out. We sold the house and I moved home. With my mom and dad helping me with you, so I could finish college, I got an associate's degree and the job at the library. We lived with your grandparents until you were almost seven."

"The man in the library." Jim began looking up, "When I was in first grade then. That was him?"

"Yes." She admitted feebly, looking around the room, but never directly at any of the men. "While he was on leave, he learned from someone I had a son. I told him you weren't his and I had aborted his. That you were the son of another man from Vermont, and he believed me because he hadn't seen you yet. Then, he raped me again. He said I'd just have another abortion, and it didn't matter since planned on leaving and never coming back. Every day, I thank God, he didn't find you that day. Who knows what he might-"

"But he didn't." Getting back to his feet, shaking a cramp out of one of his legs. "And you did a damn fine job of raising me by yourself."

"Amen" Walt added in support.

"The book in your bedroom," Gordon queried politely, softening his interruption. "It's from that day in the library, isn't it?"

Jim reached over to hold Gordon's hand for a movement and nodded yes.

"I hid behind it when he tried to find me. I guess he was looking for a bigger threat." He turned back to his mother. "We moved right after that happened?"

"Yes. He never went to Vietnam." She lowered her gaze again. "Nor did he die in combat. It was a lie I told you, because it made sense at the time with so many young men losing their lives over there. I took the easy way out to avoid having you repeat the question."

"Where did he go, Elizabeth?" Walt asked finding his voice.

"I never knew, but he never came back again. I found out later though he did enlist in the marines, he never actually fought in the war. He had been stationed in South Korea and reenlisted, so he could stay. Allegedly he was studying martial arts at a Dojo who rarely allowed Americans to train with them. After his second enlistment ended, he never came home. We all figured he had decided to live there instead, or hoped, until yesterday."

"I'm sorry Walt for lying to you." The sincerity shone in her visage as she turned to face him. "That's who called late last night."

"Wait, he called you?" Jim interjected. "What did he say?"

"He said I did a good job raising our son."

A lightning bolt of a gestalt raced up and down Jim's spine, leaving him with only one thought.

"Mom, he's the killer."

She nodded solemnly.

"I think so too, but I couldn't be sure at first. There are so many men right here who are upset by your work, so threatened by any attempts to help women socially they'd resort to violence. Something about the way you and Gordon were saved in the alley made me wonder. He didn't interfere when Gordon got hurt, because he wanted to witness his boy in action. I think every man wants his son to be a capable fighter, and he only stepped in when things got dire. It stuck out in my mind for some reason, and then he called. Now it all makes sense, and even if I'm wrong, he fits all the requirements of this killer and should be questioned. I had Walt bring me here first thing this morning, so I could tell you both at once. I'm so sorry, Jim, had I realized sooner-"

"I might be dead," cutting her off. "Like it or not, that man probably saved mine and Gordon's lives, but we've got to stop him. He's out of control and his anger is getting worse."

"I'll get that call traced from your mother's house." Walt offered with a protective tone. "Maybe we can narrow down where he's staying. Maybe."

"This might help." Elizabeth dug into her pocket book and produced a small photo. The edges were aged and frayed, but the image was intact.

Jim took the old photograph from her. This was his father, looking at his own features in the man's face and eyes. The likeness mesmerized him for a moment, but anyone would still see his mother in his visage as well.

"How come you never showed me this before?"

"You never asked me to. Not as an adult, and I wanted to wait until then. Now, I'm sorry I hid all this from you."

"Momma." Jim explained kneeling on one knee in front of her. "You did the right thing by choosing to raise me by yourself. You like the way I turned out don't you."

"Of course, I do." She touched his bruised face softly with one hand.

"Do you think if that man was a part of my life, I would have been any better off? In any way?"

She shook her head no.

"Hell no." Walt added for affect, to which all nodded in agreement.

"Then you should harbor no regrets. You are not responsible for this man turning out to be a psychopath. He's not even blaming you, but honestly blaming himself for pushing you away by raping you. He was wrong and that's why you wouldn't let him be in our lives. Now, he's punishing other men for his crimes, it's classic projection. You can see that can't you?"

She nodded yes again. Jim stood up.

"I'll take this photo to Carmine and Hanson, and fill them in with what we know now." Jim addressed Walt directly. "Take her with you. You can't leave her alone, and nothing could be safer than a police station. My father could be the killer, and he knows where she lives, she could be in danger. Can you stay with her 24-7 until we find him?"

"Absolutely, without question." He agreed. "I'll park the cruiser over a block or two, so he'll think she's by herself. Then if he does show up, element of surprise in my favor."

"Excellent idea." Jim stated his mind racing at the possibilities. "This man, Walt. He may be a world-class fighter. You can't take any chances with him, especially not on my behalf. If you have to-"

"I will." Walt cut him off so neither had to address it out loud. "He's not getting anywhere near your mother."

Jim nodded as he looked him in the eye. The two men bonded over of their concern for a woman they both cared for deeply. A fact they now clearly understood about each other.

"Let's get going."

"Oh, your keys." Elizabeth dug into her pocket book once again as she struggled a bit to get up, but was quickly steadied by Walt's hands. She produced the keys to Jim's Mercedes, and placed them in his hand.

In her eyes he saw a trust unlike any Jim had ever seen in her before. Facing the psychotic nature of his father, she had newfound faith and respect for her son as a man among men. It was a shame he didn't have time to enjoy the revelation.

He gave her a hug, and leaned back holding her shoulders.

"We'll find him. I promise."

"Jim?" Gordon's voice pulling his attention back to him. "You listen to your own advice. You know he's dangerous. Be extra careful is all I'm gonna say."

Leaning over, he kisses him, and runs his hand through his hair ever so gently.

"I will. I swear." He said so confidently Gordon felt assured. "We've got a lot to talk about still, like who's giving up their place and the rest of the book story I promised you."

Gordon smiled widely. Suddenly, the challenge ahead was lessened by the fact they were now in this together, as one. And that, was a powerful feeling.

THIRTY

Dave Hanson hated doing shit work, but the headway being made lessened the smell. Walt Hawthorne called in the name of Jim Whistler's father that morning, and within minutes quality information on their first real suspect, Robert Sheffield, came flooding in.

Where the hell was Frank? He always answered his phone for him, or at least texted him back. Dave considered calling Carrie, but he thought that might be tacky. All he could do was focus on the work.

As he continued reading through his military records, one thing seemed to be a reoccurring theme, violence. He got into a violent confrontation with someone every six to eight months like some internal clock. At first, he played the hero, which mitigated the offenses in the eyes of his command, even completely overlooking some of the incidents.

Three weeks after arriving in Korea, he managed to save his commanding officer in a bar fight. One of the other Marines made the mistake of calling him C.O. in public, making him a target in town. Later that evening, several locals attacked him with knives. Sheffield found himself as the proverbial *right man, in the right place, at the right time,* to score himself serious brownie points and kick a little ass.

A little more than what the average person would consider kicking ass; he killed two men with a beer bottle, and three others with the knives he liberated from the first two. They were most likely Vietcong, and initially outnumbered the soldiers eight to four. The original first lieutenant who blew the C.O.'s cover was stabbed to death in the melee. A third Marine survived being stabbed multiple times. The commander himself received a severe gash in his arm, but reportedly took out the last attacker himself with a pool cue to the eye. You don't want to piss off Marines. It's not healthy.

Not only did he sway the admiration of his C.O., but also a revered martial arts master, impressed with the selfless way he defended his comrades. The master invited him to study at one of the most prestigious Dojos in Asia. Only a handful of foreigners have ever been allowed to train among them, and Robert Sheffield became one of them.

The dojo taught an advanced version of Kempo developed by the native priests. A small, very religious oriented sect, who taught family and the place of men in ruling their village. Women were to be protected and honored, but men made all decisions. Apparently, his views fit right in.

Several other altercations littered the record of his first four-year enlistment. No other fatalities, but he crippled a man he caught beating a woman with a stick on a sidewalk downtown. The Korean authorities almost charged him, but the Dojo came to his rescue. They convinced a judge the honorable thing to do was protect the woman from an evil man of no character, who was not the woman's husband, an important distinction in the case. According to eyewitnesses, Robert only resorted to violence when the man assaulted him directly. He walked away with an even bigger reputation as a man of honor.

When his tour of duty ended, he made a pact to re-sign only if he stayed in Korea. The Marines didn't need as many men in Vietnam any longer, but kept up the number watching the 38th parallel, so they okayed the deal. Also, for the last six months before Sheffield's re-enlistment, he got into no physical conflicts. That didn't last long.

Two months later he got into it with a couple of Ranger's on R&R from 'Nam. The soldiers still hadn't relaxed, when Sheffield made a few comments about their jungle combat skills are not the same as true competence in hand-to-hand fighting. Well, you don't want to tell someone who's survived being shot at for the past three months, they don't know how to fight.

The report said the three of them destroyed half a city block worth of street side cafes. The clash became so impressive the local cops wouldn't interrupt it, and allegedly brokered the betting. Sheffield showed far more skill, but fought two battle hardened men who feared no single foe. The confrontation lasted over twenty minutes, before the military police arrived. The officers taking the bets talked the M.P.s to let them continue as long as no one else interfered, and no weapons were introduced into the fight. It went on for another ten minutes.

Another soldier at the scene said to be a trustworthy source claimed; they never hit Sheffield once, and that he only struck them every 15-30 seconds when they left an opening. His style so tactically thrilling they were using them as entertainment, no one wanted to break it up. Until one of the two soldiers, frustrated his blows never landed with any force, grabbed and broke a chair on Sheffield's back. Regardless of having blocked most of the impact of the strike, he went down hard. They proceeded to beat him with a renewed vigor, and the remains of the chair. The MPs finally stepped in, after resorting to firing shots to get the Rangers' attention.

Sheffield suffered a concussion and two broken ribs, and a major blow to his reputation with the locals. He had been beaten down in front of a crowd.

Hanson shuffled the papers to continue reading, only to find the reports taking a dark turn. Within three days, both of the Rangers turned up dead. A lot of people, including his own command, believed Sheffield murdered them, but there wasn't any proof and no witnesses. The hair on Dave's neck stood on end as he read the cause of death in both cases; their throats were slashed.

Studying the picture of Robert Sheffield in his marine uniform, he couldn't ignore the resemblance to Doctor Whistler. The dark hair and eyes, similar facial structure, and comparable builds. However, one glaring difference stood out to him, their eyes. Doc Jim always looked at you with attention, concern or compassion. You could feel he honestly cared about you, valued what you said, and made anyone comfortable talking to him in mere moments. None of that was in this photo. These eyes were dark and soulless.

Sheffield became a target for every Ranger on leave. In his final six months he fought seven more men on base and in town, and each time the outcome grew more savage. The first few were knocked unconscious, but the next few received broken arms, ribs, and a leg or two. The last one sealed his fate on two levels.

A friend of one of the two dead Rangers ambushed him off base with his standard issue eight-inch Bayonet. Sheffield, not impressed, produced a short sword he evidently carried at all time for protection, measuring over ten inches, and they went at it.

The altercation was brief, and resulted in the attacker being stabbed six times, but oddly none fatal. Sheffield escaped this duel without a scratch. The people who saw the two scrap, said he toyed with the man until he rendered him immobile. Then he moved in face to face, eye to eye, and told him the only reason he would not die that day is because of the crowd watching them. He then wiped his blade on the man's shirt, and left him bleeding profusely in the middle of the road.

The Marines ruled it self-defense, and wanted to send him to Vietnam. They planned to channel his anger into helping the war effort. Anyone this adept at fighting and killing should be sent to the front-line, but having less than a month left on his enlistment, they settled on an early release instead.

What kind of psycho is this guy Dave wondered? Soldiers got extra time tacked on in 'Nam far too often, and they decided to discharge him? Something didn't make sense, but the last entry of the C.O. he once saved, no longer under his spell, made his position obvious.

"Although the skills of Robert Sheffield would clearly be an asset to any fighting unit, his unpredictable code of honor made him an undesirable as a member of the U.S. Armed Forces." They gave him a general, under honorable conditions discharge and released him from active duty.

After his release, the details become sketchy to say the least. One unconfirmed source claimed his Dojo expelled him. He had disgraced himself by using a ceremonial sword in combat, and other violations of their code. After leaving the Dojo, he turned to a local drug warlord, becoming an enforcer for the area's crime syndicate. The mob boss protected him from the law better than the Dojo or the U.S. military. The whispered rumors of the American slasher who worked the dark side of town were prolific. Despite the fact that they were never officially proven, tales of brutal mutilations and intimidation followed any mention of his name locally.

Eventually the syndicate's head honcho himself turned up with his throat cut, and the reports from Korea ceased.

Dave couldn't find any record of Sheffield in the United States until 1977. Did he stay in Asia the entire time working for the neighborhood crime ring? How many people might he have killed in that time? It was a simple unattainable fact, and it bothered him he would never know, far more than it should.

In 1977 Robert applied for and got a driver's license in San Francisco, California, yet there were no work records. No tax filings. No official documents of any kind since then. Did he change his identity, switch to an alias? It had been roughly

30 years, that's a long time for a man to remain off the public radar entirely. Did he take an assignment for another criminal outfit, or bounce from no name job to no name job? More digging needed to be done, and this is when paperwork didn't bother him, when progress is being made.

He stopped at the desk of the duty officer on his way by.

"Hey Steve," he said holding out the photo from the 1977 license. It was old, but newer than his Marine photos, and showed his civilians haircut which was similar only longer, but not by much. "Get this copied, and put out an A.P.B. for this guy. Robert Sheffield late 50s now, so looks should have aged. He may be using an alias, and he's to be considered extremely dangerous."

"Is this the one who's whacking the abusers?" Steve asked looking over the picture. "Doesn't look like much."

"Extreme caution." Dave repeated firmly. "This man is a world-class martial arts expert and may be armed. I want you to be very clear in the bulletin. Extreme caution."

"Yes, sir. I'm on it. I'll get it out right away."

Before the young office left his sight, his cellphone rang.

"This better be you Carmine," he stated out loud as he answered the phone. "Hanson?"

Dave met Carrie McKenna on the same day Frank did. They were already partners when she came on board as the coroner. He took his shot almost immediately and got blown out of the water. She delivered rejection so deftly, you'd swear she just complimented you. Such a remarkable woman by any standard of judgement, he still held a tinge of jealously she preferred Frank. But, if he was not the one for her, there was some solace in her choosing his best friend in the world. She could have done far, far worse.

In the two years he's known Carrie, she always maintained a calm clear focus on everything. Defiantly at ease standing among dismembered bodies, and discussing absolutely disgusting details of a crime scene with a candor that lessened the impact of things most people only see in their worst nightmares. He never heard her raise her voice once, or do anything even remotely out of control. Normally the epitome of grace under pressure, but here and now on his phone, she was raving like a lunatic.

"Carrie. Carrie. Slow down. What the hell are you talking about?"

THIRTY-ONE

Carrie grew concerned. When a man is twenty minutes late without calling, especially one with a cellphone, it naturally causes a woman who cares about them to worry. Not only was Frank held up in some way, he wasn't responding to her attempts to call or text him. What could he be keeping him so busy, that he couldn't take half a minute to reassure her he's safe?

Standing outside the lobby of the hospital, near the emergency room entrance for almost a half hour now, she tried to remain rational. He knew she didn't bring her car to work, and was relying on him for a ride home.

Ten minutes is not an issue. At fifteen, she called him. No answer. After twenty, she texted him for a second time. Still, nothing.

In her mind, she wondered if this is what Sarah couldn't handle? Those moments when you have no idea where he is, and that any day could be his last just because of his job. She got upset with herself for letting the paranoia in.

Damn! She had more faith in him than that to allow herself to fret over a few measly minutes. So many logical explanations for the delay ran through her mind, like spending some unscheduled time with Joey. No, she thought, he should be in class. Truthfully, she couldn't even be sure for a fact he went through with his plan to apologize to the woman from high school today or not. If the meeting went bad, he might simply be sulking, regrouping before facing another woman.

"Come on, Frank. Let me help. I want to be the one you tell your problems to, don't shut me out," she murmured softly to herself checking her watch again.

Calm down, she told herself. It had only been twenty lousy minutes, but she couldn't shake the feeling that something was wrong. Call it a bond, psychic ability, or woman's intuition, but something had gone awry and the question of 'how bad' dominated her thoughts.

There was no way she would involve Dave, and seem like a worried little girl. She believed in Frank and his abilities. They were part of what attracted her to him, so cool under fire, and quick when shit hit the fan. He didn't over react and make things worse, but that didn't erase the tremors along her spine.

She began to call a taxi, when she spotted Jim Whistler slipping out the automatic doors leading outdoors. She chased after him.

"Doctor Whistler!" she hollered to attract his attention. He turned, and after recognizing her, stopped and waited for her to approach. Catching up to him, she composed herself before speaking. "They're releasing you already? That's great."

"My injuries are mostly cosmetic at this point." He answered pleasantly. "Not much they can do for bruises that time won't cure."

"I'm glad you're going to be okay. Have you seen Detective Carmine today?"

"No. As a matter of fact, I'm about to head downtown to talk to him and his partner Hanson. I believe I know who the killer is."

"Wait, really? Who do you think it is?" her control slipping as the chill in her bones grow colder.

"Apparently my father is not dead, is back in town, and he fits the profile perfectly right down to the martial arts, and a history of violence."

"So that's why he saved you. He was followin-" She stopped in mid-sentence; her eyes opening wide to show the new connection in her mind. "Oh, my, god."

A lump paralyzed her throat, as the possibility revealed itself to her.

"What? What's wrong?" Jim's empathy noticing the alarm on her face.

"If he's been following you, and you've been here all day, then who did he follow today?" She theorized aloud, the panic growing deeper in her voice.

"I don't understand. What are you saying?" Jim asked perplexed.

Impatiently, she grabbed him by the shoulder and began to drag him towards the parking lot.

"You need to give me a ride. This is very important. I would never lie to you, I'm a member of the police force," fumbling with her phone.

"But, I'm about to head to the station."

"No!" nearly screamed. "We have to go to Frank's house. Right now! Let's go."

"Hold on a second, Miss McKenna. I think it's more important that we go to the station first." He argued.

"Listen to me," fire raging in her eyes. "A long time ago Frank was involved in a date rape, and I talked him into apologizing to her. He planned to go *today*. So, if the murderer didn't follow you *today*, then-"

"Holy shit." Involuntarily cutting her off as the thought became clear to him. "He might be following Carmine instead."

"Where's your car. We have to go; Frank may be in danger."

Jim led her on a short sprint to his Mercedes parked nearby. She struggled with her cell, attempting to dial as she hurried through the lot. They jumped into the car. As she fastened her seat belt, she spit out directions.

"Washington Ave near Taylor. Let's go. Let's go." trying to contain herself, and waiting for the other end of her call to answer.

"Dave, its Carrie. I think Frank's in trouble. You need to meet us at his place right away. I'm with Doctor Jim."

A pause left the car silent, as she listened to his reply.

"Don't fucking tell me to calm down, Dave. There's something in Frank's past that would make him a target, and if the killer followed him today, he would've found out about it. Now, I haven't been able to reach him for over thirty minutes when he was supposed to pick me up. So, get in your fucking car and get your ass to his house, NOW! Doctor Whistler and I are leaving from the hospital now, and if we beat you there, I will never forgive you. Do you understand me!? Now move!"

Carrie didn't even bother to hang up the phone, throwing it on the carpet near her feet. The tires squealed as they pulled onto the street, and sped away.

"Please let me be wrong. Please let me be wrong," Digging around in her purse and mumbling audibly. "Son of bitch."

And with that, she dumped the entire contents of the handbag on the floor of the car. She stirred briskly through the pile searching for something. Then from somewhere within the small molehill of items covering the floor-mat, she produced a small 9 mm handgun. Holding it up to her face, she insured it was loaded, and cocked it.

"Oh, Lord. Please let me be wrong."

She wrapped both hands around the gun, and held it to her forehead, and ignoring the fact of a weapon in her hands, launched into a quiet prayer.

Jim never said a word. He learned long ago when to trust a woman's instincts. The hugged a turn as he shifted gears.

THIRTY-TWO

Dave bolted out the door of the police station. Frank's place was only a mile or so away, and he could be there just as quickly as any other officer. Besides, he didn't want to call out the troops for Carrie's intuition, but he didn't want to ignore it either.

Like Frank, he loved his car, but Dave had more expensive tastes and lost his belief in America's ability to make a good sports car years ago. He owned a beautiful black BMW 533i he bought used, and got a great deal on. He fancied himself like the car, fast, agile and powerful. Right now, the acceleration and top speed were most important.

The coupe screamed out of the lot with full lights and siren blazing. People always did a double-take when they saw him fly by with the single cherry rooftop LED flashing. The siren blared so loudly you couldn't hear the rubber squeal as he took the corner at the end of the street, already doing over forty.

The two of them often argued as to who had the superior car. Which is faster, handled better, dominated many of their conversations. Maybe, and only maybe the IROC produced a greater top speed, but it couldn't match the overall performance of the Beamer. The handling, the ride, and the air of sophistication couldn't be matched by a Trans-am. Of course, Frank disagreed.

The tires chirped again taking a hard power slide onto Wilson Ave, now less than half a mile from Frank's apartment. He calculated to arrive in two minutes, as he accelerated to over sixty MPH as he weaved his way through downtown.

Dave drifted sideways through the intersection with Taylor Drive near the edge of the business district. A touch of panic struck him, as he felt the rear-end break loose for a second. It corrected itself, grabbing the pavement with a vengeance. The car skidded violently in the other direction, and he found himself fishtailing at roughly fifty miles an hour in a crowded section of town.

The back end swung out far enough to jump the curb, the slight jolt nudged the car back on the road. But, not before the tail clipped a parking meter launching it across the sidewalk, scattering pedestrians, and crashing through a storefront window.

Inside the store, a few frightened shoppers took refuge from the hail of glass sprayed by the meter's trajectory. They scrambled behind racks and displays to protect themselves. They all managed to evade any serious injury. It's not every day that a parking meter comes sailing through the display window of showroom you're shopping in. They'd have a hell of a story to share with someone, and a better conversation than the one he would surely have with the captain about the same events.

"Fuck! Fuck! Fuck!" He yelled out loud as he battled to regain control. The fishtail reversed now, and he slid over the center-line and into oncoming traffic, ramping up the danger to another level.

The back-end swerved out into the approaching lane causing several cars to swerve to avoid hitting him. He made a last effort to cut the wheel back to the other side to move away from the opposing motorists.

One automobile traveling in the opposite lanes steered away from Dave's BMW but screeched to a stop, only to have a small SUV rear end him. Not a major collision, but certainly enough to ruin their day.

There's a point when you're about to have an accident, when you realize you are no longer in control and you are going to crash. Dave accepted this fact. The car swung wildly back to his own side of the street, snapping the steering wheel from his hands. No longer in charge, one thought occupied his mind, prepare for impact.

He looked up to receive the bad news, as he sped towards the back of a parked semi-truck unloading some goods. Fortunately, whoever was offloading the truck were currently inside at the time. With his last thoughts of protecting himself, Dave dropped the seat back as far as it could go, and slammed on the brakes.

The demolition went in waves. First, the hood crumbled as soon as the front end smashed into the truck's Mansfield bar, peeling the hood back like a sardine tin until hitting the motor which slowed the momentum only slightly. The windshield exploded above him, showering the interior with flying glass. Finally, the nose of the BMW hit the back wheels of the semi as blunt force became reality.

If not for fear dampening all his expectations, the sudden stop of all that forward motion would seem amazing. How a two-ton car came to an abrupt halt by running into an immovable object, but there were two issues with this: One, Dave was in the middle of a high speed crash and not processing time in his head properly, and what he thought was the end, was merely a break in the action of less than a full second; and two, this meant the truck was done absorbing the forward motion and energy from the physical impact of the collision, the dissipation of the remaining energy was now up to the car. Which when then the crumbling began.

His whole world kept getting smaller as the impact began to crush the entire front end. The back of the trailer passed directly over his head as it tore the car's roof off the frame. Shards of glass showered into the passenger compartment, but the large pieces mercifully flew over his slumped body without striking him. A few fragments cut into his skin as they shot at him from the side windows, but he worried most about his shrinking car.

As the car shrunk, the firewall was driven backwards like a tidal wave of twisted steel capturing both his legs under its onslaught and drove them into the seat. The sound of strong metallic alloys compacting around him was deafening. The collapsing fire wall met up with the reinforcements of his perch. It broke completely off its rails into the back seating area, but not soon enough to save Dave's legs.

In an instant the pressure snapped them both like twigs. The fact that it happened quickly brought a small relief as the sports-car came to a rest tucked neatly under the back of the semi. His limbs were painfully pinned between the damaged seat and the metal tsunami the engine pushed into the rear seat. Then came the ricochet.

The whole car reverberated backward slamming Dave into a dashboard now only inches from his face. The blow stunned his senses, but paled in comparison to his broken legs being jerked around with no place to go. Everything went still.

The smell of radiator fluid assaulted his nostrils. His mind was spinning. The blow to the head wasn't that severe, but his crippled legs were trapped awkwardly by the crushing of the vehicle. He began fading in and out from the pain.

Dave opened his eyes, but the shade of the trailer left him in the dark, or did he black out? The searing agony in his lower extremities altered his judgment. As he lay there helpless, he realized his injuries would not be fatal. It would be only a few more moments before the torment in his legs caused him to lose consciousness altogether, but he couldn't stop thinking that if Carrie was right, he had just let down his best friend and partner. And that hurt the most.

242

THIRTY-THREE

Frank had been awake for a few minutes now, but grasping the situation, did not move or open his eyes. He needed some time to work the cobwebs out of his head, and prayed Dave might come looking for him. Both his landline and cellphone rang several times, but he laid still trying to regain his strength. When or if it comes down to one last-ditch effort, he wanted a fighting chance, because he'd probably only get one, if he's lucky.

He listened to the man move about the apartment. The man showed plenty of self-control as he waited patiently for Frank to wake up, so the party could begin in earnest. He was inspecting the things on his desk and the counters, as if putting together a profile of him based on his belongings.

Who the fuck is this guy, and how the hell did I let him gain the upper hand, he asked himself? He evaluated how bad a position he left himself in, and the diagnosis didn't look promising.

The cool air on his skin told him he was still naked, and that remained as the highlight of his analysis. The remainder of his assessment went steadily downhill.

He found himself bound to his own kitchen table, his body spread out like someone about to be drawn and quartered, with his legs hanging off one side. He tried not to think about why, although he was fully aware of the reasoning. Besides, compared to the setup and the finale, the pony ride would be the easy part. His limbs were tied very securely with what felt like pieces of his clothing. Each leg restrained in two different places to the tubular columns that supported the top, once around the ankles, and again around his thighs as close to the hips as possible. This eliminated his ability to bend at the knee to gain any advantage. Son-of-a-bitch is talented. This was not the first time, but he couldn't recall the others being tied up so well. Was this some sort of perverted respect for Frank's abilities requiring an extra layer of thoroughness? So at least this man doesn't think of himself as superman. He acknowledges his limits, realizing he is probably more level-headed than he hoped. Exploiting his emotions to his favor may not be possible.

His hands reached just over the far side of table. They stuck out over the end allowing the attacker to tie the wrists down to the table legs below, effectively removing any chance of him using them. If he can work it loose silently even a tiny bit, he might be able to grip the edge when the time came.

His old table had brushed metal columns and a linoleum top with a metal frame. After calculating the weight at less than seventy-five pounds, he acknowledged it was still more than he could lift from this position without any leverage. He was sure the old thing would break in half at the split for adding the leaf, if raised off the ground even a few inches, then use his weight to push it past its breaking point. He thought it might give out and separate, if he toppled sideways, but questioned if that would be enough of an impact. Either plan would still leave him tied to the two halves, and judging from the knots digging into his skin, he'll need more time than he had to wrestle free from the table. And if all those things went well, he would still end up fighting a maniac with a large knife while wearing his birthday suit. Hopefully, Frank thought, he'll slit his throat first.

Frank's head lay on his chin, facing forward. Directly in before him lay his kitchen counter top and stove. After managing to break loose, the nearest weapon was his butcher's block full of various knives, only three or four steps from him. He started doing math in his head, maybe five seconds to smash the thing apart, at best fifteen to twenty to untie himself of the bindings, and another two or three to reach the kitchen counter. Fuck, he thought to himself, there's no way of earning that much time without this man hearing, if not seeing his every move. His balls folded forward under him and his body-weight rested on them, after being thrown on top and dragged backwards into his current position. One more thing to weaken his leverage come the moment of truth.

He tried not to react as the assailant began tapping something metallic impatiently against the linoleum tabletop. The son-of-a-bitch was standing right in front of his face. Attempting to wake him up, the man slid a long knife under Frank's neck, pressing upward with the flat of the blade. Frank mustered all his will and tried to pretend to be unconscious still. The cold steel made his heart pump violently. This was no everyday cutlery, but something akin to a small sword. It wasn't but a foot long, but supported the weight of his head and neck without bending. Whoever made that blade, spent some time doing so.

"You can open your eyes, Carmine. I can tell that you're awake from the difference in your breathing." The voice spoke calmly, bringing a lump to Frank's throat.

He opened his eyes cautiously, and focused on the small saber pressing against his Adam's apple. As he slowly raised his line of sight, he noticed the handle decorated with some sort oriental design proving this man is the murderer they sought these past few weeks. The United States Marine Corp tattoo on his forearm only served to confirm his suspicion.

The arm appeared to be solid and well-toned. His gaze rose to the man's shoulders, and up to his face, as he finally got his first look at his abductor.

Surprisingly, he found himself looking at a man significantly older than himself. Not sure why that surprised him, but it also gave him a little hope. The man stood about Frank's height, so there would be no size advantage should he find a way to break free of his confinement.

His dark eyes and black hair struck him as oddly familiar as he studied his face. He produced a sick smile as he looked down on him secured to the table. Frank estimated him to be at least in his fifties, but in better shape than most men half his age. The man's visage projected wisdom, even if his soul was so twisted you could smell it.

"Not what you expected?" He asked in a disturbingly calm fashion.

"I was hoping you'd be smaller," almost too honestly.

The murderer's laugh was honest, but brief.

"So, this is the home of detective Frank Carmine. Veteran police officer, x-husband, part-time father, and rapist?" looking around. "I guess they don't pay detectives much."

"About forty-five K a year to start," praying the conversation would buy him sometime. "Got some seniority now, so I make a little more these days. Minus the alimony and child support, of course."

He withdrew the short sword from under Frank's neck, and laughed.

"Is that all you get to serve and protect, no wonder they can't find any good cops?" Flashing a menacing smile.

"Yet, they hired me anyway," trying to keep the mood somewhat jovial.

"How old are you, Frank?"

"Thirty-Seven."

"Ever been this close to dying before?"

"Not under these circumstances. I got shot once a few years back. Felt pretty dam close at the time." With the humor part their conversation over, he hoped the truth about his experiences might buy some time.

"I saw the scar. What happened? Punctured lung?" sitting down in a chair bringing himself down to Frank's eye level. He oozed confidence as he lowered himself down, crossed his legs in a regal fashion, and placed his ceremonial dagger across his lap in a deliberately overt manner.

"No. The angle was left to right, missed the lung and logged in the ribs. They had to dig it out. Small caliber fortunately."

"Drugs?"

"Domestic dispute."

He laughed out loud for a moment, and then settled down with a smirk that reeked of impending violence.

"How ironic," leaning in with his twisted smile.

"You got a name? Doesn't make any difference now, you might as well tell me."

"You may call me Robert. I suppose knowing my name will make it more enjoyable when you start begging."

He likes to be called Robert, he thought to himself. Not Rob, or Bob, or Bert, but the full formal, given and authoritative name. Anal-retentive bastard. Frank was running out of time.

"Did the others beg?"

"Oh, yes," He gushed confidently. "They all begged."

"So, there were others that you killed?"

"Of course, but we won't have time for that now. To count them all would take more time than you have left in this world."

"Sounds like you have a long list."

"Longer than anyone else you've ever dealt with."

"And they all begged?"

"Only the ones I allowed to see it coming."

"So, if I don't beg, do you let me go?"

"You'll beg, unless you like being fucked in the ass."

"I can't say for sure, but I'd probably prefer that over being shot again," as he continued to stall.

"A fair point. So, do you enjoy being fucked in the ass, Frank?"

"Never tried it. How about you?"

As soon as the words left his mouth, he realized his mistake. Robert sat up straight in the chair, and anger flashed in his eyes. He touched a nerve and may have erased whatever time he gained so far. More importantly, he might have found a weakness.

"So why the ritual?" trying to find a subject he would discuss, as he tried to discreetly wiggle his legs to make some space in the knots binding him.

"It is important that you experience the hopelessness an abused woman feels, and the shame of not being able to say no."

"So why me?" playing dumb as another stalling tactic. "I don't abuse women, and I like to think I'm a good father." He added, hoping that fact might mean something to him.

"Do you think I choose people at random, Carmine? You're a rapist."

"You followed me?" realizing he confirmed his own guilt.

"Let's pretend I'm psychic. I had a hunch, and I was right. You destroyed Amanda's life."

"She's married to a good man, with two healthy kids. What's wrong with that?"

"You crushed her dream of a better life. It will haunt her forever, and when she can't live the way she hoped, she'll begin to take it out on her children. She'll blame them instead of you. Your action will affect no less than two generations in her family."

"So, this is all about kids. I have a son, Joey. He's a good kid."

"I'm quite aware. I enjoyed his baseball game with you the other day. He played well, although he needs to keep his glove on the turf when he's fielding ground balls."

"We've worked on that. He's getting better, but he's not there yet." Using every bit of strength within him not to over respond to this news. This motherfucker knows his son and where to find him.

"Your girlfriend's quite beautiful. What's her name again, oh yes, Carrie. Nice upgrade you made there."

"That was not planned in any way. My wife and I couldn't work together anymore."

"This isn't about your current life. This is about what you did to Amanda."

"You did follow me, you fuck." he spit out angrily, before he thought to hold his tongue. His outburst only aroused his captor.

Robert stooped down to eye level, and slid the large knife carefully under his windpipe. This time, pressing the sharp edge of the cold blade against his trachea.

"Watch what you say Carmine, or the party will end before it starts." He said glaring at him only inches from Frank's face. Searing rage filled the man's eyes.

"Fuck you. You're not going to just kill me. I think you like fucking men in the ass don't you, Bob?" He spurted out venomously with more balls than brains. "Where'd that come from, huh? Was Daddy gay too? I heard it might be genetic."

He withdrew the small saber from beneath his neck and punched Frank in the kidney. The blow knocked the breath out of his lungs.

"You don't know what I've been through! Or what happens to a family when the man forces the woman to leave with a child! A boy!"

He pummeled his side three or four times in the same spot. The blows extinguished most of the fight left in his body, but fired up his mind. Fuck this guy, if he's going to kill him, and if no other options presented themselves, he would at least force the bastard to make it quick.

"Is that it? You fucked up your family? What'd you do to your son?" Frank spit out between coughs.

"Don't you talk about my son!" Punching him again in the same kidney. "He turned out just fine! You hear me?!"

"No thanks to you, no doubt. All of this could have been avoided, if only you were honest with yourself about wanting to suck dick. You closet homo."

The killer went berserk, beating on Frank's side until his entire rib-cage went numb.

"I am not a faggot!" He bellowed over and over while repeatedly striking the weakened place in his abdomen until he was sure the flesh would tear open. "That was her fault for leaving! She failed him! She's a woman! What does she know about raising a son!?"

He stopped long enough for Frank to have a coughing fit. At this point, he almost expected to cough up blood, but surprised as he only started to drool profusely.

"So, that's it, huh?" He spit out, with what little breath he could muster. "You beat up your wife, and she left, and she raised her son by herself without you?"

The assassin stopped cold and glared at him. His eyes darkened. He pulled the sword back as if to cock it like a gun, but Frank went right on in a slow confident manner, punching the soft spot he had found in the man's psyche.

"So, you fucked up, and instead of taking responsibility you're gonna punish every other guy who's fucked up. Is that it, Bob? Am I close?"

He didn't have to say a word. The raging fire in his eyes spoke volumes, revealing his mental struggle as he decided whether to end Frank's life right then and there. Even though Frank considered death a distinct possibility, he kept laying it on thicker.

"Well fuck you, *Robert*. My kid ain't fucked up. If you fucked up your boy then you should kill yourself, before he finds out what a piece of shit his old man is."

"YOU DON'T TALK ABOUT MY SON!"

Frank faced his last stand, but didn't care, resigning himself to going down fighting, if only verbally. He was going to make this bastard do him quickly, not fuck him and gut him like a pig.

"Come on do it, you fucking pussy! You can't even kill me like a man, because you *want* to fuck me first! We got your come out of the last guy's ass. You love it! Is that what you gave your son?! A taste for dick!?"

His words enraged the murderer so violently, he was visibly shaking. "I'll cut your fucking tongue out, you...!"

Before he could finish his threat, the dead bolt for the door to Frank's apartment rocketed across the room along with the doorknob, as the frame exploded in a hail of splinters. The shredded door opened easily.

Robert struck a defensive position with the saber, turning his body to face whoever was capable of performing this feat of strength. He found himself astonished to learn the force that blew the door open was his son, Jim Whistler.

Carrie rushed through the door with her handgun out in front of her. Running into the room, she stopped only steps away from an armed killer now focusing on her.

"Drop the knife!" She screamed in a voice completely foreign to Frank.

Carrie McKenna was a coroner. She never received the training of a full policeman, only a few basic pistol classes and shooting lessons, but none of the advanced guidance on how to subdue a suspect, which would have taught her not to stand that close to a perp. Robert kicked the broken door lock along the floor, and her eyes followed, it was all he needed.

In the instant her eyes strayed, he struck out with the sword slicing her arm badly as she fired the weapon harmlessly into the wall, before dropping the gun. She wailed loudly as the blade cut into the thick of her left forearm. The tone stung Frank's ears.

"Never take your eyes off the opponent, bitch."

Frank gained his thirty seconds. Deep inside he found more strength to save Carrie than he had for himself. Why could he draw on every muscle fiber of his entire frame for her life and not his? That didn't matter. Frank's rage focused into a power surge allowing him to lift the table completely off the tile. Rising not the few inches he prayed for, but nearly straight up, before he drove it down, along with weight of his body. Just as he hoped, all four legs gave out and the table-top split in half, leaving him tied to two large, but separate pieces.

The 9 mm weapon fell on the hardwood and bounced towards the open door. Jim scooped it up off the deck as Robert turned his attention to the commotion in the kitchen, breaking his own rule he just admonished Carrie for only seconds before. Recognizing three assailants and a handgun tipped the odds in their favor, he would have to act fast to keep

Frank from joining the fight. He raised his menacing weapon up ready to land an easy death blow, he thought, watching the detective as he struggled with the bindings holding him to the two halves of the table. But, as he stepped forward, a shot rang out whizzing past his ear close enough for him to feel, stopping him in his tracks.

"That's far enough, *Dad*." Jim Whistler stated sarcastically hoping the colloquialism would help bring him under control.

He lowered the saber and turned to face his grown son. After staring at him for a long moment, judging the threat he now faced, he took a deliberate stride forward.

"Don't make me shoot you." Jim warned holding up Carrie's Glock, still smoking from the last discharge.

Robert smiled and tucked the blade into the backside of his belt. Frank worked furiously to free himself from the remains of the table.

"You won't do that will you, James?" he began adopting an eerie calm voice. "I'm your father. If you were going to shoot me, you would have shot me when I was about to end this rapist cop's pathetic life."

"You had no problem raping my mother. You're a pathetic rapist!" Jim spit back at him. "Get on your knees."

"No. You'll have to kill me, son." Taking a deliberate step towards him.

"Waste him!" Carrie said, trying to stop her wounded forearm from bleeding.

"Yes, James. Waste me. Don't I deserve it?" Moving forward again.

"I will if I have too." stepping backwards, letting his actions undermine his statement.

"Aim here, in the forehead. It'll be quick and sure." Titling his head towards his son as he strode closer. "Or shoot me in the chest, so I'll *suffer* more."

"I'm warning you. I'll take you out." Jim said as the gun began to tremble slightly in his hand.

"Then shoot me, James. Kill me. I murdered those men who liked to hurt women. I killed them. It's all my fault, right down to the way you are, you know..." pausing to twinkle one hand in the air disparagingly before taking another step.

"Detective Carmine is right. I deserve to die, and you should be the one to do it. Go ahead son, you have every right, but you don't have it in you. Your mother made you weak. Go ahead, SHOOT ME!"

Jim looked into the twisted face of his father, and could only see the resemblance. The similar features, and the anger that created him. Is that why he always harbored a need to protect, rebelling against his own hidden nature? Is that why he wanted to help heal? Because he was conceived in violence? His father was everything he worked against his whole adult life, why shouldn't he just shoot him? No one would care. No one would complain. There wouldn't even be a trial. They'd call him a hero, but not what Jim considered a hero, and he retreated yet again.

"I don't want to, because I'm not like you." He explained. As he moved back to keep his safe distance, he stepped on a piece of the broken door-lock and stumbled ever so slightly, creating yet another opening for his father to exploit.

The gun went up a few inches, and Robert struck out. His left hand pushed the Glock to one side as Jim fired, but too late to do any damage. He used his momentum to deliver a vicious punch to Jim's sternum driving him backwards, and causing him to drop the weapon in an effort to use his hands to stabilize himself as he fell. Only the wall behind him saved him from falling over entirely.

He tried to bounce back, but Robert made the most of his stolen moments of concentration, and with a straight kick to his stomach doubled him over in pain. His follow-up, a spinning roundhouse to the head sent Jim sprawling over the end of a couch and onto the floor near Carrie in a daze.

"I expected more from *my son*."

As his son fell to the hardwood, Robert wasted no time bolting out the door. Frank, still working to untie his legs, watched in horror as she scrambled across the room, snapped up the handgun and ran into the hallway.

She turned to face down the corridor in the direction he fled, but he had already disappeared out of sight. Rocking back on the balls of her feet, he witnessed her trying to decide if she should go after him.

"Carrie, no!" He shouted from his place on the tile, still wrestling with the strips of cloth holding him to the table. "Don't follow him. It's too dangerous. Call it in now."

She raced back into the room and grabbed the old landline phone off the wall.

"Dispatch, this is Carrie McKenna. We're at Frank Carmine's apartment building at 56 Washington Street. The killer he's been tracking just tried to take him out. He just left the building on foot. He's a white male, black hair, dark features, mid-fifties, six-foot, around two to two hundred and twenty pounds, and he's carrying some sort of short sword with him. So, he is armed and dangerous. He's wearing a blue t-shirt, and khaki type pants. Get out an APB now! Are we hurt?"

Carrie glanced around the room. Jim Whistler leaned dejectedly sat on the couch still dazed, mentally punishing himself worse than the beating his estranged father had just given him, as Frank continued to extricate himself from the last of his bindings.

"We're okay, but send an ambulance anyway." somberly and hung up the phone, and placed the gun on the counter.

She knelt next to Frank, who gazed up at her trying to hold the blood in from the slash in her arm with her opposite hand. He sat up quickly and using one of his former restraints made out of his own clothing, wrapped it around Carrie's wound stopping the flow, before tying the makeshift bandage firmly, yet gently.

They studied each other for a long moment, Carrie with her arm covered in crimson from the bleeding, and Frank stark naked in a pile of what used to be his kitchen table and clothing. They couldn't find words in the moment. Instead, they hugged wordlessly with a level of passion they had never experienced before. Exhausted he let himself fall back against the floor again still holding her in his arms, all but oblivious to Dr. Whistler recovering his senses nearby. He thought he would never see her again, let alone hold her, and the warmth of her pressed against him now was the best feeling of his entire life. She hugged him tightly. Neither of them, nor Jim said a word. Frank simply held her and fully enjoyed this tiny moment of pleasure, in an otherwise fucked up day.

THIRTY-FOUR

Frank stood on the sorry little porch of his apartment, trying to settle down his emotional swings. His mind careened in circles between fury, desire for vengeance and thankful to be alive. Taking deep breaths, he never noticed how satisfying breathing fresh air could be, or how amazing the sun felt on his skin. A lot better than dirt would have. The sensation washed over him like a renewal of his soul, so near to being set free against its will. Funny, water used to give him this feeling, but for him, that sanctuary had expired forever.

He was pissed off. How did this bastard get into his house? Did talking to Amanda leave him in such a daze, he left the door unlocked? Did he break in? Can he pick locks, and then locked the door after he got inside? The questions came faster than the answers. How much did he learn about his family, and their habits? Would he hurt a child? Frank tried to push himself out of his head.

They immediately sent people to take Joey out of school, and Sarah too if she wanted their protection, but he got far too close without noticing. He let his guard down, and that pissed him off. Of course, he was grateful he survived the whole event, and indebted forever to Carrie and Doctor Jim?

The minuscule pieces of info he gleaned from *Robert* didn't amount to much, and for all he knew at this point, the killer might have lied about all of it. But, something in the way he gloated over the specifics made Frank believe him, although he couldn't reckon on anything he learned today being of any actual value. The few straws of information he got out of him are most likely true, as killers usually don't lie to their victims who they think will never speak to anyone else ever again. However, any real benefit was yet to be decided.

For the amount of blood, Carrie's wound looked worse than it turned out to be. Part of him was more upset over her injury, than the details of his own ordeal. She refused go to the hospital for stitches. Butterflied the cut herself, before the paramedics showed up. He sometimes forgot before you earn the job of corner, you become a doctor first. Carrie even set his nose for him, as he breathed through his mouth thanks to the cotton pack in his nostrils. She made him promised her he'll go for an x-ray of his side sometime tomorrow, but due to the maniac's focus on his kidney, he didn't break anything in his midsection. Not any bones at least, but the muscle spasms in his abdomen some thirty minutes after the fact did bother him. That cannot be good.

She wanted to talk, but he needed a few moments. So here he stands, alone with his thoughts on the four by eight-foot slab of concrete his apartment complex called a patio. Doing a little mental self-assessment. What's next he thought to himself as he adjusted the wading in his busted schnoz? Son of bitch threw a helluva punch when he had you pinned down. This man must not escape again. He's too dangerous. If he found so much as the slightest possibility of claiming "in the line of duty" this guy was going to die. Frank already decided as much.

Okay, so his nose is broken, and his ribs are a little sore on one side, but he had to be ready otherwise. His animosity continued to push any residual haze out of his mind. His thankful embrace of life and all things living, remained no match for his seething desire to put this killer down.

Having his home and sanctuary violated irritated him far more than being tied au naturel to the table, when Jim and Carrie arrived. They've both seen their share of naked men, although the majority of the ones she's laid eyes on were dead.

And where the fuck was Hanson? Carrie said she called him before she left the hospital with Whistler.

Frank was not the only one questioning himself after the incident. Doc Jim sat on the couch like a wounded puppy, nearly comatose since his old man escaped. If he apologized to him one more time, he might slap him to break him out of it. He froze, so what. It's not every day you learn your father is a multiple murderer. At least nobody died here and now, but this was not over.

He sorted through the facts in his head. So, this man, this assassin, *Robert*, is Jim Whistler's father. Obviously, he has some issues dealing with his boy being gay. How is he not proud of a son who became a well-respected doctor, and protector of battered women? Was he upset because he turned out homosexual, or because he wasn't around to try to prevent it? Is he himself gay and pissed that Jim embraced his homosexuality and made a success of himself? Did he envy his own child for successfully living a lifestyle he wanted for himself, but could never be honest or brave enough to try? Society really needs to get fuck over homosexuality. Who gives a fuck who someone loves?

Glancing over his shoulder, he spotted Carrie preventing Torres from coming out on the balcony. They traded a few sentences, and the captain nodded in agreement. She turned, heading for the sliding doors to the small patio.

The rush of cool air hit him the moment she opened the door, and stepped out on the deck. She wore a more solemn face than only minutes before, as she closed the pane behind her. It amazed him how he could switch gears in an instant, going from raging about the events to worrying about whatever just removed the smile off Carrie's face. If she hurt, he hurt. He loved this women, pure and simple, and he needed to tell her. Frank swore to himself, from this day forward, he would do everything in his power to keep her happy.

"I found out what happened to Dave," In a tone that foreboded harsh news. "He wrecked his car over on Taylor Drive racing over here."

"Holy shit. How bad is it?" More than glad to discuss something other than himself. Why is it always easier to talk about someone else's problems?

"Broke both his legs. He lost control and slammed into a parked semi. If he hadn't managed to duck before impact..."

"Fuck. He was racing like that for me."

She nodded yes. "Some of the fault is mine as well. When I called him, I sort of threatened him. I told him; I better not beat him to your place."

"Shit, Carrie. Dave, always drove a little crazy. He put too much faith in that 'Beamer of his. So, he's gonna be alright? Nothing serious?"

"Captain Torres said they were bad breaks. Two places on one leg, three on the other. One of our guys shooting radar along the way clocked him doing over sixty on Edgewood, but they think he slowed down to maybe thirty when he hit the truck. Gave the shoppers at Peterson's furniture store the scare of a lifetime by sending a parking meter through the storefront window."

"He always did like to make scene." Trying to manage a smile knowing Dave would recover, but it wouldn't come.

He turned back to the railing, and studied the view of the river a few blocks away. You had to peer between buildings, but he could still see it all in the way your eyes sometimes fill in the blanks. That explained life right there in a nutshell. You can never see the whole picture, but if you can read between the lines, the image will still seem complete.

"Dave's gonna hate desk duty the next few months, and I can't blame him."

"Are you okay?" Carrie asked, putting her gentle hand on his shoulder and leaning up against him just enough to transfer her warmth.

"No. Not really." Frank tried to explain. "I'm mad, glad, and grateful I'm still breathing. I'm fucking everything all at once, and I'm having a hard time trying to separate them. So, my plan is to channel it into pure anger. I can use that."

"Don't let your rage blind your instincts. What do you feel about this guy?"

"I think he's gay, but for whatever reason wouldn't let himself act on it. Maybe he's mad Jim's able to do it so successfully? Doesn't matter. We know who he is now, and that means 48 to 72 hours."

"You don't think he'll run?"

"Hell, no. He's not finished yet. He may want another shot at me, or possibly Doc Jim now, but he's not done."

"He followed you this morning, didn't he?"

"This morning, to Joey's game the other day, who knows how long he's been following me, and maybe even you? Either he's fucking psychic, or watches Sarah's fucking news reports, and learned the rest by spying on me. I have to give him credit for keeping tabs on the people in charge of finding his ass. He's definitely a psychopath, but he's not stupid."

Carrie rested her chin on Frank's shoulder and slid her arms around him, he wasn't the only one who needed a warm touch. He turned to look at her.

"You need to calm down, Frank." With that calming voice of hers, and look of caring and sincerity. "With Dave out of commission, you have to find this guy. So, you have to relax, think clearly, and take this fucker out."

He smiled inside at the reassurance of her words, and her tacit approval of his preferred solution. Regardless of his belief in his own skills, his assessment of the outcome became significantly murkier from what he would have predicted two hours ago. Just his honest opinion on what he faced next. She was right. He needed to pull himself together, because their best chance to catch this maniac is now. This bastard gained a thirty-minute head start, while he moped about getting his head straight, more than enough time for to this sick fuck to plan his next move. He wanted to strike while the iron was hot.

He ran his fingertips along the outline of her cheek, and as he gazed into her eyes, for a moment, every trouble and pain disappeared. The whole world became only the two of them.

"I need to tell you something," He began without taking his eyes off hers. The deep radiant green that pushed the world away for him. "In case I never..."

Then the sliding glass door opened, and the moment vanished.

Captain Torres slid through the open door gingerly, closing the slider behind him. He'd always tried to boss him around over which one went for the management job, but this time the edge was missing from his voice. For all his venom, he cared about his ace detective, and he needed him.

"You all right, Frank?" He started in a voice that conveyed his sincerity. "Fucking close call there, buddy."

"Yeah, too close. I'll be fine soon enough. Thanks, Paul."

Neither he, nor Carrie were consciously aware of the fact they were still holding each other's hand.

"This is what Hanson was working on when Carrie called him. Seems he had the goods on Whistler's father this morning, and spent most of the day compiling everything he found. Guy's a full-blown psycho, but worse, he's a trained one."

Torres handed him the folder.

"Who trained him?"

"The Marines first, then some martial-arts cult in Korea during the Vietnam war. After they kicked him out near the end of his enlistment, for a murder they couldn't pin on him. Tell me this doesn't sound familiar; the dead guy had his throat cut."

"Jesus Christ." Frank murmured almost despondently.

"After they booted him, and despite him being an American, he became an enforcer for a local syndicate for maybe as long as ten years, before returning to the states. We're waiting on some stuff from the west coast, but looks like he did a lot of freelancing for various crime organizations out there. High priced contract shit, all cash. They chased his profile for years without finding him. There's virtually no printed record of him being back in the country except an old driver's license from the 80s he never renewed. That was the last time he played ball with society as far as we can tell."

"Christ, thirty years. Where the hell's he been all this time?"

"I hate to speculate, Frank. I don't like the theories I come up with."

"That is a *long* time to be living under ground." Carrie interjected. "It probably cut down on his social life and normal human contact."

"My first thought as well," Torres suggested. "Not exactly fertile soil for a stable mind set."

"Can I keep this?" Holding up the folder.

"Sure. That's why I brought it. I know you want to get right back on this guy's ass." Realizing the bad pun, "Sorry, poor choice of words."

They examined each other's somber game face. Quietly acknowledging the fact, they both understood the other a lot better than they pretended. Maybe they actually cared for one another.

"I'm telling you straight up, Paul." Frank stated evenly. "This guy is a cold-blooded killer and has been for decades. If I get half a chance, I'm putting this fucker down."

Torres paused a long time soaking up the statement, before nodded slightly in reluctant agreement. "Make it look good." Then turned opening the slider to go back inside.

Frank and Carrie followed him back into the living room of the apartment. Fragments of the table littered the floor of the kitchen. A lab technician continued dusting some of Frank's things for fingerprints, while a patrolman stood guard in the damaged doorway. Jim Whistler rose from the couch, eagerly waiting for some sign of what to do next. The captain crossed over to the broken door.

"The killer do this?" Pointing to the remains of the door jamb.

"Actually, that is the Doc's handy work." Frank professed happily. "Fucking awesome timing too. You saved my life, and I'll never forget it."

He stepped up to the Doc and hugged him, not letting go as he spoke. "I hope my son turns out to be even half the man you are, Jim. I mean that." He let him go, only to witness Dr. Whistler having a hard time with either the heartfelt hug or the honest statement.

"I should have shot him. In the leg or something, so he wouldn't have gotten away." Jim confessed as they separated.

"Shit happens, Doc. You may be a black belt, and a helluva fighter, but they don't train people to face down their own father as a murderer. Hell, McKenna here got closer than she should have for her own good, and was damn lucky to escape with only a few stitches." He said flatly. "But, the two of you still saved Carmine today, and an untold number of people down the line."

Jim nodded begrudgingly, acknowledging at least that much. Carrie lowered her head in shame. Torres lifted her head with one hand to look her in the eye.

"Don't do that, McKenna. You were never trained like a street cop, but your instinct was dead on balls accurate and if you hadn't figure out what you did..." He trailed off, not wanting to finish his own train of thought.

"So, do you want a temp partner, and I don't mean Carrie?" Fairly certain what his answer would be.

"Hell no." Frank jumped in. "She needs to be off the front line."

"I can handle myself." Jumping in defensively, though most of her didn't want to go face to face with a killer ever again, especially this one.

"Not what I mean, McKenna." Torres explained. "I want Carmine to have experienced back up when he lines up against this guy next time. Someone with trigger time, and battle experience."

"I don't want anybody yet. Give me twenty-four hours to track this piece of shit, and I'll call for back up when I'm ready to make my move. Then send the entire fucking cavalry."

The captain agreed, nodding. "Where you gonna start?"

"Well, Carrie will go to the hospital for me, check on Dave, and tell him I'll come visit him as soon as I can." Looking at her for approval.

"Sure." Agreeing with the plan. "I'll fill him in on the details. I'll even throw in a short, 'should have bought an American car' speech for you if he doesn't look too bad."

"I fucking love this girl." Frank spoke out loud, smiling for the first time all day. Carrie's eyes light up to hear him say it in front of everyone, in spite of the situation tempering the sentiment.

"Tell us something we don't know, Carmine." Torres tossed out. "What are you going to do?"

Frank glanced over to the doctor standing nearby waiting for a mission, or some opportunity for redemption.

"If it's alright with him, I'd like to take Doc Jim here with me, and go talk to his mother. I need to learn as much as I can about that father of his."

"He's not my father." He spit out, angrily. "He's just a man who raped my mother. I'm good with anything that will put that bastard down once and for all."

They all nodded silently, each of them more than a little pleased to see Jim Whistler finally showing his anger.

THIRTY-FIVE

It should have been a beautiful drive, as the restored Chevy IROC cut through the late afternoon sun. The magic of the rays filtering through the old trees lining the road, ever since they cut the original trail through the forest over four hundred years ago. Old Route 12 ran up the east side of the Thames River as it wound through a series of sleepy old towns in eastern Connecticut. The waterway itself is fed by several smaller rivers until they all merge into one, and make their way to Long Island Sound. The secondary highway has long majestic curves, making the drive more of a pleasure than a chore. On any other day a therapeutic ride through the country, but not today for Frank Carmine and Jim Whistler.

They were different men in most ways; Frank somewhat brash and outgoing, Jim more laid back, with quiet confidence, but they also had a lot in common too. Both men are successful in careers helping people, and passionate about their professions. But right now, each of them is thinking about one man, Robert Sheffield. In that regard they stood unified, after developing a hatred for the man for their own intimate reasons, with the real-world implications of those feelings affecting them differently.

Frank barely kept his seething emotions in check. He wanted to find this man in the worst possible way, which required all his concentration to stay focused on the hunt, and not the kill. Disregarding the oath, he swore to protect and serve when becoming a police officer, he now prayed for a chance to end this murderer.

Jim's psychological reasoning swirled around his head at a hundred miles per hour. This man is his biological father, and possibly the reason he is gay? Proof exists of the genetic possibilities, and Sheffield's actions show some sort of latent homosexuality that he is fighting a losing battle with, and will never accept. His treatment of his mother became the basis for everything driving him into the field of helping women, or did those experiences cause him to establish his own biases of girls being weaker and needing protection? He never once considered the plausibility of this theory before today. He always thought finding his father would put to bed so many unanswered questions about his personal development, and never imagined the discovery would open up a whole new can of worms about his motivations in life.

What bothered Jim is his anger. Almost ashamed his rage didn't come sooner, it surged through him now. Why didn't he get mad when he murdered those abusers, or did he unconsciously approve when he only killed wife beaters? Like taking those lives didn't matter, as if they couldn't be rehabilitated. Surely a man who abuses women can be rehabilitated, but Sheffield is a cold-blooded killer. Setting aside any appreciation for the man for saving his and Gordon's life, he is not redeemable. You hate to look a gift horse in the mouth, but he is a psychopath. His thoughts continued to race.

Frank on the other hand began to develop some clarity, now that he identified his suspect. He knew his name, and what he looked like. The profile isn't complete yet, but he already learned his skill level, and it fell within acceptable levels of engagement. His mind started scheming things to say to strike out at Sheffield's fragile psyche in hopes of gaining an upper hand physically. As much as he hated to admit it, he didn't want this to come down to another physical battle, because if he is honest with himself, he may not possess the combat skills to win. What he did acquire was years of experience with trash talk and how to push people's buttons. Nobody fights well when they get angry. They think they do, counting on the Adrenalin rush to make them faster and stronger, when in truth it makes them sloppy. His blood pressure and adrenaline settled down as he planned his strategy. He smirked inside after deciding to overcome his own anger by focusing on finding Sheffield. Everything is coming together. A few more personal details, and Frank might be able to figure out where he is hiding. He only needed a handful of childhood memories, and a smattering of details about the things that made him happy as a kid or teenager, and the portrait is complete. And when the profile is done, so is the killer.

Jim worried he might freeze if it came down to him and his father again? Would he take the next step if necessary? Can he pull the trigger, or at least fire in a non-fatal way to immobilize him? He couldn't even shoot him in the leg last time, which never occurred to him in the heat of the moment. There is something about holding a gun that makes the outcome seem fatal when other possible outcomes exist. If Robert Sheffield, his own sire, is a complete psychopath, then some remnant of those unwanted violent genes must be somewhere deep inside him. He needs to find and access them within himself should the situation force itself on him a second time.

The irony of it all was Jim being upset about some of the same issues that drove his father to his rampage, like the fact his father did not raise him. Granted his mother prevented Robert's influence, he understood why now, but often wondered about it as a child. What he didn't understand was raping a woman he claimed to love. How could you take something so sacred like that from someone you allegedly worshiped? He never loved her. He only wanted her, pure and simple. An angry, young, self-centered narcissist taking what he wanted by force, as he fought in vain to prove he wasn't a homosexual to himself. A vast ocean of difference exists between showing your feelings and disproving your natural desires.

Jim remembered the few feeble attempts when he tried sleeping with women. They were exceptional ladies too, but his failures left him hollow. There was no emotion, just the physical act. His inability to feel passion and love with a woman is what convinced him of his homosexuality. The first time he experienced sex with another man felt so much more honest and fulfilling. The genuine intimacy allowed him to revel in all the emotions missing during his physical encounters with females. What most of society did not consider normal, became essential for him. He did not like calling it, making a choice, because this was his true nature. Being gay is a naturally occurring biological fact, although a minority among humans, and he was gay.

As they drove along, Jim read Hanson's report on Robert Sheffield out loud, outlining his long history of violence in and around his time in the service. Twenty-five years in the life of a murderer condensed into around ten pages. Neither man spoke during the breaks in the narrative. They both waited to finish the entire summary before giving their thoughts to the other, but took full advantage of the pauses to let their own imagination roam.

This son of a bitch had what Frank called "the taste", a full-blown case of blood-lust. When nothing compares to the rush of the kill, you keep killing. He firmly believed; no psychiatric treatment can cure a man under its influence. You put down a dog once they've tasted blood, or they'll go for more.

Could he be cured, Jim wondered? Should they even try? He's over fifty years old, and has been doing this for thirty of them. The more his death toll rose as the report went on, the less he cared what happened to him, which bothered him in a strange way. It went against everything he believed. Related or not, the possibility of killing another man scared him. Would he develop a thirst for blood of his own if he killed this man, regardless of how much he might deserve such a fate? NO. He is not like him. Sure, he has his genes, but he also has his mother's. He is not a killer, but a sworn protector. He still hadn't decided if he could end this man's life, but came to the conclusion he would not stop anyone else from doing so. Robert Sheffield's life has been one of pure violence and murder, and those crimes against civilized society forfeits any rights to life he once owned.

The teachings of Frank's Catholic upbringing bounced around in his head now. Thou shalt not kill, but the church organized the crusades and massacred thousands simply for believing in another god? How many died for not following the church's doctrine? Frank was reaching. He wanted to execute this man, and he was already trying to rationalize it. The two men whose lives he had taken before were on the spot decisions to save himself or others. Those never worried him. They seemed justified. Granted the ten commandants doesn't say "Thou shalt not kill unless you're about to be killed", and each time those shootings were rated "righteous kills." This one would be premeditated. He didn't want to bring this guy in. He craved in a most unhealthy way to exterminate him. The psycho violated his life, and his family's. He learned his son's name. Frank couldn't let him live and sleep at night. With the shallow remnants of his church indoctrination haunting him, he made up his mind. Maybe, God rates on a curve, and he won't be sent to the same hell as this piece of shit, for taking him out? There would be a lot he needed to account for on judgment day, but he started to feel this would be the big one. You Francis Louis Carmine did willfully plan to, and murder Robert Sheffield. How do you plead? Not as guilty as that motherfucker!

"And this concludes the official story of my father." Rather solemnly as he finished reading the file, and closed the folder. "Not exactly the role model I was hoping for."

"You can't pick your parents." Frank added supportively, relieved Jim's comments snapped him out his religious upbringing. "Besides, you turned out better without him."

"Thank you." Humbly appreciating the honest compliment.

"Listen, Jim... I should, or want to apologize for saying 'let's go find your fucked up father'. I know you have nothing to do with him. It just came out wrong."

"Apology accepted, Frank. Although, the statement is correct. Robert Sheffield is technically my father, and clearly very fucked up."

"Is that your professional or your personal opinion?"

"Both. He should be locked away for whatever is left of his life. At this point I can't see any realistic path to rehabilitation. It's not like he killed someone thirty years ago and he's finally remorseful, he's been actively doing this the entire time. He's been at this too long."

"Do you think he likes it? The killing?"

"I'm not sure if he enjoys what he's doing, or needs it. Transferring his own guilt on to others, allows him to rationalize killing them. It keeps him from directing his judgment at himself."

"I think that was true in the beginning." Frank explained. "But now I think he likes it. Plus, I think he knows his time is growing short, like a dying animal. They go back to their spawning ground. The fact he learned you were never put up for adoption, was all the justification he needed for this wave of killings. Like a new focal point for his rage, but if he didn't use you as the excuse, I think he would have found another reason. This is what he does now. If he couldn't come up with his own rationale, he'd probably hire himself out to terminate other people's problems, whatever served his blood-lust."

"That's a solid theory, Frank. I can see the logic in it. Every time he kills, he gets a reprieve from his own hatred of himself, and he definitely hates himself, because he thinks being gay is an abomination. You can thank a few thousand years of religious teachings for that thinking. "

"I think he might be getting tired of all this as well. He's lived on the run or outside the mainstream for twenty-five years now, and may have been killing for a living, or pleasure, the whole time. That is a long time to live like that. He came back to his roots, like a sturgeon returning to its original breeding ground. This is when killers are at their most dangerous. Each individual act of murder gives them less relief, and they either step up the frequency, or get reckless in the hope someone else can stop them. I'm hoping for the second option."

"You want to kill him, don't you?" fully knowing the answer, unsure if Frank would say so out loud.

"Man to man, and of course I'll deny it especially in court, but if I find the slightest justification when I catch up to him, and I will catch up to him, I have every intention of taking him out."

"I don't blame you." nodding and looking out the window to avoid eye contact. "I think the only thing stopping me from shooting him at your apartment was the fact he saved my life in the alley. Like I owed him something for that, and for Gordon too."

"So now you're even. What about next time?"

"Next time," he began slowly. "I'll at least shoot him in the leg."

"Good enough for me. We cannot let him escape again. It's possible, he might have done someone this afternoon out of anger for not getting to finish me off."

"What do you hope to gain from speaking to my mother?"

"I need a little more information, and I can track this bastard." gripping the wheel tighter. "I hope to learn some personal things about him, and I'll know where to start. Did he like the river or the woods? Did he like crowds or was he more comfortable alone? Even some of the places he liked to hang out at or visit. Just a few details from back in the day, might point to where he'll be now."

Jim studied Frank Carmine, and for the first time, saw the quality mind hidden behind the brash exterior.

"You're a good cop, aren't you?"

"Yeah, but we need more. Too many idiots out there for us to catch them all."

"Your partner, Hanson. He's pretty sharp too."

"Who Dave? Oh, hell yes. He's gonna be better than me when he finishes fine-tuning his instincts. He's the one who can read between the lines in the paperwork. Shit, he's the one who found all the intel on your father."

"I'm sorry he broke his legs in the accident. Will they assign you a temporary replacement when you go after... Let's call him Sheffield. For my own sake, I need to stop calling him my father."

"Consider it done. Yeah, I wish Dave had my back going into the hunt phase, which begins right after I speak to your mother. There is nobody I'd rather have backing me up in any situation. I'm gonna miss him on this one."

"This, man, Sheffield. He's very dangerous. Getting a temporary partner might be a smart idea."

"I appreciate the concern, but they may not share my vision on how this one should end."

A long moment of silence hung in the air after Frank's statement.

"Turn left up here at the light, and follow the road down towards the water. My mother's house is only about a half mile from the river."

"They posted a cruiser at her house in addition to Sheriff's Deputy Hawthorne who she's dating also staying with her. She seems like a hell of a woman your mother."

"She is." Jim said smiling for the first time all day. "She sure is."

"I wanted to say something else," he paused. "Straight up, because I'm not good with compliments. You're a good man, Jim. I mean truly one of the good guys. I have known a lot of men, civilian and police, but the work you do, and the people you help, not to mention the success you've had in your field, really puts you above ninety percent of the men I've met in my life."

"Thank you, Frank. I bet you don't receive as many compliments as you deserve either."

"Your mother should be proud of you, and you have nothing to worry about as far as Robert Sheffield's genes. You are the polar opposite of that murderous piece of shit. I always leaned towards the environment over genetics school of thought, and your mother obviously gave you a positive environment as a child."

"It was a point of pride for her, and she'd be pleased to hear you say so. Turn right here and go up the hill."

Frank guided the car onto the quiet lane.

"Go two blocks up and hang a left onto Riverview Court. It was a great house to grow up in. You can see the river from my old bedroom. I lost touch with most of my childhood friends over the years. My best friend, Teddy moved out west after high school."

Frank glanced down the side street, and slammed on the brakes. Jim nearly hit the windshield. He quickly turned and slipped down the smaller avenue.

"What? What?" almost frantically.

"Whose cruiser is that?" he asked as they neared the sheriff's department SUV parked down the cross street. "Is it Hawthorne's?"

"I don't know," his tone expressing concern. "But that is definitely my mother's car behind it. Is that a bad thing?"

"Probably not. Just want to know who's here." Frank said lying as his stomach turned over in knots. Goddamn intuition raged out of control so badly, he could barely contain the spine chills as he groped for a logical explanation as to why seeing the cars triggered his gut. "They might have parked them both down here to make it look like they're not home at all."

Frank whipped the car around and sped back up the street trying not to drive too fast as to give away his suspicions. His intuition for trouble is almost never wrong, but there's always a first time. At least he hoped so.

"Sure, that would make sense." Jim agreed, but all too aware of the change in Frank's mannerisms.

THIRTY-SIX

The IROC cruised up the street where Elizabeth Whistler lived. As they cleared the last turn, another sheriff's department car came into view, sitting in front of her house on the opposite side of the road. They pulled to a quick stop nose to nose with the cruiser, alarming the two deputies so much that they drew their weapons and leap out of their vehicle pointing them at the two of them.

"Easy," Frank warned Jim. "I spooked them."

"Out of the car." The first deputy, a thin but fit man with dark hair in his early twenties, ordered approaching the driver's side of the Camaro.

Frank got out in a steady deliberate manner, keeping his hands in view. Jim did the same, holding them up while trying to keep calm as his day continues to reveal new surprises as it unfurls.

"Detective Frank Carmine from New London. This is Doctor Jim Whistler, Elizabeth's son. Sorry for the scare."

"I.D. now." The second officer, a thick-built blonde in his forties demanded while keeping his weapon pointed at them.

He carefully opened his jacket revealing his gun and badge on his belt line. The local cops lowered their weapons, as he reached into his inside pocket for his full detective credentials with a photo. The larger and older officer examined them.

"Shit Carmine, you trying to get shot?" The veteran deputy questioned annoyed, putting away his handgun.

"How long have you two been here?" Skipping right past the officer's comment.

Jim finally lowered his arms and the men all congregated at the cruiser.

"About two hours now." The dark haired one replied.

"Have you scoped out the house yet?" Frank asked.

"For what?" The blonde inquired, "They're not home. Haven't been here all afternoon."

There it was, the stomach-turning details he was afraid of, and the explanation for the brutal fire of intuition burning in his gut.

"But their cars are on Roberts Drive," Jim interjected wide-eyed, recognizing a breach of protocol. Then addressing Frank, "You knew something was wrong, didn't you?"

He turned as if he was going to charge into the house. Frank quickly grabbed him by the belt.

"Jim, wait." He said sincerely. "You cannot run into that house unprepared. He's probably armed. We need a plan."

"What the hell are you talking about?" The older deputy argued. "They're not even home."

"Look dipshit, both Hawthorne's cruiser and Mrs. Whistler's car are strategically parked down the next block." Frank took out his gun and chambered a round. "Whenever you're assigned a surveillance stakeout the first thing you do is survey the *entire* layout. Where's the access? Where's the escape? And find out if the person you're here to watch over is fucking here or not. They've been here the whole time and you two morons didn't know."

"Well shit," The first officer explained. "We came in from the north side and never saw Roberts Drive."

"You idiots couldn't protect a fucking dollhouse. So, help me, if anything happens to my mother, I swear to God..." Confronting the deputies in anger.

"Easy, Jim." Frank stopping his charge by stepping between them. "How many exit doors are on the first floor of the house?"

"Only two. The front and the back door near the kitchen, and they face each other through the main hallway." Jim answered trying to focus. "The only other way out would be the hatchway to the cellar."

"Listen up, here's the plan." Frank began taking control of the situation.

"Who the fuck put you in charge?" The first deputy spit out. "This ain't your jurisdiction."

"Hold on," The older deputy trying to defuse the situation. "I know Walt, I'll call him and see if he answers."

They wait as he tries calling. He pauses stoically while the phone rings, but it only rings. He hangs up the phone.

"It went to voicemail."

"In the middle of the afternoon, right after a violent event they were advised of?" Frank pointed out. "Yeah, we're going in."

He checked the name tag of the younger deputy. It read "Clark".

"Clark. Alright, Clark, you're coming with me hothead. We'll go front door. What's your name?" Speaking to the second officer.

"Miller." The blonde replied.

"Okay, Miller. You got back door. Jim can go with you. We'll come through the front loud. See if you can come through the back door quietly. We'll do a room to room until the whole house is cleared."

"Should I have a gun, Frank?" Jim now fully aware of the possibilities facing them.

"What do you guys have?"

"Just a shotgun." The elder deputy responded.

"Give it to him." He ordered flatly.

"We're not giving some civilian one of our guns." Clark shot back.

"At this point I trust Doc Jim here a lot more than you two." Turning to Miller. "He's gonna be your back up do want him unarmed?"

The deputy looked at him intently. The determination on Jim's face would have impressed a stone. Satisfied, he reached into their cruiser, grabbed the shotgun from its bracket on the dashboard, and tossed it to Jim.

The veteran officer gave him a full once over, sizing him up. "You know how to use that thing?"

He cocked the pump action with one hand.

"Mossberg. Twelve gauge. One in the chamber. Five in the stock." Jim spoke calmly as he tried to prepare himself mentally.

"Good enough for me." Miller added mildly impressed. "One quick thing, always remember to hold the weapon in such a way so you can shoot at any time. Keep your finger on the trigger guard until you mean to shoot, and lower it only if one of us are in your line of fire."

Jim nodded in resolute agreement.

"Call it in and let's go." Frank instructed. "If I'm wrong great, but if I'm right every second counts, so we're not waiting on the backup."

Miller sat back into the vehicle and called in for support. Clark crossed over to Frank.

"Just because you work in the city doesn't make you better than us." Clark spit out defiantly.

"Listen hothead. You do what I say, when I say it. This ain't no fucking bar drunk, or domestic dispute. This guy is a trained killer, first by the Marines, then by some rogue martial arts cult in Korea. He's highly skilled with weapons, and even better with his hands. He's already murdered a half dozen men here in Connecticut in the past few weeks. I am authorizing you to shoot to kill, that's how fucking dangerous this guy is. Now, I've been doing raids like this since you were in high school and if you question me again, so help me God, I'll shoot you myself. So, stay alert and do as I say, and if you get me killed, I will haunt your family until the end of time. Do you understand me?"

"We're on our own for at least five minutes." Deputy Miller informed them, getting out of the cruiser, pulling out his gun out again, and this time chambering a round.

Frank turned to Jim.

"I don't want you to follow him through the door. You are our safety valve. He won't expect you to be here, but he should expect a fourth cop if he's familiar with procedure. Your job, if necessary, is to prevent him from leaving if he gets past us. That's all, got it?"

Nodding in agreement, he swallowed hard. He trusted Frank now, and if he thought Sheffield was in the house, he believed him. He started praying that they had gotten there in time, as he tightened his grip on the shotgun.

"Let's go." Frank commanded. "Stay low and away from windows. Keep your eyes on the house at all times. He may be waiting for us. Fucker could be watching us right now."

He cocked his gun and led them in a light trot across the street towards the old Victorian house. A wrap around porch went completely around the first floor of the large house.

Frank and Clark took up positions on either side of the steps leading to the front door as Jim and Miller disappeared out of sight moving towards the back of the house.

Frank crept up the stairs slowly and positioned himself on one side of the door. Officer Clark followed him up onto the deck, and crouched on the opposite side.

They could hear voices inside the house. No, only one voice was doing all the talking. Frank recognized the voice in an instant. He would never forget it. He whispered soberly to the young officer.

"It's him."

THIRTY-SEVEN

Elizabeth Whistler felt protected with Walter Hawthorne. A sizable man over six feet tall and two-hundred and fifty pounds, who spent time in the military, and served as a sheriff's deputy for almost twenty years. The kind of man who made you feel safe. His biceps were the size of her thighs, she thought as she held on to him coming up her back porch. He was smart too. She would have never thought of parking both cars over one block to give the appearance of her not being home. They weren't aware if Robert knew what her car looked like, but she liked the ounce of prevention. After all, he learned the location of her house, and phone number. Walt looped his arm through hers, elevating her sense of security.

Walt decided to move the cars after they got word Robert attacked Detective Carmine in his home. She experienced a swell of pride knowing Jim played a part in saving the detective's life, regardless of him getting away. He prevented the death of a policeman, and that counted for something. Especially one who appeared to be a good cop, dedicated and hard-working. Walt heard of his exploits, even though he worked three or four towns away. He is a respected police officer, and Jim saved his life. She raised her son into a righteous adult, by not to letting Robert participate in his life. Who knows how his anger would have affected Jim's development, or what he might have become under his influence? She finally acknowledged to herself with complete authority she did the right thing raising him alone, without Robert Sheffield.

She pulled out the keys to the backdoor as they made their way up the back steps to the rear balcony. She always loved the back deck. You could see the Thames River from her loveseat. She used to sit out there and watch the water go by to work out something troubling her, or simply relax in the awe of nature. The river seemed so reliable, streaming steadily towards the ocean. Sure, it would overflow its banks every April, but never enough to reach her house. Her house near the top of the hill sat far from flood plain. It would show a little anger, settle down, and go about its business of flowing south to the sound again. Almost like people when they blow off steam, calm down and go about their lives. Well, most people.

"I'll get that." He said taking the key chain from Elizabeth.

Not sure if his actions were chivalrous or cautious, they comforted her nonetheless, as he unlocked the door for her and led her into the house. She entered the kitchen, while Walt turned to lock the door, and set her keys down. When he turned around, it was too late.

Robert Sheffield stood holding Elizabeth with his short sword to her larynx. An evil smirk on his face, almost gloating over the ease in which he gained the upper hand. Tears streamed from her wide-open eyes, now full of fear. Her worst nightmare had come to pass.

"You must be Walt?" Robert cooed with sinister intent positioning himself behind her as not to give him an angle for a shot as he pulled his service revolver from his holster.

"Drop it, Sheffield. You've got nowhere to run." Walt spoke with authority knowing full well this murderer held the cards now. Between the two of them, he was the only one who cared about Elizabeth.

"Oh, I am done running." He stated casually, moving the blade to the side of her neck. "Did you know, Walt, opening this artery below the ear is far more fatal than cutting the throat? Oh, sure, when you slit the trachea you get that great choking, gurgling sound that gives you a warm feeling only an apex predator experiences, but you can survive a throat cut if it's not deep enough. All you need to do is slice it open right here," Running the sharp edge up and down her the bulging vein as if trying to shave her, "and it would take a surgeon's best efforts to save her even if he was standing in the room with us."

"You don't want to kill her, Sheffield. You're just using her as a shield. I'm the real threat here."

"You? A threat? I could have dropped you the moment you came through the door, but where's the thrill in that?"

"You are a sick bastard. Now drop the knife."

"And you are a fool if you think I won't hurt this woman," Producing a small switchblade in his left hand and plunging it deep into Elizabeth's leg. "Her value to me ended when she hid my son, and raised him without my knowledge."

She let out a muffled scream, dampened by her own fear. She went to double over in pain, but the saber pressing forcefully against her neck kept her upright. The tears flowed uncontrollably down her face, but she would not make a sound or cry out. No matter what, she would not give Robert that satisfaction. She fought back her fear that today might be the day she dies, along with the reluctant assumption Walt might not be able to protect her this time.

"You son of a-" Walt started.

"I don't think so," Raising the smaller knife again, halting him in his tracks.

"What do you want, Sheffield?" He asked, taking a step back in hopes of preventing another stabbing.

"I'll tell you what, Walt. I'll give you a chance, man to man. Place your gun on the floor and kick it over in the corner.

I'll put the sword down, and may the best man win. You're not gonna get a better deal than that."

Sheffield is clearly psychotic, but he means what he says. He wasn't sure if he could take him hand to hand, but accepting this madman's offer might give Elizabeth time to escape, and if only one of them were going to survive this ordeal he wanted it to be her.

"Okay, you and me." Walt agreed, slowly reaching down and placing his weapon on the stone tile flooring, never taking his eyes off the intruder. He kicked the weapon under the large industrial style oven. If he couldn't use it, he sure as hell didn't want him to have it.

"Alright, let her go," Standing up and striking a defensive stance.

"I did not say I would set her free." Sheffield replied calmly. "I said I'd give you a chance man to man, and I am a man of my word."

He switched the sword to his left hand, then grabbed Elizabeth by the hair and slammed her head into the door jamb to the kitchen knocking her out. She fell to the floor in a slump.

Walt went to charge Sheffield, who turned brandishing the sharp blade in his direction, stopping him again.

"Uh, uh, uh. Not until I say go." Smiling widely. He dragged Elizabeth by the hair depositing her on the far side leaning unconscious against her refrigerator. He casually sauntered back to the middle of the room, flipped his sword into the sink, held his arms out wide, and calmly said, "Go."

Walt pushed the table to one side of the room, thinking his larger frame would need more room to maneuver.

"You don't know shit about fighting, do you Walt?" Sheffield taunted as he sized him up moving in slightly closer.

"What makes you think that?" Looking for an opening.

"Your only advantage is your strength." He explained as he closed the gap between them with an assured conviction.

"Maybe, just maybe, if you actually got a grip on me, you might have had a faint chance. The close quarters worked in your favor, but you moved the table out of the way. You gave away your one possible advantage. This is going to be a very short fight, Walt."

"You keep telling yourself that." Waiting for Sheffield to make a move. His best strategy was to let him strike first and act defensively. "Until you believe it."

Sheffield laughed out loud, inching closer, as his smile disappeared from his face, replaced by a twisted game face.

"You ever been fucked in the ass by a man, Walt?" He questioned coyly.

Walt was not listening to his taunts anymore. He was in fight mode. He watched Sheffield's body for any indication of which limb he might lead with, his feet or his hands, or would he risk a full out charge?

"I think you're going to like getting fucked, Officer Hawthorne." He said confidently staying just beyond arms reach. "But not nearly as much as I'm gonna enjoy fucking you."

"I'm sure you would," He spit out defiantly. "That and killing people seem to be the only two things you enjoy."

"What real man doesn't enjoy fucking and killing?"

Sheffield stomped one foot on the kitchen tile, and Walt's eyes followed. He did the same with the other, and his eyes moved to that one.

"You're making this too easy, Walt." Speaking in a manner that truly unnerved him.

Sheffield hoisted his left foot again. Walt turned to anticipate an attack with the left, but his attacker deftly shifted his weight, and struck him solidly in the face with his right foot driving him across the room into the hefty oaken table.

Surprised by the speed and strength of Sheffield's attack, he barely managed to catch himself from falling down with a death grip on the table. He was in trouble. This was going to be the fight of his life, as well as Elizabeth's, and he was not off to an auspicious start.

Sheffield moved in quickly following up by stepping on the back of Walt's right calf forcing him down to his knees. He then spun his whole body for momentum, and delivered a crushing blow with his elbow to his temple sending him sprawling on the floor in a stupor.

Walt tried to raise himself, still too dizzy to focus. His vision wavered from the shot to the head, and his equilibrium was gone. Holding himself up in a kneeling position took all his remaining energy. He tried desperately to keep himself between Sheffield and the unconscious Elizabeth, who slept unwillingly on the floor beside him.

"I told you this would be short, Walt." And with that, he landed a vicious straight kick into his head driving it into the refrigerator behind him. His skull reverberated inside and out, as he fell on the cold tiles fighting to stay conscious.

The world spun around in circles for him, as the darkness came and went. The pain wracking his body paled to the thought of leaving Elizabeth to this murderer's will. He had failed her. He couldn't even raise his head off the floor.

Sheffield crouched down beside him, and put a hand on the dent left in the refrigerator by Walt's head.

"Hard-headed to the end, eh Walt? Look what you did to the fridge." Both teasing and taunting him.

He pulled him up by the hair to show him the indentation, but he couldn't focus through the swirling obscurity beginning to overtake him.

"You'll have to be punished for that. No dessert for you." And slammed his head into the tile floor.

Walt couldn't even see the ceramic flooring inches in front of his face, only the sensation of motion, the sudden stop, and then darkness.

THIRTY-EIGHT

Elizabeth Whistler came back to consciousness slowly. Her head throbbed from Robert knocking her out, while her injured thigh swelled around the knife wound, and pulsed in time with her rapid heartbeat. The bleeding stopped, but a stiffness took over and spread throughout the leg. This was aggravated by the seated position she found herself in, with her arms raised aside her head, and wrists tied to the wide handle of the oven. Afraid to open her eyes, she sensed movement close to her, and a loud slapping sound. An angry muffled voice filled the room. She didn't want to look, if she kept her eyes closed then none of this is really happening. Maybe the gag in her mouth was all in her imagination, but the taste of musty cotton and day-old dish soap confirmed her reality. It felt like she died and went to hell.

"How's that feel, Walt?" Robert taunted him over his muffled objections. "What'd you say? You want it harder?" and the slapping got louder.

His actions became all too obvious to Elizabeth as to what was transpiring in her own kitchen. She didn't want to see Walt like that, but she couldn't stop herself from opening her eyes enough to peer around the room clandestinely.

Walt's naked body spread across her large oak table with his legs bound to the posts on one side, and his hand lashed to the opposite end. Bruises covered his body from head to toe, and blood dripped from several slash wounds in his midsection and shoulders. What she feared most of all was occurring right before her eyes.

Robert, now wearing Walt's sheriff's uniform shirt as he vigorously sodomized him less than six feet away from her, acted more like a crazed animal than human. She tried to turn her head away, but couldn't as she observed this man reaching depths of depravity, she couldn't even fathom.

He smiled as he repeatedly rammed him from behind. Walt's blood seeped from his wounds as he continued to taunt him. Pure evil emanated from his eyes as he enjoyed every agonizing second humbling Walter over and over again. He reveled in the misery he delivered with every stroke. It excited him immeasurably. She wished he had killed her now. As she turned her head away in disgust, Sheffield perceived her movement.

"Elizabeth. You're awake, and just in time. I'm about to come."

She refused to meet his gaze, keeping her head turned and eyes shut.

"Don't you want to watch?" with evil candor.

She shook her head "no" violently. This isn't happening, she thought. This cannot be happening.

"Come on, Elizabeth. This is the best part. I'll even call it the climax since there's a lady present."

She screamed a muffled scream through her gag, shaking her head with reckless abandon. The tears were coming so heavily she tasted them soaking through the dishrag gagging her.

Sheffield finished and wiped his penis on the deputy's shirt he wore. Walt said nothing. After being beaten so savagely he didn't know why he was still conscious. He had been so humiliated in every way, and now this in front of the woman he loved. All hope left his soul, as he prayed Sheffield would make his death quick.

"I can see why you like him, Elizabeth. He's a pretty good fuck." He proclaimed crossing over to the sink to retrieve his ceremonial short sword.

Her vision blurred from crying so hard, and sobbed uncontrollably. What had she done to deserve this? What could Walter have possibly done to be treated like this? All he did was love her. Is that such a crime, for a man to care about her, and treat her nicely? Was it too much to ask in her lifetime to find an honorable man of quality, only to have a demon she once cared for take it all away? She found no humanity left in this man who fathered her child in anger. Only a monster stood before her now.

She looked up with animosity, shaking her head to clear her tears. Robert stared her in the eye as he lifted Walt's head, placed his blade under his outstretched neck, and with one swift movement cut a deep gouging slash across his throat.

The blood flowed immediately, gushing from the wound in sheets, spraying across the table, and drenched the tiles below.

"Watch him die, Elizabeth. Witness the life draining out of him. Nothing in life is more fascinating than watching it end. If you pay attention, you can almost tell the exact moment when the soul leaves the body."

The blood began to pool on the floor. She wretched silently, but fought back the urge to throw up. With the cotton muzzle in place, if she vomited, she would probably choke herself to death. She let her anger rise up, and pushed down the bile in her throat.

Robert ran his fingers through Walt's blood, then put them in his mouth.

"In some cultures, they believe that by drinking the blood of a slain enemy you gain their power and steal their soul." licking the thick red liquid from his digits. "You want to try it?"

He drew one finger through the crimson pool on the table and crossed over to her. Squatting down in front of her, grabbed her by her neck to steady her, and smeared Walt's life fluid on her lips.

"It'll make you stronger." smiling at her.

Something within Elizabeth Whistler's mind broke completely. She no longer cared if she died, and kicked him in the balls, landing a second blow to his chest knocking him backwards on his ass. Her legs continued to kick at him even after he fell out of their reach, laughing. Her blows lashed out at the space between them until she was too tired to continue.

"Must be working already." and burst into a demented laughter that sickened her.

She reached down deep, fighting the gag, and screamed so loud it managed to push the rag from her mouth. As he rose to his feet, she stared at him with an intensity that was palpable.

"If it is the last thing I ever do. I'll see you are dead and buried, and on your way to hell." She spit out with all the venom and hatred of a lifetime of angst thanks to this man.

"Look around, Elizabeth." now laughing heartily. "This is the last thing you're going to do."

Frank reached up, and turned the doorknob ever so gently, finding it unsecured.

"Shit." He whispered. "Fucking unlocked."

"Isn't that a good thing?" The deputy asked.

"No. He's giving us access, so he either knows we're coming or doesn't care because he's prepared."

Peering through the window of the door cautiously, he had an unobstructed view down the long hall straight through to the back door. He searched carefully for traps but couldn't identify anything obvious, but that certainly didn't rule them out.

Frank tried for a better glimpse into the kitchen, but his viewing angle only let him observe the far corner. He could make out Sheffield's voice, but couldn't distinguish the words. Elizabeth Whistler's voice sounded faint and weary, but she was still alive. Then the fresh blood on the floor pooling towards the hall came into his view.

"Shit." He mumbled, sliding off to one side of the entryway. "I think he killed Hawthorne already, but I can hear Mrs. Whistler still."

"How do you know he's dead?" Whispered the young deputy now having a little more respect for Frank's experience.

"There is way too much blood on the floor for her to be talking still, so it can't be hers." Frank explained in a low voice. "I think he's saving her for last. Here's the plan. We throw open this door and count to ten. Any booby traps will have gone off by then. We fire a few shots into the house. Don't aim for the kitchen. We want to draw his attention, and hopefully your partner will drop him when he goes for us. Okay."

The young deputy nodded in agreement.

On the back porch, Jim Whistler and the officer Miller took up positions on opposite sides of the rear entryway. They overheard Sheffield speaking to Elizabeth. The elder cop carefully snuck a peek into the room.

"Damn." Keeping his voice down. "He's already done Hawthorne."

"What about my mother?" Hoping his speech didn't quiver, and give away the fear he battled to control.

"She's tied to the stove. He's only taunting her so far."

The deputy reached up and tried the door knob.

"It's open." He murmured to Jim, and stood to take another peek inside the kitchen.

"Hawthorne just moved. If we go now, we may be able to save them both of them."

"Carmine said to wait." In a hushed, but firm tone, now fully believing in Frank's skill and experience.

"We don't have the time to wait." Miller spit out as he crouched in a ready position.

Jim backed away from the door for a better angle, and made the sign of the cross as the deputy turned the knob as quietly as possible.

"He's a few feet away and only has a big knife." steadying himself. "Here we go."

And with that, he pushed the door open and stepped inside.

Frank watched through the window preparing to make his move, when the back door swung ajar.

"NO! NO! NO!" He shouted.

Deputy Miller stormed into the kitchen, only to be met by a shotgun blast from the right side. He never saw the weapon hidden in the chairs of the neighboring dining room, and aimed at the door with a tripwire. The discharge torn through his lower midsection exposing his internal organs as he fell to the floor lifeless. Jim tightened his grip on the shotgun, while aiming at the open door. He had no plans to enter the house yet, but the six shells in his Mossberg said nobody was coming out.

"Ah, cops. So predictable. He could have shot me through the window, but he had to play hero."

Sheffield squatted by the dying officer. He picked up his pistol and tossed it out the back door.

Jim almost pulled his trigger reflexively as the gun sailed past him and landed on the lawn, but recovered himself at the last second.

"Shit! I thought you were the fucking hothead!" Frank threw open the door and ducked back around the door jamb for cover. He started to count out loud. "1, 2, 3, 4, 5, 6-"

"We're clear, let's go! Fucker took out Karl!" The young deputy declared, storming into the front hall.

"Not yet, FUCK!"

Frank dove flat on the porch under the windows of the living room, and as a precaution, covered his head with his hands. He would not regret that decision.

"Cover your ears. This is going to be loud." Sheffield warned Elizabeth. "Oh, you can't, sorry."

There is probably a point when you realize sadly you have fucked up in a fatal manner. You understand you're going to die, and will never get a chance to explain why to anyone. Today, two good men who swore to protect and serve their community, experienced that feeling only moments apart from each other.

Deputy Clark stormed through the foyer into the hallway striking a defensive pose with his gun held out with conviction in front of him. He gawked at his fallen comrade, his abdomen torn asunder and strewn all over the floor near the rear entrance. Only then did he notice the thin wire pressing against his heavy police boots. The younger officer had just enough time to follow them with his eyes, around the post of the stairway, and back down through a hefty cast iron foot scraper by the open door. Dangling from the string were the keys to the two grenades, pressed up behind the ornamental metal out of sight, that now rolled towards him in slow motion. He never said a word.

The blast painted the entire room with the young cop's mangled body. Pieces of which soared out the entry door showering the yard twenty-five feet from where he stood a mere second before. Glass shards showered Frank from the shattering of the large picture windows.

"Fucking amateurs," he lamented as he scrambled to peek inside, and survey the damage.

The hallway was now impassable, as the grenades blew a gaping hole through the floor from wall to wall, and halfway down the main passageway through the house. The detonation destroyed the base of the stairwell and made any entrance through the front door and corridor impossible. A second doorway from the forward parlor led into the hall as well, dangerously close to the kitchen, but he was out of other options.

Frank dove threw one of the newly opened window frames landing on a couch. He tried to stand up and slipped on the dislodged cushions throwing him off balance. Over compensating, he hit the deck hard jarring the gun from his hand. He gasped in despair as it slid across the rug, and into the massive hole left by the explosion.

He steadied his anger at himself and searched the room for a weapon. Spotting the fireplace, he retrieved the iron poker and positioned himself against what remained of the wall, near the opening to the hall. It wasn't a gun, but it was strong and solid in his hands.

"Hey ass pirate!" Frank taunted. "Do you know who this is?"

"Detective Carmine." Sheffield sang out almost musically, as he placed his blade on the counter. Stepping into the dining room, he ripped the shotgun from its hidden perch, and removed the trip wire from the trigger. "So nice of you to drop by."

"He's got a shotgun!" Elizabeth screamed, no longer timid or shy.

"Spoilsport." He whispered to her antagonistically, accompanied by a sadistic grin.

"I knew those deputies weren't gonna be much help." Frank called out trying to keep his attention focused on him.

"I wouldn't say that," he joked casually. "They were kind enough to take out the booby traps for you."

"That was not the plan, but you can't tell these hotheads shit. So how do you want to do this?" hoping to give Doc Jim the element of surprise if Sheffield thought he was the only one left.

"I suppose I'll leave the choice up to you, Carmine." he countered. "Personally, I'm a hands-on kind of guy."

"Yeah, I've seen that. You're real tough when a guy's taking a bath."

"You act like exploiting the enemies' weakness is a bad thing. I thought you spent time in the service?"

"If you mean fucking a marine in the ass. No, my military experience didn't include that." trying to work on his anger.

"You should try it sometime, Frank. You should feel the amazing sensation of power in that position when you use it to punish another man."

Outside the back door Jim inched cautiously towards the door holding the shotgun at the ready. He struggled to narrow down an exact fix on where Sheffield stood, as he kept moving from the edge of the hallway to deeper within the kitchen. His voice bounced differently each time he spoke. Frank noticed that too. He would to have to rely on Jim, planning to give him a chance by working on Sheffield's anger to create an opening, and prayed he'd take the shot this time.

"Mrs. Whistler, are you okay?" he bellowed.

"No." She shrieked from her spot of captivity, bound to her own stove.

"I'm gonna get you out of this." sticking to his lone survivor narrative.

"Hey, Frank." Sheffield started. "What's to prevent me from taking her out right now?"

"Because where's the challenge in that? Knowing you, she's hog-tied to something in the kitchen. Only a closet fag who likes little boys would shoot a woman who's tied up. Especially the mother of your child. Oh, that's right. He's gay too. I guess it is genetic like they say."

"Careful what you say about my son, Carmine!"

"Your son's a doctor no thanks to your psycho ass. Shit, he's twice the man you are Sheffield. At least he can admit he likes cock."

Jim inched to the doorway and peered around the corner. His estranged sire stood near the archway to the kitchen eyeing the hallway as he spoke, leaving his back to him. His mother glanced up and recognized him. Fear filled her eyes as he put his finger to his lips to ensure her silence. She nodded, and summon her inner strength to remain quiet.

"He's just confused. We Sheffield's don't like cock. We enjoy humiliating other men."

"I'm not a Sheffield!" Jim yelled squaring up just inside the door and aiming the shotgun, undoing his own element of surprise.

Sheffield blocked the gun upwards with his, and the blast blew through the ceiling, showering them with splinters and plaster. He butted him in the gut with the stock, he countered with an upward motion smashing the Mossberg out of his hands with the barrel of his. It flipped end over end, skittered across floor, and fell through the hole to the basement.

At the sound of the gunshot, Frank immediately started running through the dining room into the back hallway. This was it. All he could hope for is that Jim wasn't dead or wounded.

The doctor latched on to Sheffield's shotgun and tried to kick out one of his legs, but he sidesteps the attempt and pushed him backwards with the leverage of the rifle they both held onto fiercely.

Frank had no idea how close to the door the two of them stood wrestling for control over the firearm, and when he came barreling through the doorway into the back hall, he ran right into Sheffield's back. He drove the pair across the kitchen towards the table where Hawthorne's lifeless body remained tied.

Jim let go of the gun. He grabbed his estranged father by the lapels of the shirt, fell on his back and using his feet, launched them both over the table, only to have them land on Frank who crashed into the cabinets and stove.

Elizabeth braced for the possible impact. The force of detective Carmine's body broke the oven's handle freeing her. But he also lost his hold on the fireplace poker, and it sailed under the dishwasher out of sight. Now at least freed from the range, she quickly back-peddled away from the two men sprawled out beside her.

Frank took the brunt of the fall, and his aching back assured him of that fact. He needed Doc Jim to do his part now, needing a few seconds to recover from his awkward landing.

At least the impact separated the shotgun from Sheffield, coming to a rest in front of Elizabeth. She reached out for the rifle, but Robert grabbed the barrel and tossed it across the room and out the back door, bouncing down the rear steps. This was about to get ugly now.

He tried to kick her in the face, but only caught her shoulder, but with enough force to send her sprawling face first towards the far corner of the room. Lifting her head, she peered down the gap between her refrigerator and the wall, and sitting there like an old friend lay her old straw broom. The sight of which brought an odd smile to her face.

Sheffield slid through the blood now covering half the tiles, and leg whipped Jim felling him to the floor like cutting down a tree. The Doc blocked the punch that followed, and rolled backwards and up to his feet.

Sheffield did the same, as Frank finally found his legs. His back hurt, but he figured with Jim's help they should be able to take this piece of shit down once and for all.

The three of them, covered in blood, squared off for the final round of mortal combat. Jim struck a defensive stance by the hallway, with Frank deeper in the room by the oven, and Sheffield midway between the two of them. An ominous smile returned to his face.

"Looks like it's just the men now. Reminds me of a little skirmish I had in Korea with a couple of Rangers back in the day." he bragged with a gleam in his eye of a madman in his glory.

"I heard you lost that fight, butt boy." stepping forward to attack.

Sheffield counter attacked putting him on the defensive. As he blocked a barrage of punches, Jim stepped in and side kicked his father into the table. He still managed to strike Frank in the ribs with an elbow, and push him into the Doc giving them space again.

"So, there will be no honor in this fight?" Sheffield questioned as if he held some sort of moral high ground.

"What makes you think you deserve any honor?" he asked his father flatly.

"You don't even have any fucking pants on!" Frank added as they charged back in.

Sheffield was loving every minute of this, and the longer it took the more frustrated the two partners grew. They'd land a shot, but he would deliver two. They were all slowing down, and when you slow down you get sloppy.

Unlike Sheffield, the two of them still nursed previous damage to their bodies. Frank from the beating at his hand that morning, and Jim from the melee in the alley earlier in the week, and they began to take a toll. Even Sheffield's broken finger he gave him didn't seem to slow him down, not in the way their injuries were.

Whenever possible, Sheffield hit Frank in the face jarring his fractured nose or in the back where he crashed into the stove. Jim's weak spots were his ribs and recently cracked skull. Every shot the skilled maniac landed on them seemed to be a higher quality than the blows they dispensed upon him.

The battle raged on violently. Frank struck a clean blow to Sheffield's jaw, knocking him backwards. Jim tried to follow up with a straight kick, but Sheffield trapped his leg under one arm, and retaliated with a devastating punch to Jim's groin dropping him to the floor. And, before Frank could close the gap, delivered a vicious mule-kick to his midsection rolling him over on back in obvious pain.

Jim lay helpless, and Frank's own reflexes and power were fading. He attempted to grab hold of Sheffield. As the bigger man, he stood a good chance of out powering him on the ground, but he gave up too much momentum.

Sheffield swung him around slamming his lower spine into the protruding edge of the counter. The pain shot straight up his vertebrates and buckled his legs. He got his hands down together in time to block a knee to the balls, but by bending down, he left himself open for the other one as his kneecap struck him square in the nose.

His head rocketed upwards; his optics became a blur. The room began to spin, and the five or six punches that followed were all Sheffield needed to take the fight out of Frank. He grabbed him by the shirt and threw him on the tile floor beside Jim who desperately struggled to get to his feet. His injuries only let him get as far as his hands and knees, leaving himself unguarded for a crushing coup-de-grâce ax kick from Sheffield. In a movie, this would have impressed him, but here and now, in his own life or death struggle, it only served to shattered his remaining resistance.

Jim's ribs audibly cracked from the blow. He rolled over on his back in agony. The pain blurred his vision, making it hard for him to catch his breath. The broken ribs made every simple inhale a laborious chore. It was over. They had lost.

"You two are pathetic." he announced standing over them breathing hard. "My faggot son and the cop who rapes women. I can't decide which of you to kill first."

Frank and Jim stared up at Sheffield gloating as he lorded over the two of them with a smug expression of victory. Their swirling vision distorted his facial features, except the sickening smile spread across his face. After retrieving his ceremonial sword from the counter top, he started chanting childishly as he pointed back and forth between the two, morbidly deciding who would die first.

"Eeny, meeny, miney, moe, catch a tiger by the toe. If he hollers, let him go. Eeny meeny miney..."

"Moe." Came Elizabeth Whistler's stern voice from the other side of the kitchen.

Sheffield turned to find her kneeling in a perfect firing stance, wielding Hawthorne's black .38 revolver. She fired a shot silencing them all.

The bullet tore through his left thigh and drove him backwards to the door.

"That was for Detective Carmine." She spoke calmly rising to her feet and stepping closer. She steadied the gun like Walt taught her, and a second discharge rang out.

This one ripped through the meat of his right shoulder removing another of his favored limb from the battle. He dropped the sharp sword he wielded in that hand, and propped himself up against the counter with the one arm that still responded to him.

"That was for villainizing Jim for being gay." before capping off another shot.

This time, the slug struck him in the other shoulder as the blood splatter coated the door behind him. Miraculously, he managed to stay on his feet defiantly.

"That was for all the men you killed here in Connecticut." She fired again.

This one tore into the thigh of the other leg dropping him to his knees, but he wouldn't give her the satisfaction of so much as a whimper.

"That one is for all the people you've killed elsewhere." She stated, then firing yet another time.

This time to the groin, the bullet shredded Sheffield's manhood and bravado as he finally cried out in pain.

"That one is for Walter you bastard!"

Jim reached out to grab his mother's leg, worried about her future psyche if she followed through with killing a helpless Sheffield. But, before he could latch onto her, Frank seized wrist, pulled it back, simply shook his head, no.

She moved in close and put the barrel of the pistol against his forehead. "This one is for me you piece of shit. Your days of haunting my life ends now."

"Go ahead, Elizabeth." Sheffield encouraged her, fighting through his pain of his fatally damaged body. "Do it."

"I don't remember asking your permission." She retorted firmly, and pulled the trigger.

The shot echoed through the house.

EPILOUGE

"Holy Shit! Looks like a fucking war zone." Captain Torres exclaimed as he forced his way through a maze of reporters and the uniformed officers holding them back. He passed some of the remains of the first deputy under a set of sheets on the lawn, as he made his way to the porch, where the paramedics were still examining Jim and Elizabeth Whistler sitting on a loveseat, with Frank sitting alone in a nearby rocking chair.

He looked inside the entryway and saw the gaping hole in the floor.

"Jesus Christ, Frank. How the hell did you survive all this?" he inquired crossing over to them.

"It has become clear to me today that I deserve a raise." He replied, hardly even looking up at him.

"What the fuck is going on here!" Stammered a large man in his fifties storming up the front steps. "I got a perp back there with a half dozen holes in him, including one at point-blank!"

"Capt. Torres, meet Sheriff Dawson, Essex County." handling the quick introduction.

"Who shot the guy like that?" Dawson's voice belaying his frustration.

"That piece of shit killed three of your men today." Frank asserted jumping up. "What do you care how many times or even how he was shot? It's over! He's dead!"

"This ain't even your jurisdiction hotshot." Dawson countered. "And with three dead officers, I want a damn good explanation as to why."

"I can't say what happened to Hawthorne. He was..." Looking at Elizabeth and editing himself, "Already expired when I got here. But, as for the other two assholes, they're dead because they don't listen, and I blame that on shitty training!"

"You better watch your mouth, Carmine. I've got three dead men because of you."

"That is not true." Jim retorted, standing up in Frank's defense, holding his ribs gingerly all the while. "If they had done what Detective Carmine said they'd probably still be alive."

"Who the fuck are you?" he spit out in Jim's direction.

"That's enough, Dawson!" Frank warned, getting in the big man's face. "Doctor Jim here is the only guy who pulled his own weight here today, and his mother turned out to be worth more than both those morons you had watching the house!"

Elizabeth Whistler managed to crack a tiny wry smile acknowledging Frank's support of her skills.

"I'll tell you right now, I'd rather have these two back me up, than anyone on your squad next time! They're alive because they did what I said and stuck together, something your hotheads didn't know shit about!"

"You better back the fuck up, Carmine!" Dawson demanded angrily. "Or I'll run you in myself."

Torres grabbed his colleague, and pulled him away from the sheriff.

"Easy Frank." He interjected, stepping between the two. "Don't get yourself in trouble."

"Oh, he's already in trouble." ratcheting up his voice another notch. "He's out of his jurisdiction, and thanks to him three of my men are dead. You're going up on charges, Carmine!"

"That won't be necessary." A voice boomed from behind them.

They all turned to see the two men in suits now standing with them. Both were solid, well-built men in their forties. The slightly taller of the two spoke, while producing a badge and credentials.

"My name is Detective Rizzo. This is my partner Detective Harris, State Police. We're taking over this investigation." He stated with Stoic authority.

"Says who?" Dawson fired back.

"The constitution of the state of Connecticut." He answered firmly. "Look, Sheriff. I realize you lost some men today, but it is painfully clear both the doors were booby-trapped. Now, I'm familiar with Carmine here. He's an honest cop with a great record, and there is no way in hell he would send anyone through a rigged door like that. You may have to accept the fact that your men performed poorly here today."

"Who the fuck are you to tell me they performed poorly?" he shouted.

Rizzo calmly moved face to face with the local.

"So, help me God, if you swear in front of this woman, who has been through so much in her own home, one more time I will arrest you, and you will spend the night in the state pen." He spouted firmly without raising his voice. "We are in charge now, Sheriff, and there will be a full investigation."

"I'll run my own damn investigation." he proclaimed defiantly.

"If you interfere, or corrupt one iota of evidence, I will see to it you are locked up. Now get out of my face, and see what you can do about crowd control."

"You arrogant son of a-"

"Don't say it." cutting him off. "Not one more word. You won't be popular in lockup."

Dawson gave him an angry stare, then pushed past the two state cops, and stomped down the steps clearly disgruntled.

"Hey, Carmine. Is this yours?" Harris asked holding up a cellphone. "One of the reporters answered it. There's a hysterical woman on the line asking about you."

"Oh, shit that must be Carrie." Frank snapped the phone out of his hand, and moved to the other end of the deck for some privacy.

"Carrie McKenna?" Harris' eyes lit up. "The coroner?"

Capt. Torres nodded, yes.

"Nice." Harris slipped out inappropriately.

Rizzo smacked him lightly in the chest and gave him a shut the hell up, because now is not the time for that look. He crossed over to Jim and his mother and knelt on one knee before them.

"It seems in the middle of all this havoc, we have forgotten who the real victims are here, and I would like to apologize for that right up front." Rizzo began. "Walter Hawthorne was a pillar of this community, and he'll be missed by a lot of people."

"Thank you." she mumbled.

"Now, regardless of Sheriff Dawson outbursts, I am in charge from here on out, and this is how we will proceed. After we take you to a hospital and ensure any injuries you sustained are under control to the highest-level modern medicine will allow, then and only then we'll go over what happened here today. I will talk to you ma'am, your son here, and Detective Carmine, and if the stories match and I'm fairly certain they will, then this investigation is over. Personally, I don't care which one of you shot him or how many times. I'm just glad that murderer has been stopped."

"I did it." Elizabeth said speaking up. "I shot him."

"Well ma'am, considering all you've been through, I'm sorry your weapon only held six shots."

Jim reached over and took his mother's hand. She turned to face him and produced a reserved smile.

"I'll tell you one other thing, Mrs. Whistler." Rizzo continued. "I am well aware of the quality work your son has done on behalf of at-risk women, and you can rest assured that you raised a good man. I only wish you had more."

"Thank you, sir." She managed feebly, looking at Jim with admiration.

"You don't call me sir today, Ma'am. I don't deserve it in this house, but it sure sounds like the two of you do. We should thank you."

"We appreciate that." Jim spoke with gratitude in his voice. "But, if those other two deputies had done like Frank said, it wouldn't have gotten this bad."

"I believe you're right, Doctor Whistler, and all the evidence I've seen or been briefed on so far, agrees with you." He stood up. "Now, my men will escort you to the emergency room in New London, and we'll talk tomorrow. You two ever considered becoming cops?"

Jim chuckled ever so slightly, but stifled it, seemingly mindful of his discomfort. Elizabeth turned with motherly concern, as he grimaced from even the small exertion of a laugh.

"You should call, Gordon." she reminded him gently.

"I can tell him it looks like we'll be roomies at the hospital again for a while." he winced and held his side as he spoke.

"Have told you how much I like Gordon? I hope you two stay together."

"I'm so sorry about Walt." He assured his mother. "I liked him too."

Jim leaned over and kissed his mother on the cheek, only to grimace in pain, which led to a small coughing fit that aggravated his misery exponentially.

"Harris, tell the medics bring the stretchers up here on the porch for these fine folks," Rizzo instructed. "I do not want these two walking another step today if they don't have to."

He turned to fetch them without saying a word.

"What you two did here was impressive. Truly impressive." he added.

They nodded solemnly in agreement, and leaned on each other to wait for their ride to the ambulance.

"I'm okay, Carrie." Frank repeated on the far side of the veranda for the tenth time. "Some cracked ribs, and my nose again... Doc Jim and his mother have similar injuries, but will recover in the long run... No, Hawthorne didn't make it..."

There was a long silence on both ends of the call. After a moment, she went on with her concerns.

"Yes ma'am, I promise will not drive myself, and will ride there in an ambulance."

He couldn't focus on what she was saying. All he could think about was how much this woman meant to him now, and how close he came to losing everything. She deserved to know.

"I love you." startling her into silence for the second time in the conversation.

"Did you just..." She stammered.

"Yes. I said, I love you, Carrie."

"I love you too, Frank." her voice finally returning to that breathy wonder that stirred his soul. "I'll meet you at the E.R."

He hung up the phone, as the EMTs started take the Whistlers down the front stairs to the waiting EMS transports.

"Hey!" He yelled running down the stairs to catch up, then doubling over as his own bodily damage reminded him of their existence. "Hold on a second," as he composed himself. "I want to tell you two something."

The paramedics stopped, and he offered an outstretched hand to both of them. The two of them each took one of Frank's hands in theirs, and there was a long pause as they waited on him to speak. His expression already speaking with volumes of sincerity and gratitude.

"I just wanted to say, to each of you, sincerely," taking a beat. "Thank you."

Neither of them spoke. They gripped his hand tighter and smiled what sad smiles they could muster at the end of day like today. He bent over and kissed their hands once each, and grinned warmly. He let go, nodding earnestly, and let the medics roll them away.

An expression of relief came over his face, as he watched them place the Whistlers into separate ambulances. Torres appeared beside him, and put his hand on his shoulder supportively.

"You sounded like you really meant that, Frank." as the EMS vehicles disappeared from their view.

"I did, Paul. I most certainly did."

~Fini~